FROM A

WHISPER

TO A

SCREAM

FROM A
WHISPER
TO A
SCREAM

CHARLES DE LINT

WRITING AS SAMUEL M. KEY

A TOM DOHERTY ASSOCIATES BOOK
NEW YORK

FROM A WHISPER TO A SCREAM

Copyright © 1992 by Charles de Lint

Preface copyright © 2003 by Charles de Lint

This edition edited by Patrick Nielsen Hayden.

An Orb Edition
Published by Tom Doherty Associates, LLC
175 Fifth Avenue
New York, NY 10010

www.tor.com

Library of Congress Cataloging-in-Publication Data

Key, Samuel M.
     From a whisper to a scream / Charles de Lint writing as Samuel M. Key.
       p. cm.
     ISBN 0-765-30434-1
     1. Children—Crimes against—Fiction. 2. Serial murders—Fiction. 3. Photographers—Fiction. I. Title.

PR9199.3.D357 F76 2003
813'.54—dc21

                                                    2002035454

This book, written under the name Samuel M. Key, was originally published by Berkley Books in October 1992.

First Orb Edition: January 2003

Printed in the United States of America

0 9 8 7 6 5 4 3 2 1

FOR
ANDREW VACHSS...

A LIGHT IN THE DARKNESS

WITH SPECIAL THANKS TO JOHN
MAJOR FOR TECHNICAL ADVICE

PREFACE

Sometimes the darkness calls and I find myself approaching it. Not because it has any sort of appeal to me, but to try to understand it.

One of the ongoing themes of my work is the effect that preternatural encounters have on the ordinary person. Mostly, the darker sections of my novels arrive from the human psyche, with the magical elements playing against that shadow. The Otherworld, however, contains as much darkness as it does ambiguity and light, and to ignore it strikes me as telling only half the story. Hence the books I wrote under the pen name Samuel M. Key.

From a Whisper to a Scream originally had a working title of *Niki* and was the first full-length Newford novel. (*The Dreaming Place* came before it, but at just under 50,000 words, it strikes me as more of a novella.) In retrospect, considering the somewhat whimsical tone of most of the Newford stories up to that point (later collected in *Dreams Underfoot*), it seems a little odd to me that I'd choose such a dark story as my first novel-length excursion into the city. However, I remember at the time that I hadn't thought the story would be as dark as it turned out to be when I actually sat down to write it.

When my first "horror" novel, *Mulengro*, appeared in 1985, readers picked it up expecting the usual de Lint novel. *Mulengro* has many of the elements that readers have come to expect in my work, but it also contains somewhat graphic descriptions of violence and its aftereffects which some readers found disturbing. I can well understand that some people prefer not to read horror fiction, so one of the reasons I decided to create "Samuel M. Key" was so that readers could differentiate between the types of fiction I was writing. The Key books would be the darker ones. No secret was made of the fact that the pseudonym was mine, since it was merely a device to let readers know in advance that they could expect a darker story between the covers.

If you'd like to know more of the origins of Sam Key, please visit my Web site at www.charlesdelint.com/faq.htm.

The Sam Key books are dark, and at times, graphically rendered novels, *From a Whisper to a Scream* as much as any of the others. Though ultimately they reach for the light, the journey to get there becomes both arduous and harrowing in places. Much like life itself, really, reminding us to take care of each other along the way.

THE WONDER IS NOT
THAT THERE IS SO MUCH DARKNESS.

THE WONDER IS THAT
THERE IS ANY LIGHT AT ALL.

ALLEN LEE HARRIS
DELIVER US FROM EVIL

FROM A WHISPER TO A SCREAM

ONE

OCTOBER 1988

Thomas Morningstar was on traffic duty that month. He didn't mind the eight-to-four shift, but unlike most of the cops he worked with, he preferred a night foot patrol. Being stuck in a car for most of the day just made him antsy. When you walked a beat, you still felt as though you had some connection to the world around you. The stars kept you company, distanced only by the haze of lights that the city cast up into the darkness. The wind knew where to find you.

The blue-and-white patrol car, with the gold badge of the Newford Police Department on its doors, was too confining. The squawk of the radio, trapped between metal and glass, was a constant irritation. Looking out at the street through a windshield was too much like observing the world through the glass screen of a television set.

But he could be patient. This was his last day on traffic. Two days off, and he'd be back to hoofing it once more: evening shift, walking a one-armed post along Grasso Street. But before that he had to go up to the reserve to see his father.

Big Dan Morningstar was the elected chief of the Kickaha Reserve. He considered Thomas, his eldest son, to be his only failure.

"You want to be a cop, why don't you join the Tribal Police?" he demanded at least once on every visit Thomas made. "But no. You want to pretend to be a white man. You want to marry a white girl. You're ashamed of your people and that brings me shame. Why can't you be more like your brother?"

John was unemployed and still lived with their parents, but that was never brought up, because his politics were correct. Still, he, at least, understood Thomas's position.

Thomas wasn't ashamed of his heritage; he just didn't want to live on the reserve. That was the reason he had entered law enforcement, but not simply to escape. He truly believed that the only hope for his people to find a prosperous future was for them to meet white society on its own terms, to have a say in the making and keeping of its laws, while still maintaining links with their own traditions. And was it his fault that the woman who stole his heart was white? Why should it make any difference what color Angie's skin was so long as they loved each other?

He would sit on the porch of his parents' house with those thoughts in mind, but he no longer voiced them. He would keep his face stoic as he listened to his father, and he wouldn't argue. He'd long since given up trying to change his father's mind.

His mother had never expressed her feelings on the subject, but she didn't need to. Thomas could always sense her unspoken approval. It was to see her and John that he tried to come by at least a couple of times a month. Angie never drove up with him.

He thought of Angie now as he headed north on Williamson, where it cut through the Tombs, and was only half paying attention

to the driver in the vehicle ahead of him. The radio squawked, and
the dispatch receiver informed all units of a possible domestic over in
the Rosses. Thomas was close enough to catch the squeal and
reached for the microphone, but another unit beat him to it.

Just as well. He hated catching a domestic. You never knew what
you were going to walk into—a normal argument that had escalated a
little too loudly and caused the neighbors some concern, or some
wacko standing there in the hallway, waiting for you with a sawed-off
shotgun.

As Thomas straightened in his seat, some sixth sense made him
pay closer attention to the occupant of the car in front of his own.
The man kept glancing back at him in his rearview mirror, then
quickly shifting his gaze to the road ahead. He seemed jumpy, more
high-strung than was normal, even taking into consideration the nervousness that all citizens seemed to feel in the proximity of a police
officer—whether they were guilty of something or not.

Thomas made a mental note of the license plate number and
started to apply his brakes as the lights at MacNeil up ahead turned
amber. In the car ahead of him, the man's gaze met Thomas's in the
rearview mirror, holding it for a beat. Panic flickered in the man's
eyes and he suddenly stepped on the gas.

His car shot across the intersection and just narrowly missed being
struck by an eager motorist jumping the light. With a squeal of tires,
he sped off. Thomas hit his lights and siren. He waited long seconds
for the cars on MacNeil to let him through, then set off in pursuit.
Steering with one hand, he hooked free the microphone and called in
to his dispatch receiver.

"This is Charlie-car; in pursuit of a brown, late-model Buick heading north on Williamson through the Tombs." He gave the license
plate number and the few meager details of description he had of the
driver.

"Copy, Charlie-car," the dispatcher replied. "Do you require assistance?"

"Wouldn't hurt. I've got a bad feeling about this."

"Backup's on the way. Ten-four."

Thomas dropped the microphone. Letting it dangle loosely from its cord, he concentrated on the pursuit. He'd seen the Buick make a sharp right two blocks north of MacNeil as he was signing off, but when he made the turn himself, the car was no longer in sight.

Siren blaring, he gunned the engine and raced up the deserted street.

This part of the city was nightmare country. The Tombs stretched for what seemed like endless blocks of derelict buildings, rubble-strewn lots, abandoned cars, and refuse. It was home to junkies and biker gangs, homeless squatters and runaways. Citizens' groups had been screaming for years to get the city to clean it up, to no avail.

Thomas slowed down at each cross street he came to, looking sharply left and right, but the Buick seemed to have vanished into the jungle. He killed his siren, but left the cherry lights strobing as he continued on. He could hear the approach of the backup patrol cars, wailing in the distance. From the broken windows of the abandoned buildings on either side of the street, faces peered down at him as he passed. Street rats, in uniforms of ragged jeans and T-shirts, lounged in doorways, their studied nonchalance ready to be replaced by flight should his attention turn to them.

He reached for the dangling mike to call in his position, then realized he didn't know where he was. Street signs here had long since been torn down or vandalized beyond recognition. All he knew was that he was somewhere in the Tombs and he'd lost the car he'd been pursuing. He brought his hand back to the steering wheel and started to brake for the next cross street.

A flicker of sun on metal caught the corner of his eye, and he found himself hauling on the steering wheel and squealing around the corner before he was consciously aware of making the decision to do so. The patrol car shot down the side street, slaloming around the hulk of an abandoned station wagon, orange with rust, and the rotting mass of a box spring that someone had left in the middle of the road.

When Thomas reached the next cross street, he was in time to see the Buick slide around another corner. He'd closed the gap between his own vehicle and the Buick by almost three car lengths, he estimated as he leaned against the driver's door to make his turn. He burned rubber up the length of the block, his own tires squealing and sliding as he followed the Buick's lead.

He pumped the brakes as he came around the corner. The patrol car slid sideways across the buckling pavement before it came to a jerking stop that threw Thomas against his seat belt. Halfway up the block, the Buick had crashed into the back of a derelict pickup truck. The driver of the car was on foot, running across the debris-covered lot that lay between the two old tenements fronting the scene of the accident.

Thomas snapped free his seat belt and rolled his car down toward the lot. He was out of the car almost before it came to a full stop.

"Police!" he called after the driver.

The driver was almost at the far side of the lot. He was overweight, definitely out of shape. Thomas didn't think he'd have any trouble running the man down. But when the driver turned at the sound of Thomas's voice, he had a gun in his hand.

Thomas ducked, scrabbling for his own service revolver, as the first shot rang out. The No Parking sign above his head, with its spray-painted graffiti, rang with the impact of the bullet and showered him with rust. The sound of the shot boomed and echoed between the buildings.

Thomas's heartbeat kicked into overdrive and his training cut in.

He could almost hear his instructor's voice at the police academy ringing in his ears: "Don't aim; point like you're using your finger."

The revolver bucked in his hand and he saw his assailant drop. A heap of rubble hid the man from his sight.

Was he dead, or just wounded?

Thomas moved cautiously forward, giving himself plenty of cover, but it wasn't necessary. By the time he reached the downed man, he could see that the driver wasn't going to be leading any car chases ever again. He was sprawled on his stomach, the back of his head a bloodied mess. It looked as though he'd fallen backward against a low wall, but then pitched forward. His gun lay by his hand, where he had dropped it. Thomas's bullet had caught him in the face and taken off most of the back of his head on its way out.

Thomas moved forward, the adrenaline rush still whining through him. He kicked the man's gun a little farther from his hand—procedure, though it seemed stupid. This guy wasn't going to be reaching for anything.

Thomas stared at the body, his gaze caught and trapped by the gory exit wound in the back of the driver's head. Slowly it sunk in. He'd just killed a man.

This wasn't the body of some victim he'd come across in the line of duty, when he would seal off the immediate area so that the suits and Crime Scene Unit could conduct their investigation. The man was dead because he'd shot him. *He'd* pulled the trigger. And all the poor fuck had been doing was speeding. . . .

He turned away and heaved up the fast-food lunch he'd eaten a couple of hours ago. Leaning weakly against another part of the stone wall, he stared down at the undigested remains of a burger and fries. His mouth tasted like a sewer. His hands trembled as he tried to reholster his revolver. It took him three tries to get it back in.

He thought about what his father would think to see him like this. Warriors were stoic. At a moment such as this a warrior would let nothing of what he felt show in his features.

Fuck the warriors, Thomas thought.

Numbly, he pushed himself up from the wall and made his way back to his car. The first of the backup patrol cars arrived just as he was calling in to dispatch.

Although detectives from his own 9th Precinct were in charge of the investigation, Lieutenant Jacob Brewer, a Homicide detective from Headquarters Division, was also present at the scene of the crime. He was a big white man, almost as big as Thomas's father but with none of the fat. His drooping eyes gave him a sleepy look, but the look was a deception.

He divided his time between observing the investigation and talking to Thomas.

"You had no choice," he told Thomas at one point. "The guy pulled on you."

Thomas nodded. "I know."

There'd be an investigation anyway, but Thomas's own lieutenant had already assured him that there'd be no problem. It would only be a formality.

Tell that to the dead man, Thomas thought.

He and Brewer were leaning against the hood of Thomas's patrol car. The lot between the buildings was no longer deserted. Detectives, the lieutenant on duty from the 9th Precinct, an assistant DA, the medical examiner, detectives from the Crime Scene Unit, a police photographer and even some off-duty men who had just dropped by to catch the show were crawling all over the rubble. Both ends of the block had been cordoned off. The street was littered with police vehicles and an ambulance. Beyond the cordons, television crews, photojournalists, reporters, and the curious were all jostling for the best view.

It was a circus, and next to the dead man, Thomas was its star attraction. The numb feeling had gone, as had the nausea, but he was left with a kind of cold emptiness inside that all the noise and crowds weren't helping. They just seemed to accentuate the sense of dissociation that he felt.

"It gets worse," Brewer said.

"What do you mean?"

"This guy you took down wasn't just some speeder."

Thomas glanced at the man's car. He'd noticed the investigators popping the trunk earlier and a lot of hubbub going on around it, but he hadn't paid much attention to what was happening. He pushed away from the hood of his patrol car and started over to the Buick. Brewer caught his arm.

"It's bad," he said.

Thomas nodded. But he had to see. He had to know that he hadn't just taken out some guy who'd maybe had an argument with his wife or his boss and gone a little wacko—panicking at the police car behind him, pulling a gun he'd probably never fired off a firing range. He had to know. But when Thomas got to where he could get a view of the trunk's contents, he realized that he should have left well enough alone. What he saw then he knew he'd carry with him for the rest of his life.

Inside the trunk of the Buick was a tangle of bloodied limbs and bodies. Small bodies. The bodies of children. There were maybe three or four of them, but it was hard to take an exact count from his perspective because of how they lay entangled. The guy had just dumped them in there. . . .

Thomas turned away.

He got the details later. The man he had killed was Teddy Bird, a pedophile; he was unemployed, lived in a basement apartment near Chinatown. He'd been married, but his wife had left him because he'd been abusing both her and their daughter, since the girl was less than a year old. There were three dead children in the trunk of his car; evidence in his apartment linked him to at least six other missing person reports, all children; the oldest was nine.

Thomas hadn't killed a man; he'd killed a monster.

NOVEMBER 1988

Teddy Bird was buried in a pauper's grave at the expense of the city. There was no graveside ceremony, no one else present at all except for the two men filling the grave. And Thomas.

He stood and watched until the men were finished with their work; then he finally turned away. Lieutenant Brewer was leaning against Thomas's car, smoking a cigarette, when Thomas left the graveyard and stepped out onto the street. He lifted his eyebrows at Thomas's approach.

"I had to see them put him in the ground," he explained.

Brewer nodded. "I know the feeling."

Neither man spoke for a time. Thomas looked skyward. At night, the stars didn't seem close anymore. They seemed, instead, to be the eyes of Teddy Bird's victims, the ones whose bodies hadn't been found; they seemed to be the eyes of all victims who, for one reason or another, would never know peace.

It was still midafternoon, though. Thomas wouldn't see those eyes for hours; maybe he wouldn't see them at all if the present cloud cover continued. But he didn't need to see them to know that they were there.

Walking a beat didn't satisfy him any longer. A cop on the street did what he could, but all too often he got there too late to do any good. The detectives at least had the opportunity to track the bastards down.

Thomas had the opportunity of making first-grade detective coming up, but he knew it was a long shot. Racism wasn't a part of official department policy, but Newford had never had a Native American working plainclothes, and from comments he'd overheard from time to time over the years, Thomas knew there were many who wanted to make sure the department never would. No matter how well Thomas did in his upcoming exam, he needed somebody up there with the brass pulling for him. He needed a rabbi to look out for him if he wanted to get anywhere.

Brewer's presence here gave him hope.

"I went over your record," Brewer said, finally getting to the point of why he was here, "and I liked what I saw. I could use a man like you in my squad."

He took a last drag from his cigarette. A car went by, and both men followed it with their eyes until it turned the far corner.

"Interested?" Brewer asked without turning.

"What do you think?" Thomas asked.

Brewer shook another cigarette free from the crumpled pack he carried in his suit coat and lit it from the butt of the one he'd been smoking. He flicked the butt away, watching it arc and fall to hit the pavement with a flare of sparks. Only then did he look back at Thomas.

"You've got a rep for being a loner," he said.

"I can be a team player."

Brewer smiled. "I'll put the word in, then. Might take a little time." He took a drag on his cigarette, thinking. "There's an opening for Detective First Grade at the 12th. Put in some street time there and I'll work on getting you transferred to Homicide in a couple of years. If that's what you want."

Like he had to ask, Thomas thought.

"Whatever you can do," he said. "I appreciate the help."

Brewer gave Thomas a friendly bump on the shoulder with his closed fist.

"Better ace that detective's exam," he added as he walked away.

For the first time since that day he'd shot Bird, the tightness eased in Thomas's chest. He got into his car and drove home, where he spent the rest of his day off studying.

TWO

The first time he saw her was through the viewfinder of his Canon F-1. The 300mm telephoto lens brought her face up so close he felt he could just reach out and touch her. She had pale, pale skin, jet-black hair that stood up in short gelled spikes and too much makeup. Her eyes were like dark bruises, her lips a glossy red.

The makeup made her look older, but she was really just a kid, he realized, somewhere in that muddy range between seventeen and her early twenties. Her jeans were a fading black, torn at one knee and tight. She wore a white T-shirt tucked into them and scuffed Doc Martens on her feet, and she held a jean jacket tightly against her chest.

She stood under a streetlight across from him, part of the crowd held back by the police barricades. The curtain of light that dropped down from the streetlight kissed her like a spotlight, accentuating her stark black-and-white tones. The only relief was the bright red of her lips.

He shot five frames of her, just out of habit, not even thinking about what he was doing. The Canon's motor drive whirred, its shutter taking its time at the slow speed needed for night shooting. Removing his finger's pressure from the shutter release, he raised the angle of his camera so that he could focus on the graffiti high on the wall behind the girl. It was what he'd started to shoot before he spotted her. He gave the focusing ring a small clockwise turn. As the graffiti came into focus, he had a moment's déjà vu.

The wall was gray cement. Spray-painted on it was the dyslexic scrawl of a name—NIKI, the N turned backward, the paint black. The only splash of color on the wall was a pair of bright red lips, outlined with more black.

He shot another couple of frames, then lowered the angle of his camera again, panning back and forth across the crowd, looking for the girl. He couldn't find her. He straightened up and lifted his eye from the viewfinder. Closing up his tripod, he let his camera lean against him as he scanned the crowd with his naked eye.

Nothing. She was gone.

His gaze returned to the graffiti above the crowd. He'd spotted the name and those same lips in a half-dozen places over the past few weeks: on a bridge support where Highway 14 cut under the Expressway; on the sides of two buildings—one in Lower Crowsea, the other in the Tombs; three times in other parts of the Zone. And now here.

NIKI, with the dyslexic N. And the lips—not quite smiling, but not sad or pouting or any expression he could put a word to. Their expression was enigmatic, like some graffiti artist's shorthand reproduction of the Mona Lisa's smile—it said everything with just a few quick lines and a splash of color.

The girl in the crowd, he thought. Her lips carried a similar expression. Hers was a younger version, not so mature as the hidden knowledge that Da Vinci's model seemed to hint at, but the enigma was there. Remembering the girl as he'd seen her through the viewfinder, the expression haunted him.

"You about through, McGann?"

He turned to find Peter Kennedy standing beside him. They were coworkers at *The Newford Star*, photographer and reporter, but they didn't much get along. No one got along with Kennedy—not that Kennedy ever noticed. He lived in a dreamworld in which he was a star reporter who'd be joining a television news team just about any day now. He'd been saying that for about as long as he'd worked at *The Star*, which would be three years come the spring.

Kennedy did have a TV anchor's good looks: immaculate hair, broad shoulders helped by the heavy padding in his sports jackets, and strong, handsome features marred only by closely set eyes that were constantly shifting their gaze. The eyes went with his manner, which alternated between brown-nosing and abrasiveness, depending on what he wanted and whom he wanted it from.

Weasel eyes was how Jim's friend Meg described them.

They were focused on him now, waiting for his reply.

"Yeah," Jim said. "I've got all the shots I need."

Kennedy put out his hand. "I'll drop off the film for you."

Jim ignored the hand. "I do my own developing."

"Well, just make sure that you get them in on time to make the morning—"

"You my editor now?"

Kennedy shook his head, obviously puzzled.

"Why don't we let Grant worry about when I turn my work in?"

Ben Grant was *The Star*'s chief photographer and Jim's immediate supervisor.

Kennedy began one of his patented sputtering protests, but Jim moved away from him and closer to the police barricades. He could sense Kennedy hesitate, deciding whether to follow him or not, but, happily for Jim, he headed off for his car. The tension left Jim's shoulders then and he opened up his tripod again. Whenever he was around Kennedy, he just felt like hitting the man.

He finished off the roll, concentrating on some of the chief investigators on the scene, but saved the last frame for a final shot of the green body bag that was about to be loaded into the ambulance.

Hell of a thing, he thought.

Tonight's victim was the fourth teenage hooker to die in as many weeks, although the rumor mill already had it that this time around the victim was some rich kid from the Beaches, slumming in the Combat Zone's less than reputable nightclubs. Maybe the Friday Slasher was moving up the social scale, but Jim doubted it.

The police weren't giving out any information at this point, but that just lent the rumors more credence. With the other victims, the police had already made a statement, beyond "No comment," by this point in the proceedings.

Attendants lifted the stretcher and took it into the back of the ambulance. Jim shot his final frame. As he rewound his film and reached for a new roll, he was joined by one of the other photographers on the scene.

Meg Mullally was a freelancer. She was slim and attractive, with a long mane of deep red hair that would put a shampoo model's exaggerated tresses to shame. Most editors, upon first meeting her, thought she should be on the other side of the camera—until they saw her work.

Jim decided that she'd come straight to the crime scene from an evening of relaxing at home. She was wearing an old pair of jeans and a flannel shirt with its tails hanging out, and her face was free of makeup. Not that she needed it. Half the newsmen in the city had chased after her at one time or another, but she and Jim hadn't had to go through the parry and thrust of the dating game, because Jim had been in the middle of a longtime relationship when they first met. They had a friendship that was proving to be a lasting one—which was more than could be said for the relationship Jim had been in.

"Get any good shots?" Meg asked.

Jim nodded. "I liked your cover for *Time*. Nice work."

"Nice?"

The photo they'd used was one she'd taken a few months ago during a standoff between police and an armed man outside a Grasso Street nightclub that specialized in country-and-western music. The man had been holding a gun to his own head. The way he was standing, he'd blocked off the last two letters of the word "COUNTRY" that ran lengthwise beside the club's entrance.

It was a powerful image, and *Time* had run it to go with a special report on crime in the streets that took up the better part of the issue.

"Okay," Jim said. "It was great. Outstanding. Should I go on?"

"Mmmm . . ."

"Stunning."

Meg grinned. "That about sums it up."

All Jim could do was shake his head.

"How'd you ever get to be so modest?" he asked.

"It came free with my talent. Are you going back to the paper to soup your film?" she added.

"It'd break Kennedy's heart if he didn't have a photo to run with his golden prose," Jim said.

"Sounds like a good reason to lose the film."

Jim laughed.

"Well, I'll be up developing my own shots for a while tonight. Drop by for a drink on your way home if you're up for it."

"Maybe I will. You want a lift?"

"Love one. I took a cab because I couldn't find my car keys."

Jim didn't have to ask about a house key. Meg was so apt to lose things like keys that she always kept a key to her apartment on a chain around her neck.

She had her Nikon out with her tonight, and it was still attached to its tripod. Shouldering it, she fell into step beside him as they headed back through the crowds, to where he'd parked the car that the paper provided him with as one of the necessary perks of his job.

This late at night, Jim had the paper's developing lab pretty much to himself. The only other person he ran into was Phil Castleman, who'd come in to develop a roll he'd shot at an accident up where the Expressway crossed Yoors Street. A tractor trailer had turned over, resulting in a seven-car pileup.

Jim shared a coffee with Phil while he waited for his negatives to dry, then went into one of the darkroom cubicles to print up a contact sheet. Once the contact sheet was dry, he circled a couple of likely frames with a red grease pencil. Then he printed up black-and-white 8×10s of the shots he'd chosen, which he'd leave along with the contact sheet on Grant's desk when he left. After that he made color prints of the photos he'd taken for himself—some graffiti he'd shot earlier in the evening, the graffiti at the crime scene, and the five frames he'd taken of the girl in the crowd. It was close on two-thirty by the time he signed out of the building and got into his car.

He thought about just going home and hitting the sack, but he wasn't really tired and tomorrow was Saturday. Since he didn't have anything to get up early for anyway, he pointed the car in the direction of Meg's Crowsea apartment on Lee Street. She'd rigged up a little red light by the door of her apartment that shone when she was working in her darkroom. The light was on as Jim came down the hall, but flickered off just as he reached the door. He leaned on the bell.

The door opened to the length of the security chain, and Meg looked out at him. She had her hair tied back in a loose ponytail now, but that was the only change since he'd seen her earlier on in the evening. She still looked pleasantly scruffy. Giving him a smile, she closed the door so that she could take off the chain.

"Come on in," she said when she had the door open.

She headed off down the short hall that ran straight through the apartment to the kitchen in back, leaving him to close the door. He trailed after her and pulled up a chair at the kitchen table. There were 8×10 black-and-whites scattered all over it. He turned them around so that he could look at them, but they weren't much different from the ones he'd taken at the crime scene himself.

"Nothing great," Meg said, looking over his shoulder. "Do you want coffee or something stronger?"

"How about something stronger *in* my coffee?"

"Coming up."

Jim had been the first photographer to reach the crime scene, arriving before the detectives. The area hadn't even been roped off yet. The only officials present were the two patrolmen who'd found the body. He'd managed to get a few shots of the body itself—no face shots, but the paper couldn't use those anyway—but then the full weight of the Newford Police Department descended on the scene. He'd tried to remain unobtrusive, but one of the patrolmen had ushered him to the far side of the barricades all the same.

"I've got a couple there I can sell," Meg said. She moved across the kitchen to put the kettle on. "How'd you do?"

"I was the first one there."

Meg returned to the table and sat across from him.

"Let me guess," she said. "You were out shooting graffiti again—right?"

Jim nodded. "I got some interesting stuff tonight. Did you notice . . ."

His voice trailed off. He'd been leaning back in his chair, looking at the corkboard hanging above the table, where Meg pinned an ongoing and ever-changing collage of her work. He sat up straight in his chair and leaned over, his finger jabbing one of the prints.

"Can I take it down?"

"Sure. What is it?"

"I'm not sure. . . ."

But once he had the photograph in his hand, uncertainty fled. The photo showed a part of the crowd that had gathered at one of the other Friday Slasher crime scenes. Standing in its midst, just her head and shoulders visible, was the girl he'd photographed earlier this evening.

"When did you take this?" Jim asked.

"That's from last Friday."

"Do you have any prints that you shot on the other Fridays? I'm thinking of crowd scenes."

Meg nodded. "Sure. But what are you looking for?"

Jim pulled his knapsack up from the floor and dug out the folder that held the photographs he'd printed up at *The Star*'s lab. He took out one of the ones of the girl and laid it on the table beside Meg's crowd shot.

"She was there both weeks," he said.

Meg studied his photos, then hers. "Little young for you, isn't she?"

"Ha, ha." He picked up a photo of the graffiti on the wall behind the girl and laid it on the table. "I didn't see her that week, but this graffiti was there—about a block down."

Meg frowned, thinking. "A block down . . . ?"

Jim nodded.

"But tonight's killing was—"

"Three blocks north. This graffiti's been showing up in various places all over town."

"I still don't get it."

"Look at it—look at her. Don't you see the connection?"

Meg shook her head.

"Look at the graffiti," he repeated. "The wall's all in black and white, mirroring her clothes and hair."

"No way that wall's white," Meg said.

"You know what I mean."

Meg shook her head. "But do go on."

"Okay, the girl and the wall, no color. But then the lips—hers and the ones in the graffiti—are both a bright slash of color. There's some kind of connection between the two."

Meg studied the two pictures for a long moment. Finally she shook her head.

"I think you're stretching it," she said.

Jim remembered the strong sense of déjà vu he'd felt at the crime scene as he'd turned his viewfinder from the girl to the wall. But what made sense then—instinctive sense, if not logical—didn't seem quite so clear-cut now.

"Maybe," he said.

Meg rose to her feet.

"Let me get the other photos," she said.

She was a few minutes digging them out of her files. When she brought them back, they both went over them. Jim used a magnifying glass on her contact sheets, to study the frames that she hadn't printed up. Meg brewed the coffee. By the time it was ready and she'd added a shot of whiskey to each mug, Jim had finished.

"She was in the crowd every night," he said.

Meg nodded. "But that doesn't mean there's a connection. She could just live in the area."

"Could."

"Or maybe she was working."

"She doesn't dress like a hooker."

"Night off?" Meg tried.

"You think a pimp'd give one of his girls a Friday night off?"

"Maybe with the Slasher . . ."

Jim shook his head. "Pimps don't have compassion."

He pushed the photos around on the table, thinking. He hadn't worked the night of the first killing. Grant had caught that call and gone out himself when he couldn't raise one of the other photographers. But Jim had been there for every one since.

The first killing only made the local page, section three. But the next week it hit the front page. Jim couldn't remember who started up calling the killer the Friday Slasher, but the name had stuck. After the second killing, every photographer and reporter stayed close to their police scanners on Friday nights. Jim thought of the rolls of film he'd shot on those various nights, but couldn't recall the girl being in any frame.

"Maybe your first guess was right," he said.

"Which was?"

"Maybe Niki lives in the area."

He paused, realizing what he'd said. Meg just shook her head.

" 'Niki' now, is it?" she said.

He shrugged. "It's just the graffiti. . . ."

"That's okay. We might as well call her something and that's as good as anything else."

"Right. Anyway, maybe she lives in the area, but while the Slasher has always hit in the Combat Zone, so far not one of the killings has taken place closer than a few blocks from another."

"And tonight there were cops crawling all over the Zone—I know. I was out prowling myself."

"Jesus, Meg. This guy could've killed *you*."

"He didn't. But it makes you wonder. I wasn't expecting him to strike tonight. It just seemed too risky."

Jim nodded. He still didn't like the idea of Meg wandering the Zone's streets at night. And it wasn't just the fact that she might run into the Slasher that bothered him. Every lowlife in Newford gravitated to the Zone—especially on Friday and Saturday night. But while he worried, he knew it was pointless to argue about it with her. They'd been through this before. He worried, and she just said, "I've got to make a living."

"If you're this sure of yourself, you should take what you've got to the cops," Meg said now. "They've been 'on the verge of solving the case' ever since it started."

Which, as they both knew, meant that the police had absolutely no leads.

"I'm not *that* sure," Jim said. "I've just got a feeling about it, but it's nothing I can prove."

"So what are you going to do?"

"Try to track down the girl and talk to her."

Meg shook her head. "And you think I'm crazy. How long do you think that'll take? And who's even going to talk to you down there? They'll just figure you for a cop."

"I'll make up some story. I'll tell them I'm shooting photos for a show on street people."

Which was close to the truth. He *was* putting together a show using the photographs of graffiti that he'd been taking over the years. He had more material than he'd ever need. The trouble was he just didn't have a focus for it; there was nothing to link the material together beyond the obvious, which was not what he wanted to do with this show.

"Like hookers and pimps and petty criminals really want their portraits taken," Meg said.

"You'd be surprised."

Meg thought for a moment, then nodded. "Maybe not. Unless they're specifically wanted for something, they seem to like the idea of a bit of fame."

She was thinking, Jim knew, of the article on the homeless she'd illustrated in the spring for *The Daily Journal*'s Sunday section. The squats in the Tombs had as many petty criminals hiding out in them as they did honest people down on their luck.

"But I still don't know," she said. "If she *is* involved, you could end up over your head awfully fast."

"As soon as I've got anything concrete, I'll go to the cops."

Meg nodded, but it was obvious that she didn't like the idea of what he was going to do any more than he liked her prowling around in the Zone on her own. Jim shuffled the photos together with the full-face shot of Niki on top.

"Can I keep these?" he asked, indicating the prints Meg had taken that also had the girl in them.

"Sure."

"Thanks."

He put them in the folder with his own and stowed it away in his knapsack.

"So how's Jack?" he asked.

"You're changing the subject."

"No, I'm not. You just haven't been talking about him lately."

"He didn't like my hours—or rather, he didn't like how little time I spent with him, which is about the same thing."

"Tell me about it," Jim said.

That had been one of the main things he and Susan had argued about before they finally broke up. The bitch of it was, he'd gone from freelancing to working on staff at the paper for her. He'd been clearing eighty thousand dollars a year, but also putting in sixteen-hour days, seven days a week. The paper paid him forty-five thousand dollars, including perks like providing him with cameras, a car, insurance and health benefits, and he only had to put in thirty-seven-and-a-half hours a week.

After the first period of adjustment, he found he could live with it. In fact, he liked the extra time off. The trouble was, those extra hours of free time that he had to spend with Susan ended up showing both of them how little they had in common. Nights when he used to be out earning money, cruising the streets in his old Honda, following leads on his police scanner to various accidents and the like, were instead taken up with arguments that there just hadn't been time for before.

He hadn't been on staff for more than three months before their relationship died in one massive, final blowup.

"So what're you doing now?" Jim asked.

Meg sighed. "Working."

THREE

Mickey Flynn owned the Combat Zone.

Not the buildings themselves; he just got a cut of any action going down in the area—it didn't matter who was running it. He'd out-maneuvered and outlasted the Italians and had the muscle to put the pressure on anybody trying to move in on what he considered his turf. You wanted to work those streets, you gave Mickey a cut; you didn't ante up, you were out. Or you were dead. He still had connections to the Rosses, where he first got his start in the business, but the Zone was where the real money lay, and Mickey liked money even more than he did food or a good fuck.

He had been born forty years ago to a third-generation Irish family living in the shanty Irish tenements of the Rosses. Before him, none of his family had criminal connections. They might contribute to the IRA—they'd even harbored a couple of provos in the sixties—but that was a political thing. Mickey's father, two uncles, and older brother all worked on the docks, spent their wages on rent, food, and clothing for their families, and at the pub—though not necessarily in that order—and would never consider setting foot in the Kelly Street Social Club, which at the time was the principal headquarters of Pat McKenna's men—the ones that the papers liked to refer to as the Irish mob.

But Mickey had more respect for gangsters like McKenna, with their easy money and cheap women, than he could ever muster for the men in his own family. All the Flynns had were dead-end lives. Mickey wanted more.

After years of running with the neighborhood street gangs, when he was seventeen he became a bagman for one of McKenna's lieutenants. By the time he turned twenty, he'd killed six men and risen up the ranks into shylocking, extortion, and armed robbery. At the ripe old age of twenty-five, he had ousted McKenna and taken over all of his former boss's rackets.

Once he'd consolidated his holdings in the Rosses, he moved his base of operations out of there—an area which, with the sudden influx of Vietnamese and Caribbean immigrants, had degenerated, so far as he was concerned, into nothing more than a ghetto—to the downtown core. He survived a handful of indictments and two grand juries and watched with amusement as his Italian counterparts went down one by one, while he continued to prosper.

These days his principal competitors were all, as he could so eloquently put it, "Just a bunch of fucking foreigners." He could deal with the Japanese yakuza and the Chinese tongs, because they kept mostly to their own parts of town and knew well enough what to leave alone. But the city was also riddled with Vietnamese, Colombian, black, Hispanic, and Caribbean crews, all jostling for a piece of the action.

Mickey stayed on top, but it was getting harder and harder every year to stay there. He spent most of his time in his Lakeside Drive penthouse, which took up the top two floors of the Harbour Ritz, a hotel that he owned through the convenient distancing of a holding company in Barbados, and let his lieutenants do the legwork.

He indulged himself with rich foods and his drug of choice, Tullamore Dew Irish whiskey, until his body had acquired elephantine proportions and his face was redder than his hair had once been. But it made no difference to the men who worked for him, or the showgirls that he bedded, that he was an obese alcoholic. Mickey Flynn was as ruthless today as he had been when he fought his way to the top; crossing him was a risk that few would willingly take. For all the modern accoutrements that his criminal activities had acquired, his power remained rooted in violence and fear. Other mob bosses might defer the dealing of retribution to their underlings, but Mickey was still known to pull the trigger himself on occasion.

On the night that the Friday Slasher claimed his fourth victim, Mickey was sitting in the plush main suite of his penthouse. A highball glass half-filled with whiskey stood on the glass table beside him. He had his feet up on a leather ottoman and the television on, the sound coming from four speakers strategically placed about the large room to give the optimum sound without necessarily being intrusive. He was alone except for one of his lieutenants.

"This is bullshit," he said as they watched a videotape of WOKY's eleven o'clock news broadcast for the third time. "They had over thirty cops tracking up and down the Zone tonight and they still let the fucker put it to them."

Billy Ryan lit a cigarette and made no reply. He was a tall man, with a rangy build and short, curly red hair, who had just turned twenty-seven in July. His cherubic features were more those of an altar boy than a gangster. The word inside the Flynn mob was that Mickey had taken to him because Ryan reminded him of himself at the same age. He was certainly as ruthless. Unspoken was the question of how long it would be before he repeated Mickey's own treacherous history and took over the business, as Mickey had taken it from Pat McKenna.

"It's doing shit for business," Mickey added.

"But no one's getting busted," Ryan said. "All the cops're interested in is taking down the Slasher."

Mickey turned to him. "Fercrissakes, will you wake up? No one's getting busted, sure, but business is down. We had half the customers in the clubs tonight than we did on a bad night before all this Slasher crap started."

"So what are you saying, Mickey? You want me to get a few boys and play hero running this guy down?"

"What do you take me for? Some bleeding heart? I could give a shit about this Slasher except he's hurting business." He frowned, then added, "You know, I wouldn't put it past Papa Jo-el to be behind this."

Papa Jo-el was a self-proclaimed Creole juju man who mixed dealing crack and running prostitutes with the worship of his *loa*, the voodoo gods who live in a drumbeat. His men had been sliding around the edges of the Zone for the past few months, trying to expand their operations into the more lucrative territories claimed by Mickey Flynn. There were others that tried from time to time, gangs and individuals, but Papa Jo-el just couldn't seem to get the message.

The way Mickey saw it, Papa Jo-el just might be working some kind of phony voodoo shit, seeing as how his crew closed down the voodoo boys the last time they tried to work the Zone without coughing up Mickey's cut. Closed them down hard.

"I'll have a talk with him," Ryan said.

"I don't give a fuck what you do," Mickey told him. "Just get rid of the cops. I want business as usual and I want it yesterday."

"You've got it," Ryan said.

He stubbed out his cigarette and rose to his feet, wondering, as he headed for the door, how the hell he was going to make good on his word. Behind him, Mickey shut off the VCR with his remote and frowned as the black-and-white film that WOKY was running as its late movie appeared on the screen.

"What's this shit?" he demanded. "I thought they'd colored all these old flicks."

Ryan paused at the door. "You want me to send up one of the girls?"

"Sure. Make it the blonde with the big bazooms that I had up here last weekend. I need something soft to take my mind off of all this crap."

Ryan nodded and left the suite. That at least he could do. But this Slasher business . . . He shook his head. He wasn't exactly the biggest supporter of the NPD, but if the cops couldn't get a line on the sucker, where the hell was he supposed to start?

Well, the cops had to have something. A witness, maybe. He'd get his man in Vice to do a little extracurricular rooting through the files of whoever was heading up the case.

The elevator took him down to the hotel's sixteenth floor. He got out and walked down the carpeted hall, counting off the doors. A Do Not Disturb sign hung from the knob.

Gimme a break, he thought.

He took out a master key, which would open any room in the hotel, and walked in.

"Okay, Dixie," he said, moving toward the bed. "Time to make the old man happy."

Janet Dixon's disheveled blonde head protruded from below the covers. She sat up as he turned on the room's overhead light. Beside her, a male figure stirred, then sat up as well, staring angrily at Ryan.

"Who the—" he began, but the blonde put a hand on his arm.

"Take it easy, Tiger," she said, then turned to Ryan. "Mickey wants me *now*?"

"He's having a bad night."

"Shit."

Ignoring her nudity, she stepped from the bed and went to the closet, where she took down a silk evening gown.

"What do you think?" she asked Ryan, holding it up.

He shrugged. "You're only wearing it down the hall and up the elevator."

"Will somebody please tell me what's going on here?" the man in the bed demanded.

"Business," Ryan told him.

"What kind of business is conducted at—"

"Where the hell you pick him up?" Ryan asked Dixie, ignoring the man.

She had slipped on the evening gown, brushed out her hair and was now hastily applying some makeup in front of the dresser's mirror.

"There's some kind of computer convention going on in the hotel," she said, not turning from the mirror.

Ryan grinned. "Sounds like fun."

"He was. Don't give him a hard time."

She stood up from the mirror and stepped into a pair of heels. She crossed over to the bed and gave the man a kiss on the brow.

"I'm sorry about this, Tiger. Give me a call the next time you're in town and I'll make it up to you."

"I . . . I . . ."

"Jesus," Ryan said as they stepped out into the hallway. "Where do you find them?"

Dixie closed the door behind them. "I thought he was kind of cute. You won't tell Mickey?"

"Like he could care."

All she had to do was be there when Mickey wanted her. What she wanted to do on her own time was her business. It was a little like being a dog on a leash, Ryan thought. He wondered how it felt until he caught the look in Dixie's eyes as they were waiting for the elevator.

You and me, it said. We're no different.

And she was right. What they did for the old man wasn't the same, but Mickey had him on a leash that was just as tight as the one he had her on.

Maybe it was time to start seeing about some changes, Ryan thought.

FOUR

It had been a mistake to come back to the city. She knew that now. Something had drawn her back—a kind of gnawing at her mind—so she'd hitchhiked halfway across the country to return to the streets of this city where she'd spent the first few years of her life. She'd thought that what had drawn her back was having been born here; she'd thought it was safe because the newspapers and TV reports had all said he was dead. But they'd all been lies.

He wasn't dead. She should have realized it wouldn't be that easy.

She'd thought she could finally make a new start here—maybe even go back to school—but there wasn't a chance of that now. Not after he'd tricked her into coming back. That gnawing feeling in her head had been him, summoning her. And she could feel him still, worrying away at the shadows that lay in the dark streets outside the abandoned tenement in which she'd claimed a squat.

He wanted her. He wanted to pay her back for telling what he made her do to him when he came into her room late at night.

Her mother had taken her away—first from him, then, when he wouldn't leave them alone, away from the city itself. But her mother was drawn to a certain kind of a man, and when she turned thirteen, her stepfather started coming to her room when her mother was working a night shift, wanting the same things her real father had. When she ran away this time, she went by herself.

Five years of living on the street followed. She was wild when she first ran away. She'd do anything, so long as it gave her a buzz—drugs, rip-offs, lying about her age so that she could dance in strip clubs, prostitution—but unlike the other kids she ran with, she woke up one day and found herself just staring into the emptiness that lay at the heart of her life.

This couldn't be all there was, she'd realized then. There had to be something more. All she needed was a chance to find it. Coming back to Newford had seemed the perfect opportunity to start with a clean slate. Nobody knew her here.

At least she'd thought nobody did.

She didn't expect him to still be alive. She hadn't realized that it was his voice she heard in her head, calling her back. The same voice that whispered on the wind outside the window of her squat right now.

It was a hollow, midnight voice, carried on a night wind, a voice that only she could hear. The same voice that had told her what would happen to her if she ever told anyone about the little games they played in her room late at night. But it was colder now, and harsher. It was a voice like ice, and it cut a chill through her courage every time it spoke.

Coming back to Newford had been a mistake—maybe the biggest

she'd ever made. But she couldn't leave either. It was too late for that. No matter where she fled, he'd just follow her, and sooner or later he'd catch her and they'd be right back where it had all begun, except this time he'd really kill her.

But he'd do it slowly, not as he was killing these other girls.

That's what the midnight voice promised her in its cold, harsh whisper: a slow, lingering death.

It was only a matter of time.

She huddled in the corner of her squat, the blanket from her bedroll wrapped around her. She shivered, though the night wasn't cold. Somewhere in the building she could hear a boom box howling out some heavy metal. It sounded like Ozzie. There were voices down the hall in one of the other rooms—a quiet murmur, loud enough for her to hear that it was a conversation, but too low for her to make out what it was about. In the foyer downstairs, there was a sudden flurry of shouts, or maybe laughter.

She was surrounded by people, but she might as well have been alone in the building. In the city. On the planet.

She might as well have been dead.

But that was what he wanted, and she wasn't going to give him that pleasure. She'd come back to Newford looking for a new start, to find a haven for herself in a world grown too cold, to understand what people meant when they talked about happiness, how they could speak of it as something that didn't come out of a bottle or from taking some drug.

Now all she wanted to do was survive.

A footstep sounded in the hall outside her door, and she drew herself into a tighter ball, pressing into the corner, where she huddled as though the wall could swallow her up and hide her. Someone stepped inside, but it wasn't the bulk of her father that loomed in the doorway.

"Chelsea?" the newcomer asked. "You in there, girl?"

She let out a ragged breath. It was only Jammin'—a guy she'd met yesterday afternoon down by the concession stands that stood in a cluster where the boardwalk met the Pier. He was a reed-thin black man with the most soulful eyes she'd ever seen. Though his family was originally from Africa, two generations back, he had a Rasta-man's dreadlocks and played in a reggae band that also incorporated African soukous and highlife elements in their music. Hanging around with Rastas had given his speech a lilting cadence.

She'd been attracted to the infectious rhythms of the band's impromptu concert on the end of the Pier and had helped Jammin' haul away his gear when the cops came by to break things up. He'd ended up being an easy guy to be with, and they'd spent most of the afternoon just hanging out on the beach. Jammin' wanted her to come to the club where his band was playing that night. She'd put him off, but didn't tell him why.

What was she supposed to say? That her father went around killing people on Friday night, and she had to hide because the only person he really wanted to kill was her?

Not likely.

She could never hide anyway. Every Friday night found her in the Zone, trying to spot him before he saw her. What she'd do when she found him, she didn't know. She carried a switchblade in her back pocket. She supposed she'd try to kill him. But he was the one that did the killing. . . .

Jammin' was peering into her corner. "That be you, Chelsea?" he asked.

She shifted her position and let her blanket fall from her shoulders. Still hugging her knees, she nodded, but then realized he couldn't see the motion.

"Yeah," she said. "What's doing?"

"Come by to check you out, girl," he said. He crossed the room and slouched down against the wall beside her. "You don't be looking so good last time I see you."

"I guess I just get moody. How'd you find me?"

"I asked around."

Jesus, she thought. Was she that easy to find? What if her father did the same thing? The fear that had started to fade in the presence of another person began to crawl up her spine again. She shivered.

Jammin' caught the edge of her blanket and pulled it over her shoulders again, resting his arm around her. She snuggled gratefully against him.

"It don't be so cold," he said, "so why you got the shakes? You be shooting some bad shit?"

"I don't do drugs."

Not anymore.

Jammin' just shook his head. "Living in a place like this, girl, you gonna catch some fever—catch it bad."

"I'm okay."

If she just ignored the icy sound of the midnight voice that was whispering outside on the wind. Jammin's presence helped.

"How'd the gig go?" she asked.

"The club was full, mon—lots of brothers and sisters come to hear The Jah Men play. You should be coming, too. Feel the rhythm. Nothing like dancing to make the blues go 'way."

The wind called her name and she shivered again.

"Maybe I will," she said.

FIVE

At two A.M., the 12th Precinct was still in an uproar. The general duty area was crowded and noisy as various detectives and off-duty officers, brought in to handle the crowd, interviewed derelicts, hookers, pimps, and whoever else they could round up who had been on the Zone's streets at the time of the killing. Outside the precinct building, the media had gathered like birds of prey.

Although the case belonged to the 12th, the detectives who'd caught the first squeal were now working with Homicide Lieutenant Jacob Brewer, who'd come up from Headquarters and commandeered the precinct lieutenant's office to talk to the investigating officers. The calm inside Lieutenant Coonan's office was relative. Through its glass walls, Brewer and the two detectives he had with him could watch the hubbub of activity, but the noise was thankfully muffled.

Detective Second Grade Thomas Morningstar was grateful for the break from the chaos that had started with the discovery of the Slasher's fourth victim and showed no signs of letting up. He'd been on the street since early evening, and he was beat, but he knew it would be a long time before he saw his bed. He'd phoned his wife as soon as he got back to the precinct, but she'd already known he'd be late getting in.

"I heard about it on the news," Angie had told him. The sympathy in her voice helped give him his second wind.

The shit hadn't really hit the fan until they got an ID on the Slasher's latest victim. Up to that point they'd thought they were working on the latest installment of some wacked-out john's hard-on for teenage prostitutes. It hadn't been a pretty situation, but—the cynic in Thomas had thought—the pressure that came down from the Commissioner's office had seemed aimed more at impressing the media than at an honest desire to solve the crime. Nobody cared for the situation, and they were doing their best to track down the perp, but the push for immediate results still appeared moderate to Thomas.

The victims were all of a kind—slim girls, ranging in age from number three, who'd been sixteen, to number one, who'd been twenty. They were all blonde, though one of them had been a dye job, and they were all hookers, working the Zone.

Until number four.

Leslie Wilson wasn't a hooker, for all that she'd been dressed like a tramp and cruising the Zone. No, what they had here was the daughter of Charles Wilson—Mr. Real Estate, a big wheel from the Beaches who rubbed shoulders with city council members and other political hotshots. It was his little girl, out for a night's slumming, who'd ended up being in the wrong place at the wrong time earlier tonight.

In Coonan's office now, Brewer lit up a cigarette.

"What went down tonight still doesn't kill the psycho john theory," he said.

Frank Sarrantonio nodded in agreement. Sarrantonio was Thomas's partner, a detective first grade. He was a stocky man in his early forties, who kept himself in shape through a strict regimen of weight lifting and other exercises. With his hair greased back and the cheap suits he wore, he was taken for a hood as often as a cop.

"The Wilson girl might not've been a hooker," Brewer went on, "but she sure as shit was decked out like one. There's no way the perp could've known the difference." He sighed wearily. "I just don't get it. We had the place crawling with blues and suits. How the hell did he pull it off without anyone seeing him?"

To date they had made very little headway in the case, but then they had next to nothing to go on—just the bodies. Each one had died in exactly the same manner. The medical examiner laid it out for them: bruise marks around the throats of the victims showed that the perp had pulled them in close, then gone in with the knife, blade edge up, straight into the stomach, ripping up through the chest cavity. A sharp knife, the ME told them. A very sharp knife—and big.

The perp had to be big, too, from the spread of the bruises on the victims' throats, and strong, to hold them in their panic and wield the knife the way he did.

So they were looking for a big, strong guy who carried a big sharp knife, and they were coming up empty whichever way they turned, though Thomas, Frank, and other officers of the 12th had clocked in hundreds of man-hours since the first victim had been found.

The usual sexual offenders had been swept up for interrogation, with a concentration on those with a given name of Nick, Nicholas, Nicky, or any permutation thereof, because of the odd graffiti found near a couple of the crime scenes. That line of inquiry met with a complete lack of success. When the same graffiti was also discovered in parts of the city not associated with the crimes, they put that part of the investigation on a back burner.

Mostly their time had been spent tracking down and interviewing possible witnesses, as well as the friends and associates of the victims. Finding family for the latter had been a hopeless cause until the latest victim.

"I was two blocks from where it went down," Frank said, "right about the time Wilkes estimates the girl died, and I didn't hear a squawk."

Brewer nodded, then jerked a thumb at the chaos that had taken over the general duty area. "You know what this means?"

Thomas knew, but he let his partner reply.

"We start at square one and go through it all again," Frank said.

"You've got it—unless one of you hotshots can come up with something we haven't thought of yet?"

"Maybe we should hire Papa Jo-el to use his *gris-gris* to find the killer," Frank said.

Brewer cracked a tight smile. "Right."

"Actually," Thomas broke in, "I heard an odd rumor about Papa Jo-el tonight. Word is some of Flynn's crew seem to think that the killings might have something to do with the voodoo crowd trying to muscle in on their turf."

Frank nodded in agreement. "I heard that, too, from one of my snitches, but I don't buy it."

"Why not?" Brewer asked.

"What's it getting him? If Papa wants a gang war, the fewer cops he's got prowling through the area, the better."

"But it's got to be hurting Flynn's business," Thomas said. "Walking through the Zone tonight, I hardly saw any of the regular traffic at all—just the diehards."

"Look into it," Brewer said. "I want every angle that makes even a grain of sense covered, and then I want you to start hitting the ones that don't make any sense."

Thomas and Frank rose to their feet. As they reached the door, Brewer called Thomas back.

"Go ahead," Brewer told Frank. "This'll just take a minute." He waited until the door was closed and Thomas was seated again before he continued. "Word's come down since the Wilson girl got IDed that it'd be a good idea to have you taken from the case. I've got a feeling it's coming from the Commissioner."

Thomas nodded. He'd seen that one coming himself as soon as the victim was IDed. When it was just a problem with hookers, O'Hannigan wouldn't care who handled it, but with the publicity the case was going to get now, he'd want someone better able—read, nonminority—to represent the force when it came to dealing with the press.

Ever since he'd joined the NPD, Thomas had put up with abuse from a certain segment of his fellow officers. Although he'd come to expect it, it still snuck up and surprised him. He could never get used to it. Time and again his brother would ask, "Why do you put up with this crap?" The only answer Thomas could give was that he wanted to prove them wrong.

Brewer looked at him as though waiting for him to say something, but Thomas rarely spoke unless he had to. It wasn't that he was uncomfortable talking to people, or even diffident; he just found that you learned more if you waited. It was a trick he'd learned from his mother. She rarely spoke, but she knew how to listen, and there was nothing that went on around her of which she wasn't aware.

"People like to talk," she'd told him once. "If you wait long enough, they'll tell you anything you want to know."

It was a good attitude for a policeman to have, especially when dealing with lowlifes. You just sat there, waiting, patient, and pretty soon the tension would build until they got so nervous you couldn't shut them up. Thomas had worked hard at first to develop that attitude; now it was just a part of his natural makeup. But he didn't carry it too far. You had to know when to drop it, because there were relationships you didn't need tension in, like with your wife, or your partner. Or your rabbi.

"So what happens now?" he asked Brewer, knowing this was what the lieutenant was waiting for.

Brewer shook another cigarette free from his pack and lit up before replying. "Nothing. It's business as usual. Who gives a fuck what color your skin is? You're a good cop."

Without any false modesty, Thomas knew that. He and Frank had a higher solved-case ratio than any other detective team at the 12th, but he knew his recent upgrade to sergeant was due more to his rabbi, Brewer, than to the department's sense of fairness. Because there were people in headquarters who *did* give a fuck what color your skin was.

"You might be interested in knowing," Brewer added, "that your lieutenant sided with me."

Well, he would, Thomas thought. While Lieutenant Coonan was the kind of bigot who professed to have nothing against minorities just so long as they kept to themselves, he didn't give Thomas a hard time. The reasoning for that was simple. Coonan's cousin had married one of Frank's cousins, which made Frank family. And since he was Frank's partner . . .

"But the thing is," Brewer went on, "you and Sarrantonio have got to play this one by the book to cover not only your ass, but mine as well. You've got to nail that sick fuck or we could all be out on foot patrol in the Tombs."

Thomas nodded. The threat of being demoted was an exaggeration; what Brewer was really saying was that all of their careers would come to a halt. Forget about promotions; forget about that choice transfer to Homicide. Just thinking about it made Thomas angry, so he turned his thoughts to the victim's father, trying to make the needed connections to put the situation into perspective.

"This Wilson guy . . . ?" he began.

"Is part of the big money that put O'Hannigan where he is today," Brewer completed. "So you see how it stands?"

"Sure."

"Anything else?" Brewer asked.

Thomas shook his head. "I'll get right onto this."

Brewer gave him one of his thin smiles. "I know you will."

"What'd the Loot want?" Frank asked when Thomas joined him in the general duty room.

Frank frowned as Thomas explained what the lieutenant had told him about O'Hannigan.

"Those fucking micks," Frank said. "You know, when my dad used to work on the docks with them, he told me that they didn't even think of us as being white. We were just wops and guineas to them, trying to muscle in on their jobs." He gave Thomas a sad look. "Sound familiar?"

Thomas nodded. He'd heard it often enough—not only directed to his own people, but to every new wave of immigrants.

"Thing is," Frank went on, "the guys that talk that way, it's just that they've let themselves get soft. You get yourself a guy like my dad was . . . He comes here from the old country and he's just burning to work hard and make good. The lazy fuckers who already have the jobs—all of a sudden they've got to bust their asses again, just to hang onto what they've got.

"You ask me, that's what makes this country great. You get a guy who's willing to put in an honest day's work, he can get somewhere and it doesn't mean shit where he's from or what he looks like. Anybody can't take the heat—fuck 'em."

Frank hitched up his pants and gave Thomas a grin.

"But enough with the philosophy shit—right?" he said. "We've got a case to break. Where do you want to start? Hauling in some old sex perps again?"

Thomas shook his head. "I think we should have a talk with Papa Jo-el."

"Yeah? And if he puts some kind of voodoo juju on us?"

"We juice him right back with a Kickaha curse."

Frank looked at him for a long moment. "You know, whenever you talk like that you sound almost half-serious."

Thomas thought of his brother John and the men John trained with in the Warrior Lodge up on the reserve. The old teachings of Kickaha shaman were taught alongside of Green Beret and Marine techniques, so that the Warriors went from sweat lodges and dream quests to learning how to break down, clean, and reassemble an assault rifle all in one day. The mystical and the practical went hand in hand, and the way John explained it, Thomas could almost believe in the supposed powers of the old shaman. And even when the metaphysical seemed improbable at best, he could still *feel* a kind of connection with the natural world around him.

He supposed it was that respect of the old ways that his brother shared with him that made him sound half-serious to Frank.

"Let's just hope Papa Jo-el feels I'm all the way serious," he said to Frank, "and maybe he'll keep his curses to himself."

Frank laughed. "Hey, wouldn't it be great if you could cook up a bunch of curses and shit that we could just lay on a perp when we read him his rights? Like it would be a kind of retribution thing: a rapist'd have his dong fall off, a pickpocket would get like a bad case of arthritis . . ."

Frank really began to warm up to his subject as the two of them headed out the back door of the precinct to where they'd parked their car, elaborating ever more fanciful curses until all Thomas could do was shake his head in weary amusement. The TV camera crews and other press never even looked their way as Thomas steered the unmarked police car out onto the street and across town to the nightclub where Papa Jo-el held court.

The Good Serpent Club was in Upper Foxville. From the outside it looked like a dive, a squat brick two-floored structure sandwiched between a pair of taller sandstone office buildings. Inside, it was just a step or two up from run-down, but that didn't seem to bother the customers. During business hours, handfuls of uptown yuppies rubbed shoulders with the predominantly black clientele in an atmosphere that was more a set designer's idea of Creole decor than the real thing. But the bands that played from the club's small stage were authentic, the drinks were mostly laced with rum and cheap, and the dance floor was always crowded.

The club was downstairs; upstairs were the offices from which Papa Jo-el ran his rackets—drugs, loansharking, and prostitution—and his voodoo church.

The club was dark when Thomas pulled the unmarked car over to the curb. The only space was by a hydrant. He flipped down the visor, so that the laminated NPD identification could show, and got out of the car. Frank was already on the pavement, waiting for him. He offered Thomas a stick of gum.

Thomas shook his head.

"So what do you think?" Frank asked, his voice muffled as he worked his gum.

Thomas looked up at a lit window on the second floor. "Someone's home."

There were two entrances. The one leading into the club was an alcove with an iron gate pulled across the front of it. A few yards down from it was a plain unmarked door. Frank tried the knob and it turned. The door swung open into a small foyer. They could see stairs leading up.

"Are we announcing our visit?" he asked.

Thomas smiled. "You think they don't already know we're here?"

Frank gave a quick look up and down the darkened street.

"What do you see that I don't?" he asked.

"Just a feeling," Thomas replied.

He went up the stairs, Frank trailing along a couple of steps below him. At the top there was a long hall with doors leading off it on either side. Halfway down, one stood open. Light spilled from it out into the hall.

"A feeling," Frank muttered.

Thomas led the way down to the lit doorway and paused in its threshold. The man behind the desk smiled and waved him inside, large gold rings glinting on his fingers. He was a small black man, skin so pale it was hard to tell he was black unless you knew. His hair was brushed back from his high forehead in a thick, dark wave. He wore a tailored beige suit jacket over a white T-shirt.

"I've been expecting you," Papa Jo-el said.

"What?" Frank asked as he followed Thomas into the room. "You got a snitch at the 12th?"

"The *loa* told me you would be coming."

"Yeah. Right."

They took seats across from the desk. Papa Jo-el leaned his elbows on its scratched wooden surface and cupped his chin.

His real name was Joseph Eli Pilione. His priors sheet placed him as a native of New Orleans, where he'd been arrested a half-dozen times, no convictions. Since his arrival in Newford, he'd made a quick rise from the small-time racketeer he'd been in New Orleans to his present more elevated status of mob boss and voodoo priest.

"What can I do for you, officers?" he asked.

His voice had an accent that Thomas could never quite place.

Frank turned to Thomas. "His *loa* didn't tell him that as well?" he asked in a stage whisper.

Thomas gave an almost imperceptible shake of his head, knowing that Frank would get the message. He did. Leaning back in his chair, Frank chewed his gum and took in the office's sparse furnishings. There was a safe in one corner, a beat-up sofa against another wall. With the desk and chairs they were using, that was it. The walls were bare, plaster flaking in the corners. The overhead light didn't have a bulb in it. The illumination came from the tarnished brass lamp on the desk.

"There's been another killing over in the Zone," Thomas said.

Papa Jo-el nodded. "I heard. It was on the news. You don't think I had something to do with it, *mon cher*?"

Thomas shook his head, but didn't speak. For long moments there was only the sound of Frank chewing his gum. Papa Jo-el finally stirred, sitting back in his chair. He indicated some papers that were on the desk.

"I have work to do," he said.

"Flynn's people seem to think you're responsible," Thomas said finally.

"Don't be stupid. What would be the point?"

Thomas glanced at his partner.

"You tell us," Frank said. "The way these girls are buying it looks an awful lot like some kind of ritual killing. You know—like, say, voodoo?"

"Voudoun is a religion, not a cult," Papa Jo-el replied. "Our ceremonies do not include sacrifice."

"Of people," Frank said.

Papa Jo-el paused, then nodded in slow agreement. "Of people."

"Well, we all know you're trying to muscle in on Flynn's turf. His boys think you're trying to lay some voodoo shit on them with these killings."

"I told you—"

"Yeah, yeah. We heard you. Your religion doesn't kill people." Frank paused for a beat. "But how about your business?"

Anger flickered in Papa Jo-el's eyes. He turned to Thomas.

"I don't have to listen to this," he said. "Unless you have something constructive to say, I'm afraid I'll have to ask you to leave."

"The point is," Thomas said, "Flynn's people think you're responsible. You know as well as I do what happens when Mickey Flynn decides someone's putting the screws to him."

"So you're warning me?" Papa Jo-el asked, eyebrows raised.

Thomas shook his head. "We're here to ask you if you have any ideas as to what's going on."

"You see," Frank added, "we've got a sick fuck out there on the streets. One way or another, we're going to stop him from killing any more girls."

Papa Jo-el ignored Frank. His eyes, so dark they seemed black, fixed their gaze upon Thomas.

"I believe you are sincere, *mon cher*," he said.

"Now what's this shit—" Frank began, but he broke off as Thomas lifted a hand.

"What can you tell us?" Thomas asked.

Papa Jo-el gave a small shrug. "I don't think you're ready to hear what I have to say."

"Try me."

A smile touched Papa Jo-el's lips, but it never reached his eyes.

"You look for a man," he said. "For a man who walks the Zone with

FROM A WHISPER TO A SCREAM 61

a knife in hand and murder in his heart. But what stalks the night streets is a *guédé*—a spirit of the dead. An evil spirit, what we call a *baka*."

"Oh, fercrissakes," Frank said.

The other two men ignored him.

"You know how that sounds?" Thomas said. He spoke softly, without expression.

Papa Jo-el nodded. "To one who is blind to the ways of the invisible world, it has the ring of madness."

"But you believe?"

Papa Jo-el's gaze never left Thomas's features as he slowly shook his head.

"No," he said. "I *know*. If you would stop your killer, you must look to how you can lay the dead to rest."

"So now what?" Frank said as they got back into the car. "Are you going to tell me you're half-serious about that crap as well?"

Thomas shook his head. "But the thing is, he's serious. I know a con when it's being laid on me. He believes what he's saying."

"Which was crap."

Thomas looked out through the windshield at the darkened street. He thought of his brother, of the Kickaha shaman on the reserve, of that feeling of connectedness he sometimes felt with the world around him, the sense that there *was* an invisible world, sensed, felt, but not seen. Unless, perhaps, you were a shaman. Or a voudoun *houngan*.

He wasn't as close to it as his brother. He wasn't even sure it wasn't something he just wanted to believe in, rather than something that actually existed. But there was *something*. . . .

"I'm not sure," he said softly. Then he shook his head and gave Frank a grin.

Frank chuckled.

"The guy really had you going there for a minute, didn't he?" he said.

"He was definitely . . . persuasive."

"What we need to do is grab some shut-eye and meet this thing head-on with a fresh perspective in the morning."

Thomas glanced at his watch. "Who's going to feel fresh with only three or four hours of sleep?"

"Hey, you take what you can get."

Thomas nodded. Frank was right. You took what you could get. But he couldn't help wondering, did that include the cockeyed advice of a known con man?

If you would stop your killer, you must look to how you can lay the dead to rest.

He'd never been able to fully accept the pacific spirits of the land as his brother had. The *manitou*, the little mysteries. But somehow he'd never had trouble believing in evil. People. Places. Even spirits. . . .

How the hell *did* you lay the dead to rest?

SIX

There were three of them, lounging on the front stoop of the Grasso Street tenement in the afternoon sun, as Jim McGann walked by. Two were girls with jeans artfully torn at the knees and rump; both wore white T-shirts. One had short blonde hair; the other was a brunette, all curls and tangles hanging past her shoulders. The boy wore baggy black shorts and a muscle shirt. He had five gold earrings in one ear, one in the other. His dark hair was pulled back in a pony-tail and was longer than that of either of his companions.

Two blocks west of the Men's Mission on Palm Street, this whole area was prime panhandling district—a fact that made Palm Street's name all too apropos, never mind that the street took its name from Allan Palm, a Newford city council member from the thirties.

"Spare change?" the blonde asked.

Jim showed them a wallet-sized picture of Niki instead, one that he'd printed up this morning at the paper, before he hit the streets.

"Do you know her?" he asked.

"What are you? A cop?"

They were all so tough, Jim thought. Fourteen, fifteen tops, and they'd seen it all.

"No," he replied. "A photographer."

The brunette took the photo from him. Jim looked down at her fingers holding the picture. There was dirt under the nails; the fingers themselves were grubby. Charming.

"What do you want her for?" the boy asked.

"To sign a release form. I want to use the photo in a show I'm putting together."

The blonde took the photo from the other girl.

"Is there any money in this?" she asked.

"In what?"

"Being a model for a guy like you."

"Some," Jim admitted. He started to feel hopeful. Maybe the girl knew Niki and was hoping for a cut of whatever action came Niki's way. "But it's nominal."

"Shit," the blonde said. "Why don't you take my picture?"

Preening, she put a hand behind her head and stuck out her overdeveloped chest. Jim found the resulting pose so grotesque he was almost tempted to take a picture. He shook his head.

"I've already got all the shots I need," he said.

The blonde let her hand drop. Her shoulders returned to their earlier drooping posture.

"She's got nothing on me," she said.

She shook the photo disdainfully in the air between them, then flipped it back at him. He caught it awkwardly by scooping his hand through the air and trapping the photo against his chest. The kids laughed. Jim kept his temper—barely.

"Yeah, well thanks anyway," he told them.

He'd been going through variations on this routine for the better part of the afternoon now, and he was sick to death of it. Everybody thought he was a cop or—and this truly irritated him—Niki's father. Like he was old enough to have a kid that old. And of course a few had to think he was her pimp, or sugar daddy.

"What'd she do?" an Oriental girl with a skateboard under her arm had asked him. "Take off with your credit cards?"

A little farther down Grasso, near the subway entrance at Palm, he stopped to listen to a young woman with honey-colored hair playing an alto sax. He put her at about twenty-five, a slim, boyish figure in a short, black sleeveless dress and footless leotards, no shoes. There was a backpack, with a bedroll tied to it, by the wall near her feet, two sturdy walking shoes in its shadow.

The tune she was playing seemed vaguely familiar, but Jim couldn't put a name to it. Maybe she was just jazzing it up too much for him to recognize. She leaned against the side of the building, eyes closed, just playing her heart out. There were a couple of bills in the open sax case at her feet, but mostly coins.

He waited until she'd finished the tune, then dropped a couple of bucks' worth of change into the case. Her eyes flicked open at the sound of coin hitting coin. Her gaze tracked up from the case to his face. When she smiled her thanks, her whole face lit up, transforming her from simply an attractive street performer into an oddly ethereal mix of a contemporary woman and a model from some Pre-Raphaelite painting. The look was so naturally disarming that it washed away the past few hours of frustration as though they'd never been. Jim held up his camera.

"Do you mind if I take a couple of shots?"

She shook her head. "You're from out of town—right?"

With her look and sound she probably had all kinds of tourists taking her picture, Jim realized.

"No, I'm local," he told her. "I work for *The Star*. How about you?"

"Working my way to the coast," she told him, "but I ran out of bus fare." She paused a moment, then added, "You want me to be playing for the picture?"

Jim nodded. "If you don't mind. Maybe the editor'll run it on one of the local pages."

She smiled. "Little bit of human interest."

"You've done this before," Jim said. It wasn't a question.

"In pretty well every major city I've busked in since I started across the country. My favorite caption was, 'Cindy Draper, a street musician with sax appeal.' It was my own fault, I guess. I shouldn't have been wearing a tank top that day."

Jim laughed. He took a few shots of her playing through another tune, the motor drive whirring, then another couple when she didn't have the mouthpiece up to her lips, blocking the camera's view of her mouth and chin.

"You're very photogenic," he said when he was done. "The camera likes you."

"That's what they tell me."

Her voice was still warm, but he could tell that she couldn't care less about what the camera thought. Modeling wasn't her scene. She obviously loved her music too much.

"Have you got a place to stay?" he asked, then held up his hands at the wary look that came into her eyes. "I've got a friend—a lady friend—who could probably put you up for a night."

The smile came back. "No, but thanks for the offer." For a moment it looked as though the conversation had ended. She put her fingers on the sax's brass keys, but then instead of playing again, she left the sax hanging from its strap and said, "I think I need a break—I've been at this for a couple of hours now. Do you feel like having a cup of coffee with me?"

"I'd be delighted. My name's Jim," he added and put out his hand. "Jim McGann."

"Cindy Draper." Her grip was firm, her hand soft and smooth.

"It's too nice a day to sit inside," Jim said. "How about we walk over to the park? It's just a few blocks south."

"Sounds great. Just let me pack up my stuff."

She stowed away her earnings and packed up the sax. When she closed the case and hefted it, Jim shouldered her backpack.

"That thing's heavy," she said with a grin. "I should know. You sure you want to be a gentleman and carry it?"

"Hey, I'm committed now."

She laughed. Picking up her shoes, she fell into step with him as they walked south on Palm Street to Fitzhenry Park. On the park side of the street there was a long line of concession carts selling everything from hot dogs and fresh pretzels to breaded deep-fried zucchini and shish kebabs. The air was filled with dozens of savory scents, each vying for attention—as did the vendors themselves.

Jim bought a couple of Danishes and some coffee, then led the way deeper into the park, away from the noisy congregation of skateboarders near the War Memorial.

Cindy settled down on the bench they chose and leaned back, stretching.

"God, it feels great to sit down," she said. "I've been walking around all morning, and then busking for most of the afternoon."

Jim could appreciate the bench as well, having spent the better part of the day on his feet himself, following up on his fruitless quest. He put her backpack down on the pathway by the bench and sat down beside her, handing her a coffee.

"Thanks." She took a sip, then set it down between them on the bench. "So what do you do?" she asked. "Just wander around through the streets and look for neat stuff to take pictures of? And then get paid for it."

Jim shook his head. "I wish. I used to work freelance, but now my editor just hands me assignments."

"Your mission today, should you choose to accept it," she intoned in a passable imitation of the voice-over that began the old *Mission Impossible* TV series, "is to track down buskers and photograph them in performance."

"You remember that show?" Jim asked, thinking she was too young to have been around when it was on the air.

"Caught it in reruns."

"Of course."

She smiled. "And were you really assigned to take pictures of buskers?" she asked.

"Actually, it's my day off."

"So you're slumming."

"I guess you could say that."

"But normally you do—what? Fashion photography?" she asked.

"Not often and only when it's assigned, and even then I don't get to choose the models. But Meg—that's my friend who'd probably put you up—she does. She could probably use you if you wanted to make a little quick cash."

"Yuck."

Jim shrugged. "Your choice. But you'd make more in one day on a fashion shoot with Meg than you probably could in a month of playing music on the street."

"But I *like* busking."

Jim held up his hands defensively, sloshing coffee from the cup in his right. It splattered on the edge of the bench and her foot. She made a little yelping sound as she drew back her foot.

"Jeez, I'm sorry," Jim said.

She rubbed the wet spot on her foot against the leotard-covered calf and gave him a quick smile.

"That's okay. My feet could stand a cleaning. I'm going to stay at the Y tonight so that I can take a shower."

He was, Jim realized as he caught the full warmth of that smile, becoming rather quickly enamored with her expressive features. He wished there was a way to install a camera in his head for situations like this, so that he could take pictures without disrupting the mood. That was the benefit of being an artist, he thought. You lost the immediacy of the moment, but you could just file the shots away in your head and bring them to life on paper or canvas at your leisure.

"You know," she said, "when I first spotted you coming up the street, I didn't think you'd stop to listen."

That she'd even noticed him before he'd talked to her brought a foolish smile to Jim's lips. He felt like a high school kid again.

"Why was that?" he asked.

"You just looked so . . . I don't know. Grim, I guess. Or determined."

Jim nodded. "I guess I was preoccupied. I've been looking for this girl. . . ."

He pulled out Niki's photo and passed it over to her. An unreadable expression came into Cindy's eyes as she looked at the picture.

"What'd she do?" she asked.

"Nothing. That is . . ."

He hesitated, realizing that with all the experience she'd had with newspaper photographers, Cindy wasn't going to buy the artist's release line he'd been using all day. But while he didn't feel like lying to her, he didn't know what to say. As the day had gone by, he'd begun to feel that the whole thing was maybe just too much of a long shot in the first place. And just saying he tracked Niki down, what was he going to say to *her*?

"You don't have to tell me," Cindy said.

"It's not that. It's just that—well, it's going to sound weird."

He explained then how he'd seen Niki at the crime scene last night and then discovered, when he was at Meg's place, that she'd been at every one since the first victim was discovered.

"So," Cindy said when he was done. "You think she's involved in some way?"

"It's possible."

"Why don't you just go to the police?" she asked, echoing what Meg had said last night.

Jim had had some time to think it through more carefully since he'd talked to Meg.

"If Niki's not involved," he explained, "my going to the police is just going to cause her all kinds of trouble. They've been getting nowhere on the case and I've got the feeling they'd jump on anyone they even remotely thought knew something."

Cindy nodded, but didn't reply. She ate half her Danish, drank some more coffee.

He shouldn't have told her, Jim thought. He should just never have brought it up in the first place.

"I told you it was going to sound weird," he said.

Cindy turned to look at him. Her eyes were so blue he found himself wondering if she wore tinted contacts.

"I saw her last night," she said finally. "In . . . what's that place called, all those blocks of deserted tenements up north of . . . is it Gracie Street?"

Jim nodded. "It's called the Tombs, or sometimes Squatland. That's not exactly the safest place in the city."

"Safer than the Combat Zone was last night."

"There's that," he said.

"And I know that scene. There's squats to be found in every big city." She gave him one of her quick smiles, then tapped the photo. "Anyway, I saw her up there last night. She was squatting in the same building I was."

"Can you remember which one?"

"Oh, sure. But her name's not Niki."

SEVEN

Jammin' stayed with her overnight and bought her breakfast next morning at a little diner over on Williamson Street. They got there early and the place was filled with blue-collar workers. Chelsea overheard more than one snide comment as they waited for the waitress to fill their order: Jammin' got it because he was black; she, because of the way she was decked out. Although she was still wearing her jean jacket, she'd changed from her jeans and T-shirt into black stockings that came down to just below her knees, a pleated tartan miniskirt and a frilly white blouse that left her midriff bare. With her spiked hair and the clumpy Doc Martens on her feet, she knew she looked like everything that frightened the other patrons about their own kids.

They were all big, tough-looking guys, but not one of them had the courage to look her in the eye when he spoke. Screw 'em, she thought. She knew their kind all too well. They wore their conformity with smugness, like she was something that had crawled out from under a rock, but they'd still slap down twenty bucks for a quick blow job.

After breakfast, Jammin' asked her to come over to his friend George's place, where the band was going to be rehearsing, but she begged off. She washed up in the diner's claustrophobic and dingy bathroom, then walked as far as the Gracie Street subway stop with Jammin'. Leaving him there, she made her way back down the Pier, where she'd spent most of yesterday morning. She wandered in between the various concession stalls, but there wasn't any action yet. The tourists were still having their own breakfasts, and it'd still be a couple of hours before they made their way down to the lakefront.

She'd made about ten bucks panhandling yesterday before she got distracted by Jammin's band. Looking younger than her actual age, and being just naturally small, she usually did okay, and it sure beat selling her butt on a street corner. Chelsea thought of it as The Little Match Girl Syndrome. People generally seemed to take more pity on what they thought was a young, innocent girl needing a handout.

Yesterday's ten bucks had taken her just under an hour to collect. She only had three dollars left after last night's dinner. She'd have to do better today if she wanted to eat over the weekend. Sunday, for all its being God's day of grace, was usually the pits for cadging spare change from all those good Christian Samaritans.

She bought herself a coffee from the old guy who had the cart right where the Pier began, ignoring his disapproving stare. You don't look so cute yourself in that jerky apron, she wanted to tell him, but she let it be. Digging a newspaper out of a trash can, she found an empty bench overlooking the lake. There she sat, sipping her coffee and reading the account of last night's killing. Morbidly, she stared first at the photo of the crime scene, then beside it at the high school picture they'd run of the victim.

That should have been me, she thought. If Daddy'd had his way, it *would* have been her.

She shivered, feeling scared and depressed, and looked around herself. Was he watching her right now? Hidden around the corner of one of the concession stands, fingering that big knife in his pocket? But all she could see was the first scattering of tourists, a couple of bums, some businessmen.

She dropped the newspaper at her feet. Leaning on her knees, she just stared down at the picture of the girl who'd died last night.

I'm sorry, she thought.

She started as one of the businessmen sat down beside her on the bench. He gave her a smile when she turned to look at him. He was out of shape, carrying at least thirty pounds more than he should for his height. His suit looked like it was in the three-hundred-dollar range, but he didn't wear it well. She figured he was in his forties— heavy-jowled, balding, and tired. He put his briefcase on the ground between his feet.

"Got any spare change?" she asked.

He studied her for a long moment, then cleared his throat nervously.

"How'd you like to make a little real money?" he said.

Oh, gimme a break, she thought. Another upstanding citizen looking for a quick good time with Lolita.

"What did you have in mind?" she asked.

He looked embarrassed. She knew what he wanted—it was sitting there in his eyes and the bulge at his crotch—but he couldn't seem to speak.

"I . . . I thought we could . . ."

She smiled and slid over beside him. Taking his arm, she draped it over her shoulder; then she took his other hand and put it on her breast.

"Something like this?" she asked in a husky voice, slipping her hands under his suit jacket.

She almost laughed at the stunned look on his face.

"H-h-here . . . ?" he stuttered.

That was when she screamed.

"Get away from me! Get away!"

Heads turned to look at them. He still had his arm around her shoulder, a hand on her breast. But now she was pushing at his chest, acting as if she'd just been sitting there, innocent as you please, and he'd tried to molest her. A big guy who had to be a tourist—camera around his neck, wife at his side—stepped forward. Before the tourist could do anything to him, the businessman grabbed his brief-case and fled.

Her rescuer took a few steps after the businessman, but stopped when he saw he wasn't going to be able to catch the fleeing man. His wife sat down on the bench beside Chelsea, who had her hands under her jean jacket, hugging her chest. Like her husband, the woman was wearing sandals, shorts, and a T-shirt. Her dark hair was pulled back into a ponytail, and she was wearing too much perfume.

"Are you all right, honey?" she asked. Her voice had a touch of a Southern drawl.

Chelsea called up a few tears to make her eyes shiny and put a tremor in her voice.

"I . . . I think so," she said.

"Can you believe it?" the husband said as he moved back to join them. "In broad daylight. I tell you this goddamn city—"

"Sidney!" the wife said.

Sidney gave a meek nod. "Sorry." He looked at Chelsea. "How is she?"

"A little scared, that's all—right, hon? Is there anything we can do for you? Can we take you somewhere?"

Chelsea shook her head. "I . . . I'm meeting my boyfriend here. I'll be okay now."

"If you're sure . . . ?"

Chelsea nodded.

"All right then, hon. But you just be careful. There's a lot of not very nice people in this world."

"I'll be careful."

Still looking hesitant, the woman rose from the bench and let her husband lead her farther down the Pier. Chelsea could hear him saying something about if he could've got his hands on that guy . . .

She waited a few moments, then headed for the public washrooms. Once inside a cubicle, she reached into the inner pocket of her jean jacket and pulled out the businessman's wallet. There were sixty-three dollars in it.

Not bad, she thought. That'll teach that old fuck to go chasing after jailbait.

She waited until the washroom was empty, then left the cubicle. Dropping the wallet in a trash bin—the money folded up and securely stowed away between her skin and the elastic of her panties—she went back outside and looked over the beach and lakefront area with a holiday feeling growing in her mind.

It was hard to think of her father with the sun shining so brightly and all those crisp bills stashed away just waiting to be spent. Suddenly everything seemed to have a glow about it.

Maybe it wasn't going to be such a shitty day after all.

EIGHT

Thomas Morningstar was so soundly asleep that he never heard the phone ring. It wasn't until Angie shook him awake that he realized something was up.

"It's Lieutenant Brewer," she said.

For a long moment, Thomas paid no attention to the telephone receiver that Angie was holding out to him. In the Morningstar household, he was usually the first awake, and he always took the time before rising to lean on one elbow and study her sleeping beside him. He'd marvel at how good she looked, even with her auburn hair all disheveled, no makeup on that peaches-and-cream complexion, one rounded shoulder free from the sheets that would cling to the perfect curves of the rest of her form.

She was a bright, attractive woman, just a year younger than he was himself. She made half again as much as he did, working as a researcher in an office filled with good-looking, bright guys, half of whom carried a torch for her. What the hell she saw in him, with the kind of work he did and his hours, he'd never been able to figure out, but he didn't plan to raise any complaints.

He took the receiver from her and muffled the speaker end against his shoulder.

"Did I ever tell you how beautiful you are in the morning?" he asked.

Angie smiled. "Down, boy. Business calls."

Thomas glanced at the bedside clock. The luminous digits read 7:24.

"Yeah, more's the pity," he said.

"I'll put the coffee on," Angie told him.

He nodded his thanks, then turned his attention to the phone.

"Hello, Jacob," he said into the receiver. "What've you got?"

"A Mike Fisher called in to the 12th about ten minutes ago," Brewer replied. "Says he saw something last night."

The name didn't ring a bell for Thomas. "Does he have a sheet?"

"Nope. He's a clean, upstanding member of society who just happened to be passing through the Zone on his way back from work."

Thomas caught the irony in Brewer's voice. He knew just what the lieutenant was thinking. The killing went down around eleven-thirty last night—a little late for this Mike Fisher to be going home from work. Thomas could almost hear how Fisher would start his explanation: He was just passing through, you understand, we won't tell his wife, will we, because he usually didn't go home by that route, or leave so late, but he was putting in some overtime. . . .

Until it went to court, Thomas could live with holding back the details from the press and the man's wife. Hell, at least he'd stepped forward.

"When will you be interviewing him?" he asked.

"He'll be at the 12th for eight-thirty," Brewer replied. "I thought you'd want to be there when we talk to him."

"I appreciate the call."

"Yeah, well, I'll leave you to get hold of Sarrantonio and then I want both of you to get your butts down to the 12th—an hour ago."

"We're on our way," Thomas told him.

Angie came back into the bedroom just as he finished talking to Frank. He cradled the receiver and looked at her with regret. She was wearing a sloppy oversized T-shirt in place of a nightgown, but at that moment he didn't think she'd ever looked as sexy.

"You're going in early?" she asked as she handed him his coffee.

Thomas nodded glumly. "Jacob wants us at the 12th for eight-thirty."

Angie put her own coffee on the night table on her side of the bed and got back in beside him.

"What time's Frank picking you up?" she asked.

Frank had taken the unmarked car home last night, even though they'd only signed it out for the evening. It was one of the perks of working a major case—no one'd say anything about it unless he trashed it.

"Quarter past."

Angie grinned, then pulled her T-shirt up over her head.

"Then we'll just have to be quick this morning," she said.

Michael Richard Fisher, Jr., was about what Thomas had expected him to be. He was a little, weedy guy with a nervous twitch, dressed in an off-the-rack suit that hung sloppily on his thin frame. He worked as a clerk downtown in one of the office complexes on Walker Street—the Allen & Roy Corporation, the last bigwig pulp and paper industry still based in the city. Their mill was east of Newford, on the Dulfer River.

They interviewed him in one of the 12th's interrogation rooms, simply for the privacy. Thomas took notes, leaving Brewer and Frank to do most of the talking. Mostly they just listened as Fisher went through his innocent "just passing through" spiel, interrupting him only for clarification of details. When he got to the point in his story where he was following Leslie Wilson along Lambton, Frank broke in.

"Let me get this straight, Mr. Fisher," he said. "You followed Miss Wilson because you were worried about a young girl like her walking alone in the Zone?"

Fisher's eye twitch went into double time. He cleared his throat.

"Th-that's right," he said.

Frank sighed. "Look. We all know what you were doing down there."

"I—"

"Please. Let me finish, Mr. Fisher. Believe me, we appreciate your coming in to talk to us and we have absolutely no interest in pursuing what you were doing in the Zone beyond how it relates to our case. But you have to understand: If you bullshit us on this, then how are we supposed to believe anything you tell us?"

Fisher looked down at his lap. "She . . . she looked like a prostitute. . . ."

"That's right. She did. And you were looking to conduct some business with a person in her line of work, weren't you?"

Fisher nodded.

"Okay. Did you approach her?"

"No. I . . . I was still working up my . . . you know . . ."

"Your nerve."

Fisher nodded again.

"Okay. So you're following her, walking west on Lambton—about how far behind were you?"

"I don't know. Maybe a block. Just under a block."

"And were you walking more quickly at this point—trying to catch up to her so that you could talk to her, or were you still just following her?"

"Just following her, I guess. I didn't, you know, I didn't know what to say."

"So this was your first time?"

Fisher still had not lifted his gaze from his lap. "I guess. It's . . ." He looked up at Frank, then dropped his gaze again. "I saw the other girls—you know the ones that are standing out on Palm Street—but they just looked, cheap. Like you could catch a disease from them or something."

"But Miss Wilson was different."

Fisher nodded. He looked miserable. Thomas didn't doubt that Fisher had long since regretted stepping forward.

"I didn't know that she wasn't a prostitute then," he said. "She just looked . . . nice."

"Okay," Frank said. "So you're both walking down Lambton, you're trailing maybe a block behind her. What happened then, Mike?"

Thomas smiled to himself. It was good interrogation technique. You started out formal, but then dropped into the familiarity of a first-name basis. You were pals. You were on his side. When it came to the penny-ante perps, it usually made them say or do something stupid. When it came to an interview subject like Fisher here, it put him at his ease.

"Well, I was still trying to figure out what I was going to say to her, when all of a sudden she just stops dead in her tracks and turns to look at this doorway."

The detectives exchanged glances.

"What doorway was this?" Brewer asked.

"I don't know. I never went any further, because that's when—that's when this guy stepped out of the doorway. I'd already ducked into that alley beside the pawnshop, you see, because I thought she'd heard me following her and maybe I was making her nervous."

"Didn't you think," Brewer went on, "that it would have been in her best interest—considering the business she was in—to talk to you?"

Fisher's eye started its double-time twitching again. "I . . . I was just nervous. . . ."

"It's okay, Mike," Frank said, his voice soothing. "So you ducked into this alley beside the pawnshop. What happened then?"

"Well, I . . . I sort of peeked around the corner to see if she was looking my way."

"Was she?"

"No."

"And you were both alone on the street at that point?"

"I guess. I didn't see anyone else. She was standing there, looking at the doorway, and then all of a sudden this guy stepped out and he—he grabbed her by the throat." Fisher's gaze lifted to focus on Frank. "I should've done something then. I should've gone to help her. But I got scared."

"What'd you do then, Mike?"

"I ducked back into the alley and—I was shaking, you know? It was like I knew I should be helping her, but I couldn't move."

"Could you describe the man?" Thomas asked. He had his ball-point poised over the notepad.

Fisher shook his head. "I didn't see much. It was dark—there were a couple of streetlights out."

Frank nodded encouragingly.

"But he was a big guy—fat, I guess. Taller than her by maybe a head, and wide."

"Hair color?"

"It was dark—I mean too dark to see," he added as Thomas began to write down the word "dark" on his pad.

Thomas crossed out the word.

"How was he dressed?" he asked.

"I . . . I'm not sure."

"Okay," Frank said. "So you're in the alleyway. What did you do then?"

"I just sort of stood there, trying to get my courage up."

"And then?" Frank prompted when Fisher fell silent. "What happened then, Mike?"

"I . . . I looked around the corner again and she . . . she was just lying there on the ground. I guess she was dead."

"What happened to the man?"

"I don't know. He didn't come down the street in my direction."

"How did you know the girl was dead?"

"I didn't. I just panicked and ran, I guess."

Frank nodded to Thomas, who pushed the play button of a tape recorder that was sitting on the table.

"There's been a terrible accident," a tinny voice said from the recorder's speaker. "On . . . on Lambton Street, near . . . near the corner of Norton."

"Is that your voice?" Frank asked.

Fisher nodded.

"So you didn't just run—you called in to report what had happened?"

"Well, I couldn't . . . I couldn't just leave her lying there."

Frank nodded. "If everyone could be as conscientious as you've been, Mike, we'd have a hell of a lot better handle on the crimes in this city."

Fisher gave him a grateful look, but studying him, Thomas couldn't help but feel that Fisher hadn't told them everything yet. There was something else lying in the back of his eyes, something that ran deeper than his nervousness.

"Is there anything else you want to tell us about what you saw that night, Mr. Fisher?" he asked.

Fisher's twitch grew more pronounced. "I . . . it's just that I can't seem to get him out of my mind. That man . . . Whenever I think of him, I feel . . . cold, and I can almost feel him . . . I don't know. It's like he's watching me."

"You think the man saw you?" Brewer asked. "That he's following you?"

Fisher shook his head. "It's like he's inside my head . . . whispering. . . ."

The detectives exchanged puzzled glances.

"Okay," Frank said. "Let's just go back. What time did you say it was when you left the office . . . ?"

They took him over his statement a half-dozen times, but came up with no real discrepancies. They all agreed after he was gone that Fisher hadn't told the story as if he'd prepared it, but as if it had happened. But there were still problems with it.

"There was no doorway where we found the body," Thomas said.

Brewer nodded.

"And the ME said the body hadn't been moved," Frank said. "She died where we found her."

"Fisher must have been mistaken," Brewer said. "Probably the perp came up to her from a doorway further up the block."

Thomas shook his head. "There's no entrance from the alleyway where Fisher was hiding all the way to the end of the block. That's the side of the old Lawson Insurance Building. There's a foyer around the block and a back door in the alleyway. The way Fisher tells it, Leslie Wilson stopped and turned to look at the bare wall. If that's the truth, she saw something there."

"Maybe the guy was hiding in the shadows against the wall," Frank tried.

Thomas shook his head. "Think about the crime scene."

The other two men did, then Brewer nodded.

"No shadows," he said. "Not big enough to hide a man. The whole street was dimly lit, but there weren't any shadows."

"I don't think Fisher was lying," Thomas said.

Frank and Brewer nodded in agreement.

"He must have been mistaken," Brewer said. "We'll talk to him again in a day or so. In the meantime, I'm putting a twenty-four-hour surveillance on him while you two start digging. I want to know everything there is to know about Michael Richard Fisher, Jr."

"We'll get right on it," Thomas said. "Anything else?"

Brewer dug out a fresh cigarette and lit up. "Yeah. Jordin over at headquarters told me that Detective Joe Kelsey asked to see the Slasher files this morning and he made copies. I want to know why— but I don't want him knowing that we're looking into it."

That was a job for Internal Affairs, Thomas thought, but he knew better than to question the order. Brewer always had a good reason for what he wanted done—even if you couldn't figure out what it was when he first gave you the order.

"Kelsey," Frank said. "He's working Vice, isn't he?"

Brewer nodded. He scooped up his cigarette package, stuffed it into the side pocket of his jacket and stood up.

"We've got work to do," he said.

As they followed him out of the interrogation room, a uniformed officer took Thomas aside.

"Your wife called," she said.

"Did she want me to return her call?"

The officer shook her head. "She said she was going out, but she wanted to leave the message that your brother called your house soon after you left. He asked her to tell you that you've got a meeting tonight with Jack Whiteduck."

"Whiteduck?" Thomas repeated.

"That's what she said."

"Thanks," Thomas said.

"Who's Jack Whiteduck?" Frank asked.

Thomas turned to him. Brewer had already left, and the two of them had the doorway of the interrogation room to themselves. Only the smell of Brewer's cigarette smoke remained.

"Whiteduck's one of the tribal elders—on the reserve," Thomas explained.

"You look kind of stunned," Frank said. "Is this going to be a new look for you?"

Thomas shook his head. "I just can't figure out why he'd want to see me."

"Why's that?"

"He's a die-hard traditionalist," Thomas said. "He lives way back up in the hills—won't have anything to do with whites or anybody who deals with them. I didn't even know that he knew I existed."

But even as he spoke the words, he knew they weren't true. It wasn't just that he was the eldest son of the reserve's elected chief and so known, at least by sight, to just about everyone on the reserve. He could remember a day . . .

He couldn't have been more than fifteen at the time, playing a pickup game of baseball with his brother and some other kids on the lot behind the reserve's school. He was standing in left field, slapping his fist into the worn leather pocket of his hand-me-down Rawlings glove, waiting for the next batter to step up to the flat stone that

served as their makeshift home plate, when he was suddenly aware
that he was no longer alone.

He turned slowly to find Jack Whiteduck standing not six feet
away from him.

Even then Whiteduck was an old man. His skin was wrinkled, his
braids gray, but he stood straight-backed with not an ounce of fat on
his lean frame. Thomas's father had told him once that Whiteduck
lived alone, up back in that part of the reserve that was as untouched
now as it had been when the Europeans first landed on these shores.
He still ran his own trap lines in winter, fished and hunted in the
summer. He wore clothes he'd made himself: buckskin leggings,
shirt and moccasins, elaborately decorated with beadwork, quills,
and shells. On anyone else, it would have looked as if he were wearing a costume; on Whiteduck it simply appeared natural.

Even as a boy, Thomas had known that when he was old enough,
he'd be leaving the reserve. He simply hadn't told anyone yet. Knowing what his father's reaction would be, he couldn't speak of it, but he
had known. He also knew that to many of the reserve's older residents,
it would appear that he was shirking his responsibilities. Although Big
Dan Morningstar had been elected chief by the tribal council, his position could almost be considered hereditary. A Morningstar had been
chief for as long as anyone on the reserve could remember.

It was tradition. Thomas's neighbors all expected that he would
become chief when his father stepped down from the position. But
Thomas didn't want to be chief. His future wasn't tied to the reserve.
He'd heard how he was to be chief all his life—from his father and
uncles and neighbors—but he was determined to follow his own path
through life, not have it laid out for him.

He had thought that this knowledge was his own secret until that
afternoon when Whiteduck approached him.

"Wabinose," Whiteduck said.

It was Thomas's Kickaha name, the one he had been given at birth. It meant "Walks all night till dawn." Like most people on the reserve, however, Thomas used his Anglo name.

"Hello, *Mico'mis*," he replied.

While others called Whiteduck by his Anglo name, Whiteduck himself never used it. Since Thomas couldn't remember Whiteduck's Kickaha name, he settled for the honorific grandfather, not wishing to antagonize the old man. For all Thomas's need to leave the reserve and his life there behind him, he still respected the beliefs of others. He was not rude, even as a boy.

He waited expectantly for the old man to go on, but Whiteduck simply regarded him steadily for a long while. The baseball game, the lot behind the school, and the other boys on the field with him just seemed to disappear for Thomas. There were only the two of them, standing in a timeless place, locked in a moment that stood outside ordinary reality. To this day, Thomas could remember the power that had seemed to lie there in the old man's dark eyes as Whiteduck studied him, and the odd surreal sensation of being *elsewhere*. The memory of it was what kept him listening when his brother John spoke of the old ways.

"There is a war inside you," Whiteduck said finally. "It pulls your spirit in opposite directions."

He knows, Thomas had realized with panic. He knows that I want to leave. What was he going to *do*?

As though reading his mind, Whiteduck merely shook his head.

"I have known this war myself," he said. "One day you and I will talk of it."

"I . . . I . . ."

Whiteduck didn't smile as Thomas stuttered, but his features softened.

"Not now," he said. "The time will choose itself."

He turned and walked away then. Suddenly Thomas's ears filled with sound again—the cries of the boys on the field, birdcalls from the forest beyond the lot, the sound of a car rattling over the washboard ruts of the dirt road on the far side of the school building. The feeling of disorientation fled like a dream before the morning's light.

Though it felt as if he'd been away with Whiteduck in that other place for at least a half hour, time didn't seem to have passed at all on the lot behind the school. Jimmy Clearwater was still just coming up to bat. The sun hadn't moved at all in the sky. No one appeared to have noticed the old man talking to Thomas out there in left field.

Thomas played badly for the rest of the afternoon. He missed a fly ball that should have been right in his glove, and he struck out twice when his team came up to bat. He knew it wasn't his fault. His brief conversation with the shaman had shaken him, but he didn't speak of it. Even at that age, he didn't make excuses.

He hadn't seen Whiteduck again since that day.

"You figure he's planning to take up on where your dad's lectures leave off?" Frank asked.

Thomas blinked as he returned from that memory. It took him a moment or two to work out what it was that Frank had just said. Partners didn't keep much from each other; Frank knew all about the problems that Thomas had with his father.

"I don't know what he wants," Thomas said.

"But you'll go see him? You don't have to, you know. You've made your choice—nobody's got the right to tell anybody how they should live. That's something everybody's got to decide for themselves."

"It's hard to explain," Thomas said. "It's like having the mayor call you up for a meeting, even though you didn't vote for him, maybe you can't even stand him or his politics. But how can you not go to find out what he wants?"

Frank shrugged. "I guess."

What Thomas didn't add to his explanation was that Whiteduck being one of the reserve's elders wasn't really the big deal. It was the fact that he was the Kickaha's oldest shaman that made him one of the most important figures on the reserve. Not even Thomas's father as elected chief or the head of the militant Warrior's Lodge had as much clout, because everyone respected Jack Whiteduck and listened to what he had to say.

He was their spiritual leader, perhaps their conscience.

"If you want some company on the ride up to the reserve," Frank said, "I've got nothing on tonight."

"I appreciate that," Thomas told him. "But didn't you tell me you finally got a date with Tanya Lederman?"

"Well, yeah. . . ."

"I'll be okay, Frank. I'm due for a visit to the reserve anyway. You just enjoy your date."

"If you're sure."

Thomas nodded. "I'm sure. But thanks."

"Okay. Well, like the Loot said: We've got work to do. What do you want to tackle first? Fisher's background, Kelsey, or the interviews from last night?"

What he wanted and the case's priorities were two different things, Thomas thought.

"The interviews," he said.

Frank sighed. "I was afraid you were going to say that."

NINE

"This is good," Billy Ryan said after skimming through the photocopied police reports of the Slasher case that Joe Kelsey had brought him.

They were sitting at a table in the MacDonald's on Williamson out near the Expressway overpass. Ryan had the remains of a Big Mac and Coke on the table in front of him, a cigarette burning in the ashtray. Kelsey was still nursing his coffee.

The Vice detective was in his early thirties, a clean-shaven, slender man with dark blonde hair pulled back into a small ponytail at the nape of his neck. A small diamond stud glinted in his left earlobe. He was wearing worn jeans, hightops, and a black T-shirt with a dark tan cotton sports jacket over top, the sleeves pushed back over his elbows.

Working clothes, Ryan thought. Mr. Big Shot Undercover Cop.

Kelsey had been a hardworking cop with a solid rep both on the streets and with the department. The trouble was he also had a bad gambling habit, which had put him into Ryan to the tune of twenty-three large. There was no way he could keep up with the payments; but there was no way he'd roll over and put the finger on Ryan, working a little deal with the DA's office.

Working Vice was his life. He liked the contacts, liked the side benefits—free dope, payoffs, the women. He still made his collars, but now he also worked part-time for Ryan, which meant that Mickey's crews didn't get pulled in—at least not when Kelsey was heading the bust. Ryan didn't put a strain on their relationship, but he made sure that Kelsey remembered just what he owed, and who he owed it to.

Ryan straightened the photocopied reports now and returned them to their folder, then took a drag on his cigarette.

"But it's not enough," he added.

Kelsey spread his hands above the table. "That's all they've *got* man."

"You're going to have to dig a little deeper," Ryan told him.

"But—"

"That's the way it's got to play. And keep me up to date on what's going on as things develop. You still hanging out at Huxley's?"

Huxley's was a yuppie bar on Stanton that lay on the southmost edge of the Zone, fronting Fitzhenry Park. It was where the young execs picked up their coke and each other.

Kelsey nodded. "Yeah, I'm there from time to time."

"You get anything new, just drop it off behind the bar with Susie. She'll make sure I get it."

Ryan could see the protest building up in Kelsey—a you're-asking-for-too-much-this-time attitude, like Kelsey was suddenly finding himself a little backbone. His face got hard, his eyes flat. It was a look, Ryan decided, that'd just have the buttheads he usually dealt with shaking in their boots. Kelsey's problem, this time out, was that Ryan wasn't one of those buttheads. He just plain didn't scare.

He returned Kelsey's hard stare with a mild, half-amused look that made Kelsey deflate. Ryan knew just what the Vice cop was thinking: He was locked into their relationship and there was no way out—not without taking himself down as well.

It wasn't like Ryan had forced Kelsey into the situation. The asshole had blown his wad all by himself. Ryan was just there with the solution. He had had the money Kelsey needed when his world was falling apart, and just to cover himself, Ryan also had some insurance on the deal. Anything happened to Ryan at this point in the proceedings, and his lawyer would be releasing the videotape that Ryan had insisted on shooting as they made their deal.

"So what's this all about then?" Kelsey asked.

He wasn't demanding now; he was asking. Ryan appreciated that.

"Here comes the kicker," he said. "You and me, we're working the same side of the fence for a change."

A flicker of annoyance came and went in Kelsey's eyes.

"What the fuck's that supposed to mean?" he asked, but then his gaze lowered to the folder on the table between them. "This guy's hurting business," he said.

Ryan butted out his cigarette. "Mickey's not too happy with him and you know what happens to people Mickey doesn't like."

Kelsey nodded. They disappeared. No corpse, meant no charges could be laid. The perfect crime. That was the way the Irish mob operated.

"Course when we do track this guy down," Ryan added, "maybe we could see that you're there for the finish. The guy's got to die, no way out of that, but seeing how we're doing the boys in blue a favor, Mickey might let you keep the body and bring it in. You could be a hero."

Ryan watched as a look of calculation settled on Kelsey's features. If he brought in the Slasher, he'd be thinking, it could mean a promotion. A promotion meant a bigger salary. A bigger salary meant he'd be able to pay Ryan off that much sooner.

Ryan smiled. Kelsey might read it as a promise, a you-scratch-my-back-and-I'll-scratch-yours smile between partners. But all Ryan was thinking was that if that dumb fuck thought he was ever getting out of this relationship, he wasn't just a crooked cop, but a stupid one as well.

He shook another cigarette free from his pack and tapped it against the folder.

"This Fisher guy Brewer was planning to talk to today," he asked. "He's clean?"

Kelsey nodded. "All that came up when we ran his sheet was a couple of parking violations. He paid them both."

"And he's not connected?"

Ryan knew that the Italians still had their fingers in the Allen & Roy Corporation for which Fisher worked. And if it was possible that Papa Jo-el was using the Slasher to send Mickey a message, then who was to say it wasn't the wops? Sure, it wasn't their style, but one thing you had to give them, they were adaptable.

Kelsey shrugged. "Who knows? But do you think he'd come forward if he was in their pocket?"

"There's that," Ryan said, making no commitment one way or the other. "I guess I'll just have to talk to Fisher myself."

"Jesus," Kelsey began. "Don't—"

"Do something crazy?" Ryan smiled. "I'm always covered, Joe. Remember that. How about you?"

"The Slasher's working my turf. Vice's got more investigations running in the Zone than you've got operations. Anybody asks, I'm just doing my duty—looking for connections, trying to help out the overworked guys already on the case."

"Just keep yourself covered," Ryan said.

He rose from the table, cigarette dangling from his lip, and picked up the folder.

"And remember, Joe," he said before he left. "I don't like surprises."

TEN

"Now she's more your type," Meg said as Cindy retired to the bathroom to take a shower.

Jim smiled. "I didn't know I had a type."

"Everybody's got certain types they go for; the trouble is we don't usually end up with the right ones. Instead we tend to just repeat our old mistakes—over and over again."

Regret lay in her voice, but she tempered it with her own smile. Meg had never been one to brood.

"And Cindy—" Jim began.

"Isn't a repeat of Susan, God forbid."

Jim laughed. "I think you're jumping the gun a little."

"Am I?"

Jim wasn't sure. He hoped not, but then he didn't know what he was looking for right now. He wasn't even sure he was ready for another relationship, not this soon after the way the one with Susan had blown up. But whenever he looked at or even thought about Cindy, he found himself filling up with a warm glow that made him feel like he was seventeen years old again and trying to work up the courage to ask Jane O'Neill, the heartbreaker of grade twelve, Redding High, class of '76, for a date.

He never had gone on a date with Jane O'Neill, but this afternoon in the park, asking Cindy out for dinner had come out as just a natural part of the conversation's flow. He'd found himself holding his breath, until she'd smiled and said, sure. Why not?

"But I'll have to go over to the Y and get cleaned up," she'd added, "because I'm not going to a restaurant looking like this."

"You look great."

"Right." She tugged at a lock of her hair, her lips shaping a moue. "Scruffy chic."

"No, really."

"I still want to take a shower."

"Well, then why don't you do it at Meg's?"

"Oh, I don't think that'd be such a great idea. I don't even know the poor woman, and I'm supposed to just pop in to use her shower?"

Her protest was still genuine, but Jim could tell she was weakening.

"You'll really like her," he said.

Cindy shook her head and gave him a rueful grin. "You never give up, do you?"

"Not a chance."

Cindy regarded him with a long, penetrating look.

"So is she as nice as you?" she asked finally.

Be still my heart, Jim thought.

"Nicer," he assured her.

Which was how they had found themselves over at Meg's apartment an hour or so later. After a moment or two of awkwardness at the front door during introductions, they were soon sitting out on Meg's balcony, drinking wine and chatting as though they'd all been friends for years.

"You're sure you don't want to come along tonight?" Jim asked Meg now as he rose from his chair. He wanted to shower and change himself, but he had to go back to his own apartment to do so.

"Three's company and all that," Meg said, then added as Jim started to protest, "besides, I still have work to do."

On the way home Jim stopped off at the paper to develop the film he'd shot of Cindy that afternoon. After he'd run off a contact sheet, he chose a couple of the best shots and blew them up, then took them over to Grant's desk.

Ben Grant was a balding, heavyset man who looked like an ex-linebacker. He was *The Star*'s chief photographer and Jim's immediate supervisor. Unlike many of the photographers Jim knew, Grant's real passion was repairing old lenses and cameras; he had a workshop at home that would rival the best camera repair shop in the city. Jim never ceased to be amazed at how delicately Grant's big, clumsy-looking fingers could work the finest details on a repair job.

Those fingers took the photos from Jim's hands. Grant gave them a quick, appreciative glance.

"Very nice. She a friend of yours?"

"I'm working on it."

"She looks like she's worth it."

"So what do you think?" Jim asked. "Can you use any of them? I like this one the best."

He pointed out a profile shot where Cindy was leaning into a long note, eyes closed, back curved downward. You could almost hear the sax.

Ben nodded. "I'd've picked the same. We'll run it on the cover of the Living section for tomorrow's paper. Have you got any copy for one of the hotshot terminalists to write up?"

Jim handed him a piece of paper with Cindy's name and a few details about how she was supporting herself by busking on her cross-country trip.

"I know you're off this weekend," Grant went on, "but I need someone to cover a concert over at the Oxford tonight. Interested?"

"Sorry, Ben. I've got a date."

Grant looked down at the photo again.

"It's not what you're thinking," Jim said. "She didn't even know I was bringing this by."

"Yeah. Right."

The amusement in Grant's eyes reminded Jim too much of the rumors of how Lance Friedman, over at *The Weekend Sun*, had got some of his "Page Three" girls to pose for him.

"Seriously," Jim began. "It's not—"

Grant held up a hand. "It was a joke."

"And such a funny one."

"Get out of here, McGann," Grant growled, but the good humor remained in his eyes. "And have yourself a good time."

Jim had made reservations at a restaurant called Shooters in Lower Crowsea's Market area. He left his car parked at Meg's apartment, and they took the streetcar down Lee Street, since he knew he wouldn't find a parking place in the Market on a Saturday night. Cindy loved the streetcar. It was one of two lines that still remained running in the city, left over from the old days when they were pulled by horses; the other ran east-west on McKennit. The metal wheels rattled on the old tracks, and the car swung back and forth with a gentle rocking motion at each stop and start. Cindy wore a big grin the whole way down the twelve-block ride from Meg's apartment.

He'd picked Shooters because it was one of the few places in town that played jazz as background music, so he thought Cindy'd like it.

The place was a little trendy, but then the whole Market had become so over the past decade. There was a lot of wood in the furnishings, fine art prints on the walls, waiters and waitresses who introduced themselves by their first names when they took your order.

The hostess showed them to a table by the window and asked if they wanted anything to drink before their meal. Cindy ordered a glass of the house white; Jim decided to try the dark ale that they had on tap that day.

"This place is great," Cindy said after their drinks had come.

"Yeah. I thought you'd like the music."

She nodded. The Duke Ellington Orchestra was playing softly over the house sound system, and her fingers were tapping out the rhythm on the tabletop.

"I love the tunes from this era," she said. "The Duke, Goodman, all those guys. I can get into playing fusion, but I don't much listen to it."

The waitress—"Hi, my name's Jenny"—came by to take their order. They both ordered seafood: deep-fried shrimp to start with, then pasta with a clam sauce. Cindy stuck to her wine, but Jim switched to a light bottled ale.

The food was terrific, but the company, Jim thought, was infinitely better. After all the hard times he'd gone through with Susan, and then the self-imposed period of celibacy that had followed the breakup, when he just couldn't face the idea of trying to deal with any kind of romantic entanglement, he'd forgotten just how intoxicating the opening moves in a relationship could be.

For he could see this growing into a relationship. God knew, long before the end of the meal, he was head over heels. He wasn't sure how Cindy felt, but she was sending back all the right signals. In the back of his mind, he knew that she was just passing through town. She could leave tomorrow morning. But somehow, at this moment, that possibility was too undefined, too distant and vague, to be of any immediate concern.

What he liked best about being with her was how relaxed he felt. There was no pressure to put on a good show; he could just be himself. It was the same easy feeling he had when he was hanging out with Meg, except, unlike the friendship he had with Meg, the relaxed interaction with Cindy was underlaid by the barely contained fire and spark of an intense sexual attraction.

It wasn't that he found Meg unattractive. It was just that because of how their relationship had worked out, he thought of her more as a sister.

Cindy seemed anything but.

When she reached across the table to make a point and touched his hand, heat from her fingers raced up his arm, fanning the heat that had already gathered in the base of his spine. When she flicked back her hair, his gaze locked on the smooth white skin of her throat; he could almost see her pulse quickening there, just as his own was. And when he looked in her eyes, he just got lost in their flickering light-blue depths.

Down, boy, he told himself, tearing his gaze away. A moment longer and he'd be climbing over the table.

He looked out the window, hoping something could distract him long enough to allow him at least to regulate his breathing, but what he saw only served to fuel a different kind of fire. Niki was walking by.

"That's her!" he cried.

Cindy turned to look, but he was already out of his seat, hurrying for the door.

"Be right back," he told the surprised hostess as he tried to make his way through the crowd of waiting patrons as quickly as possible without jostling anyone.

It seemed to take him forever to get out onto the street, but she was still there. He couldn't remember the name that Cindy had told him earlier in the afternoon. All that came to mind was the scrawled letters beside the red lips of the graffiti he'd come to associate with her.

"Niki," he cried.

The girl turned toward him, and all the color in her already pale features seemed just to wash away. She gave him a look of such utter terror that it stopped him dead in midstep, frozen where he stood, confusion rearing in his mind.

What the hell's she so scared of? he thought.

She took advantage of his momentary hesitation and bolted. Before he could think to follow her, she was already around a corner and gone. He started in pursuit, but then knew he just had to let her go.

Something about him had frightened her and he found he couldn't deal with that. He'd never had anybody scared of him before in his life. And she hadn't just been frightened—she'd been terrified.

What the *hell* was going on here?

Before he could pursue that train of thought, he became aware of how Niki's flight and his own present confusion had attracted attention from the other pedestrians on the sidewalk. People were regarding him a little oddly, questions in their eyes that he didn't even have answers to himself. Feeling uncomfortable, he retreated back into Shooters. His mind was still all muddy and numb as he made his way back to the table. When he returned to his seat, he found Cindy regarding him with a kind of wariness in her eyes.

"What—?" she began.

"I don't know what—" he said at the same time.

They both fell silent.

Talk about screwing up a perfect evening, Jim thought. Je-*sus*. Two minutes ago they'd been lost in each other, but now there was a wall up between them.

Thanks a lot, kid, he thought to Niki.

"All I did was call her name," he said.

"She looked terrified."

Jim nodded. "You're telling me. I've never *seen* anybody look that scared before."

"And you . . . ?"

"I swear, Cindy. I never saw her before except for from a distance, taking her picture at those crime scenes. And I've never spoken to her until just now—if you can call that talking to somebody."

He felt like shit. He wished he'd never seen Niki last night, never taken her picture, never gotten this crazy idea that she could be involved with the Slasher—not if it meant that chasing Niki down had screwed up whatever had been starting with Cindy. If he'd never seen Niki, never made that crazy connection with her and the graffiti . . .

But he had. Something in the way she'd looked through the viewfinder of his Canon, and later out of the photos that he and Meg had taken, had haunted him. And still did. And something haunted her as well.

What had she *seen* when he'd called her name?

"You can't imagine what it's like to have someone look at you like that," he said.

His voice was so soft it was almost as though he were speaking to himself. He couldn't suppress the shiver that spidered up his spine.

Cindy regarded him for a long moment; then her eyes warmed, and she laid her hand on his where it rested on the tabletop.

"I'm sorry," she said. "But the way she looked at you—she was so scared. It was like she was seeing a ghost."

Jim nodded slowly. He played the scene back in his mind yet again, but this time with a photographer's eye, focusing on any details he might have missed before.

"I don't think she even *saw* me," he said finally.

"What do you mean?"

"She was looking at me, but she saw someone—some*thing* else."
He tapped his hands against his chest. "I mean, look at me. Do I look
that scary to you?"

Cindy shook her head.

"That girl's up to her neck in trouble," Jim said then. "Don't ask
me how I know it; I just do."

"I think maybe you're right."

Jim sunk back in his chair and sighed. "God, everything was just
going great." He met her gaze. "I was having a really good time."

"Me, too."

"And now it's all changed. There's this edge to everything."

"There doesn't have to be," Cindy said. "Let's get our bill and go
back to Meg's place. She said she was going to be out until around
eleven so we'll have the place to ourselves."

There was no come on in her voice, and for that—oddly enough,
considering how he'd been feeling about her earlier—Jim was grateful. He wanted to be with her, wanted the comfort of her company,
but he didn't want to complicate their relationship beyond that for
the moment. Not while he could still feel Niki's gaze fixed on him,
the terror in her eyes.

What had she *seen*?

He thought of what Cindy had said earlier.

It was like she was seeing a ghost. . . .

Jim didn't believe in that kind of thing. Ghosts were just a way that
some stupid people dealt with their dull lives. At least that was how it
seemed from his only point of reference—the supermarket tabloids.
He didn't think Niki was stupid. She hadn't seen a ghost, but she *had*
seen something that terrified her. He also got the feeling that she was
all on her own, facing whatever it was that scared her.

Nobody, he thought, should face that kind of terror on their own.

"Jim?" Cindy said.

He focused on her and remembered what she'd said about going back to Meg's.

"Sounds good to me," he said, trying to keep his tone of voice light, even though right then he felt anything but lighthearted.

ELEVEN

The money she'd ripped off from the horny businessman who had accosted her by the Pier was burning a hole in Chelsea's mind, but she didn't know what to do with it. There was no point in getting a decent meal since she was still full from the breakfast that Jammin' had bought her earlier. She could always get some new clothes, she supposed, but she didn't really need more stuff to lug around in her backpack, and if she got anything exceptional, it'd just get ripped off. A squat wasn't exactly the best place to leave lying around anything that you really cared about.

She wouldn't have minded getting together with Jammin', but all she knew was that he was rehearsing with his band at this George guy's place. She'd made plans to join Jammin' at the club where The Jah Men were playing tonight, but that wasn't until nine or so. Until then she had no idea how to go about finding him.

Nothing to do and nowhere to go. It was the story of her life.

The good feeling that had come from pulling one over on the smarmy lecher back at the Pier slipped away as she roamed aimlessly through the streets of Newford's downtown core. She wandered into Gypsy Records on Williamson Street and spent a while flipping through the records and CDs, but that just ended up making her feel more depressed.

She didn't have a sound system, not even a Walkman, to play anything on. She supposed she could pick up a cheap machine at a Radio Shack or some discount store with the money she had in her pocket, but the damn things fed on batteries, and while she had the cash to buy them now, it'd be gone quickly enough. It was hard enough to scrounge up eating money some days; who needed the hassle of trying to feed a Walkman as well? Besides, tapes cost money, too, and the player would just get ripped off anyway, so what was the point?

She tried to strike up a conversation with one of the girls working in the store who looked pretty cool, but it was just too busy to get much past asking what the record was that was blasting from the store's sound system.

"It's the first Divinyls album," the girl said, but before she could go on, some little kid interrupted to ask where they kept their cassette singles; then on her way back to where Chelsea was standing, someone else stopped her to return a defect.

While the girl was dealing with that, Chelsea wandered out of the store. The loud music combined with the push and bustle in the crowded aisles had started to get on her nerves. Outside, the sidewalk was crowded as well, so she finally retreated back to the lakefront, after first cutting over to a less crowded street.

She found herself a relatively deserted spot under the Pier and just sat there with her legs splayed out on the sand in front of her. If it hadn't been the weekend, she might have gone to see about registering for school—it'd be starting up in just a couple of weeks and she had to get moving on it—but she didn't have anything together yet. She needed a place to stay; she needed to get some kind of deal together with welfare. And then there was this crap with her old man. . . .

Just thinking about him gave her the creeps. She could see the face of last night's victim again, staring up at her from her high school photo in the newspaper—a look of accusation in her eyes.

I didn't do it, Chelsea thought. It wasn't my fault.

Suddenly, under the cries of the kids running around on the beach, the people talking and moving around on the Pier above her, she could hear the faint icy murmur of his voice, calling her.

You can't hide from Daddy. . . .

His voice seemed stronger than ever today, dark and cold like the midnight wind that had carried it to her where she'd been huddling in her squat last night. Goosebumps lifted on her arms, though the day was warm.

Shivering, she tried to put him out of her mind.

Think about what you're going to tell the welfare worker on Monday, she told herself.

Like she could do anything, with him prowling through the city, looking for her.

She should just run. Maybe he'd follow, but maybe he wouldn't. Maybe if she moved quickly enough, she could get far enough away that the cold chill of his voice couldn't find her.

She thought about the money she'd ripped off from that guy this morning, wondering how far it would take her and how far she had to go. Then she found herself wondering why the guy had been wandering around in a three-piece suit with his briefcase on a Saturday morning.

You have to ask? she thought.

He'd have told his wife that he had to work a little overtime, when all he was really working on was how he could get himself a little bit of underage tail, because the little girls made him feel so good. Just like little girls and boys made Daddy feel so good.

She could feel tears press up behind her eyes.

Jesus, she told herself. Just leave it. Just—

"Hey, pretty girl," a stranger's voice said.

She started and almost bolted before she realized that it wasn't her father, or some jerk like the guy she'd ripped off, but just a kid who'd come up on her so quietly. The sand had muffled the sounds of his footsteps as he'd approached.

The guy sat down on his ankles in front of her, rocking a little bit, to and fro, as though his body was moving to some music that only it could hear. He was probably older than he looked, she thought, as she looked more closely at him—maybe in his early twenties—but he was still just a skinny little black guy in baggy, brightly colored shorts, an armless T-shirt, hightops, and shades. His hair stood straight up in tight black curls on top while the sides of his head were shaved to just stubble about two inches above each ear.

"What's doing?" she asked.

She didn't particularly want to hang out with him, but talking to anybody just about now was better than being by herself.

"You want to buy some goods?" he asked. "I've got weed, I've got crack. Whatever you need, Jimmy's got it."

She was tempted. It was a way to cut through the blues. But it wouldn't last. All the crap in her life would still be there waiting for her when she came down, except it'd be just that much harder to deal with it.

"I'll pass," she said.

"You don't know what you're missing."

She knew exactly what she was missing, Chelsea thought.

"I said, I'll pass," she told him, irritation creeping into her voice.

"What, you don't think my shit's good enough for you?"

"Why don't you take a hike?"

"It's a public beach, girl. I want to hang out right here, nobody can tell me shit."

Chelsea sighed. She got to her feet and started to leave, but the guy caught her by the arm.

"Hey, why're you so uptight?" he asked. "I got just the thing to make you feel good. All it's gonna cost you is—"

She didn't let him finish. She just moved in close and brought her knee up into his groin. Hard. His shades shot off as he jerked his head with the sudden pain. She saw his eyes go wide, his features tighten in shock. She gave him a shove, and he toppled over onto the sand, hands cupped around his groin. She stepped forward and drew back her foot to give him a kick with the toe of her big Doc Martens, but then realized that the fight had already gone out of him.

Shaking her head, she let him lie there and walked away.

"You fucking bitch!" he shouted once she'd got a few yards away from him.

Her hand went to her purse, fingers curling around the handle of her switchblade, but when she turned around, she saw that he was still kneeling there in the sand, not making a move. It was hurt pride talking. Macho shit. His eyes looked scared.

"What a crappy day this is turning out to be," she muttered as she continued on down the beach.

It didn't get much better. She stayed at loose ends for the whole day, just wandering through the city. She found if she kept moving, the cold whisper of her father's voice couldn't seem to find her.

When the night finally started to crawl closer, she had a big, expensive meal in one of the trendy restaurants just north of McKennit. The food tasted like sawdust and she left it mostly uneaten. Her father's voice found her again, but the noise of the restaurant—the sound system with its yuppie music and all the happy little jerks who sat around her laughing and talking and mooning into each other's eyes—made it possible for her to, if not ignore, at least deal with it.

Nursing a coffee, she pretended she belonged in this place. She watched the clock behind the bar as its hands snailed toward eight-thirty. When they finally reached the magic half-hour mark, she paid her bill and followed Lee Street up through the Market.

All she wanted to do was be with Jammin'. He was the only person she knew in the city who—

An image of her father's face swelled in her mind. The wind called her name and woke goosebumps up her arms. She shivered and wrapped her arms tightly around herself.

She was suddenly aware of just how alone she was. Though there were crowds all around her, she could disappear into a crack in the sidewalk and no one'd know or even care. Except maybe for Jammin', and he'd probably forget her in a day or so anyway.

Only one person wanted her—*really* wanted her.

Look what Daddy's got for you, the wind whispered. Or maybe it was only a memory.

But he was going to find her, she realized now. He was going to find her, and this time he wasn't going to pull down the zipper of his pants. This time he was going to drag that big knife out of his pocket, the one he was using to kill all those girls. This time—

A man suddenly stepped out of the door of the restaurant she was walking beside. He looked right at her, seemed to recognize her, but she'd never seen him before in her life. Then he called out to her and everything went black inside.

"Niki!"

Panic flooded her.

Niki, Niki, Niki. . . . the midnight wind echoed.

That's not my name, she wanted to scream. Not anymore. I'm not her, I'm not her, I'm not her. . . .

But it was no use denying it. The whispering voice of the wind laughed in her head.

Nikinikiniki. . . .

The wind knew it was true. And the man who'd called out to her . . .

He'd stopped dead in his tracks, turned immobile by she didn't know what. Maybe he heard the wind that she thought was only in her head. Maybe he'd realized his mistake: He didn't know her; her name wasn't Niki.

Because it *wasn't*—not anymore.

She didn't care what had stopped him. She just stole the frozen moment and fled into the night. Running, running. Away from him. Away from the sibilant whispering of the midnight wind that carried her father's voice.

Pain stitched her side and her breath changed to a jagged rasp. People stared at her as she ran by, but no one tried to stop her. No one tried to follow.

Only the wind. Only the voice that wouldn't get out of her head.

Nikinikiniki. . . .

All she wanted to do was hide. The night was big. Surely she could find some place where he couldn't find her, where she wouldn't be able to hear that awful sound anymore.

But while she might be able to outrun a physical presence, there didn't seem to be any escape from the voice that had taken up residence in her head and was gnawing away at her courage.

Just give up, it told her. Let's get it over with.

Look what Daddy's got for you. . . .

"Fuck . . . you . . . ," she cried.

Tears streamed from her eyes, and still she ran, on and on into the endless night, until suddenly the voice was gone.

She stumbled at the mouth of an alleyway, utterly disoriented and lost, and fell sprawling onto a small mound of green garbage bags. The sweet-sour smell of the refuse seemed to coat her lungs as she sucked in badly needed air, but she didn't even have enough strength to roll over and away from it.

She lay there, panting, tears burning in her eyes, until finally her mind-numbing fatigue caught her in a grip that was too strong to break. She wouldn't have thought it possible, but she couldn't stop herself from slipping away into an exhausted sleep.

TWELVE

Frank Sarrantonio took a left off McKennit, heading north on Lambton until they reached the alleyway in which Mike Fisher said he'd hidden last night while the Slasher was taking down his fourth victim. He brought the unmarked police car to a stop and leaned a little over where Thomas was sitting in the passenger's seat, to get a better view of the alley. Neither man said anything until Frank began to inch the car farther up the street.

Thomas laid a hand on his arm. "I want to walk it," he said.

Frank put the car into park, then shut off the engine. A moment later he had joined Thomas on the sidewalk. The two men gave the alleyway a cursory glance, then slowly made their way up the street. They paused at the bloodstains enclosed by a chalk outline that were all that remained of last night's investigation, then continued on to the end of the block.

Thomas looked back the way they'd come. There was no way a man

could have run from the end of the block, back to where the murder
had been committed, in the time frame that Fisher had given them.

"It's just like we remembered it," Frank said as they started back.
"No doorways."

Thomas nodded. "And no windows low enough for him to have
dropped down onto the Wilson girl."

The only windows were enclosed in steel mesh and began, on this
side of the street, on the building's second floor, a good eighteen feet
above the street.

"No fire escapes either," Frank added.

Thomas nodded again.

"So," Frank said. "Either we've got a perp who can fly, or maybe
walk through walls—or Fisher's lying to us. I know where my vote's
going."

"Or he was just mistaken," Thomas said. "It's not as though a man
like Fisher would be used to this kind of situation."

"I suppose."

"And he did come forward. He didn't have to."

"Okay," Frank said. "But still."

"We'll be talking to him again," Thomas said as he headed back to
the car. "You can push him a little harder then—see what comes up."

The Lone Wop and Tonto, Billy Ryan thought as he watched the
Buick carrying the two plainclothes detectives pull away from the
curb. He was familiar with both of them, seeing how the better part
of his business took place in their precinct. They'd been after his ass
on more than one occasion and still had some investigations pending
that could mean trouble if the wrong person talked.

He slouched lower in his seat as the car passed him.

No imagination, he thought. That was their real problem. No
imagination and too goddamn squeaky clean. If there was anything

Ryan didn't like—and especially distrusted—it was clean cops. There was something not quite normal about them.

He watched their Buick in the rearview mirror until it turned the corner; then he straightened up in his seat once more.

He'd wanted to check out the scene, thinking the cops would be long finished with it by now. If Tonto and his pal had come a moment later, they'd have found him out on the pavement, poking around just like they'd been doing. He was just as happy they hadn't spotted him. He had nothing to hide—Christ he was alibied up to his ass for last night—but it still would have meant a session downtown, and he didn't have either the time or energy for that kind of crap. Not with Mickey on his ass.

He lit up a cigarette and tossed the match out the window.

So the cops were taking Fisher seriously. Maybe it was time he did, too.

He started up his Camaro and made a U-turn, aiming the car northward to the suburbs where Fisher lived.

There was a message from the medical examiner's office waiting for the detectives when they got back to the 12th. Thomas returned the call while Frank went to see about getting some coffee.

"The pathologist still wants to do some more on the body," Jennifer Wilkes told him when his call was put through, "but we've already got some data that might help you."

"We appreciate the call," Thomas said.

He could feel the ME's ironic smile through the phone line. "Right. Like the Commissioner's office hasn't been on our ass since the moment the body was delivered to us."

"You know what I mean."

"I guess you're feeling the pressure, too."

"Uncomfortably so," Thomas told Wilkes. "So what've you got?"

"Your perp's very strong."

"We knew that."

"Uh-huh. But maybe we weren't considering just how strong. This time around, the victim would have died even if the perp hadn't stabbed her."

"Meaning?"

"He broke her windpipe. Crushed it. Completely."

Thomas tried to think of the strength that would take.

"Just by grabbing her?" he asked.

"That's right. In the previous cases, we assumed he took his victims by the throat just long enough to hold them immobile while he used the knife. But now . . ." Wilkes cleared her throat. "The thing is, Morningstar, he seems to be getting stronger with each attack. Not just more brutal, but actually physically stronger."

"How can you tell?"

"Once I noticed where the data on the Wilson girl was leading, I went back and looked over the previous cases. What I found isn't something you'd necessarily spot unless you were looking for it, but if you go through them, case by case, you'll find that the bruises on the victims' throats become progressively more pronounced. The state of the entry wounds in their abdomens also indicates a marked increase in the force he's using to kill them."

"He's getting rougher, is that what you're saying?"

Wilkes hesitated. "That's one way of putting it. I . . . The amount of strength required for these wounds is beyond anything I've run across before, Morningstar. What we're dealing with here is a very strong, probably psychotic individual."

Thomas zeroed in on the slight emphasis she'd put on the word "psychotic."

"What makes you say psychotic?" he asked. "Given, the guy's crazy to be doing what he's doing, but it sounds to me like you're saying something else."

"Between you and me, Morningstar," Wilkes said, "what I'm seeing here is the same kind of abnormal strength that occurs in cases of extreme duress and stress. You've heard of women lifting cars to rescue their children, that kind of thing?"

"Sure."

"We're talking that kind of strength."

Before Thomas could reply, she said good-bye and cut the connection.

"What was all that about?" Frank asked as Thomas cradled the receiver.

He'd returned with their coffees about two-thirds of the way through the conversation.

"More of that stuff you don't like," Thomas said. Then he filled Frank in on what the medical examiner had told him.

"Jesus," Frank said. "This is all just Twilight Zone crap. I mean, really. You're not buying any of it, are you?"

Thomas smiled. "I'm just passing on what *I* was told, Frank."

"Yeah, but—"

The phone rang, cutting him off. Thomas picked it up.

"Detective Morningstar," he said into the phone. "Sure, put him through." He cupped the phone's speaker for a moment and mouthed "Papa Jo-el" to Frank before returning his attention to the call.

"I swear," Frank muttered as he got up and crossed over to his own desk. "They ought to start filming *Loony Toons* in here."

"What can I do for you now, Mr. Pilione?" Thomas asked after the switchboard had connected him to his caller.

"We have to talk," Papa Jo-el replied.

"I'm listening."

There was a pause, then Papa Jo-el asked, "Are you recording this conversation?" Before Thomas could reply that he wasn't, Papa Jo-el went on. "No. I see that you aren't. Very well. I'd prefer talking to you in person, *mon cher*, but this will have to do."

Thomas wondered how he'd known they weren't recording the call. Just a lucky guess, he decided. Something to add to the hoodoo mystique.

"What was it that you wanted to tell me?" he asked.

"I have done some research on your problem," Papa Jo-el replied. "Consulted with the *loa*, if you understand."

An interesting way to rationalize being an informer, Thomas thought. Just passing on the info from his gods.

He nodded to Frank to pick up the phone.

"Ah," Papa Jo-el said. "I see that Detective Sarrantonio is now on the line as well. Good afternoon, Detective."

Frank raised his eyebrows. Thomas shook his head. Not now. But he had to admit the *houngan* was starting to give him the creeps. Maybe he'd heard a click when the other receiver was picked up, but how could he have known it was Frank? Lucky guesses only went so far.

He turned his attention back to the phone.

"You were saying," he prompted.

"This *baka* you seek—it is much stronger than I had considered it to be when first we spoke. My research has shown me that soon it will walk on nights other than its death night."

Frank caught Thomas's gaze and made a circular motion with his index finger in the area of his temple. Thomas shrugged.

"What exactly does that mean?" he asked Papa Jo-el.

"A death night is the anniversary of when a spirit's mortal body has died," Papa Jo-el explained. "The *baka* you seek must have died on a Friday, so that is the night on which it can begin its return journey."

FROM A WHISPER TO A SCREAM   119

"This isn't really explaining very—"

"The spirit focuses on some aspect of its former life, *mon cher*—a place, an event, or a person. It uses that focus as a—what we call a *barriere*, an entrance way, a crossroads between the worlds. The *barriere* allows it to return to our world. Blood gives the spirit strength, and the one you seek has drunk deeply. Soon it will no longer be bound to its death night; instead it will walk any night of the week. Given enough blood and it will remain in this world forever, never needing to journey back and forth between *Zilet en Bas de l'Eau* and our world."

"Zill-ate what?" Frank asked.

"*Zilet en Bas de l'Eau*—the island below the sea where the spirits of the dead live."

Neither detective spoke then. Thomas wasn't sure what Frank was thinking at that moment, but in his own mind, the ME's words echoed in an eerie counterpoint to what Papa Jo-el was telling them.

He seems to be getting stronger with each attack. Not just more brutal, but actually physically stronger.

"Why?" Thomas finally asked. "Why does this happen?"

"Why do spirits ever return, *mon cher*? They are either summoned, or they have unfinished business with the land of the living."

Again Thomas fell silent.

"You don't believe me, do you, *mon cher*?"

"What do you think?" Thomas replied. "You have to admit it all sounds pretty farfetched."

"I think you would do well to consider what I have told you, rather than simply dismissing it."

"Right," Frank said, breaking in. "You're some hotshot mumbo-jumbo man who's helping us out just because you've got such a big heart."

"When innocents die, all men must help as they can," Papa Jo-el said.

"Bullshit," Frank told him. "Let me tell you what kind of philanthropist you are: You're the kind of guy who sells crack to little kids in a schoolyard. That's how far your caring for 'innocents' goes."

"To children," Papa Jo-el agreed. "To whomever will buy. But they are white children." Thomas knew that what was said next was directed to him: "And is that not justice of a kind? Think about it, *mon cher*."

And then he hung up.

Frank slammed down the phone. "Can you *believe* this guy? Next thing you know, he'll be calling us back and offering to exorcise our evil fucking spirit—for a price, of course. You ask me, he's behind this shit."

"Think of the size of the man," Thomas said as he cradled his own receiver.

"Okay, so he's just a little cockroach. But *you* think of the size of some of those guys he's got working for him. I've seen bears with less beef on them. And this crap about only feeding his shit to white kids—like his dealing dope's some kind of a political statement. I wish to Christ we'd had a tape running."

Thomas nodded. He let Frank rant on a little more; then he directed their attention back to the paperwork that seemed, with this case, to double itself every time they looked away from it. But he found it hard to concentrate.

Two phone calls. One based on scientific methodology, the other from what Frank called the Twilight Zone. But they were both passing along what amounted to the same message: What they were dealing with was an impossibly strong individual, one who was growing stronger with each kill.

An uneasy feeling started up in him and wouldn't go away. He didn't believe what Papa Jo-el had told them, but he was finding it increasingly hard simply to dismiss it as well.

Billy Ryan pulled his red Camaro up in front of the address of the house that, according to the photocopied files Kelsey had given him, belonged to Mike Fisher. He took in the well-manicured yard and garden that fronted the house. Some toys lay in an abandoned scatter on the wide driveway, along with a bright yellow tricycle. The house itself was an aluminum-sided bungalow with a concrete foundation and a two-car garage. The garage door was open, and he could see only one car inside—one of those station wagons with fake wood paneling on the doors. He didn't know they still made those things. The other half of the garage looked like it had been converted into a workshop area.

Getting out of his car, Ryan took the time to light up another cigarette, then sauntered across the lawn and rang the bell that was lit up beside the front door. The woman who answered wasn't exactly a plain Jane, but she wasn't going to win any beauty contests either. She might have once, but she'd let herself go. The result gave her a kind of plump motherly appearance—the way Ryan remembered the mothers had looked when he was growing up in the Rosses, before they all felt like they had to get careers.

"Yes?" she asked.

Ryan tossed the cigarette onto the lawn behind him and worked up a pleasant smile. With his choirboy looks, it wasn't hard.

"Hi. Is Mike home?"

"He's just around back. I'll go—"

Ryan let his smile widen. "Don't let me interrupt you. I can go around back myself."

He tipped a finger against his brow before she could reply and made his way around the house to find Fisher playing ball with his kid in the backyard. They made a perfect picture: father playing catch with his five-year-old son on a Saturday afternoon. Ryan felt like puking.

Jesus, he thought. With a scene like this, no wonder Fisher had to go out and get himself some hot young piece of ass in the Zone from time to time. He had to do *something* to liven up his life.

Fisher glanced up at his approach, a nervous look on his face.

"Hey, how're you doing?" Ryan said as he approached.

"Excuse me," Fisher began, "but do I know you?"

"Not exactly. But I'm hoping we can get to be pals." He smiled. "Why don't you send the kid inside?"

Fisher blinked nervously, then gave his son a pat on the behind.

"Go inside and see Mommy," he told the boy.

When he turned back to Ryan, he tried to bring a little sternness to his features. It didn't work. He still looked like a weedy little accountant.

"Are you from the police department?" he asked. When Ryan didn't answer straightaway, he went on, "Because I told the detectives there all I know. And you said my involvement wouldn't become public knowledge. What am I supposed to tell my wife?"

"How the fuck should I know?" Ryan asked. "Tell her I'm selling raffle tickets."

Fisher's nervous twitch went into overtime. "You . . . you're not from the police."

"Bingo."

"You . . . Who are you? What do you want with me?"

"Nothing to burn your nuts over," Ryan told him. "I've just got a few questions."

Fisher stood up straighter. "You can't just—"

Ryan stepped in close and prodded him in the chest with a stiff finger. Fisher's eyes went wide and got a scared look.

"I . . ."

"You know a guy called Capelli?" Ryan asked. "You ever do any work for him?"

Louie Capelli was the wiseguys' connection with the Allen & Roy Corporation. He didn't work there. He only showed up on paydays to collect the "paychecks" of the men the wiseguys had decided were on the Allen & Roy payroll if the company wanted to stay in business. It was an old scam, one that Mickey's boys ran as well wherever they could.

Fisher was shaking his head. "I . . . I've never heard of him."

"See, the way I see it," Ryan went on, "is there's a lot of wops who'd be real happy to see a certain established and well-respected member of the Newford business community have himself some cash-flow problems—you understand what I'm saying?"

Fisher shook his head.

"And I figure a guy like you, who's maybe helping them out by pointing fingers away from what they're up to, could stand to make himself a little quick spending money. Grateful guys tend to throw around the cash—am I right?"

"I don't know what—"

"Right." Ryan stopped to light a cigarette. "You don't know a thing."

"It's true, I never heard of—"

"So tell me," Ryan said. "What's this shit you're throwing out to the cops about this big fucker just appearing out of nowhere to kill that broad last night?"

Perspiration covered Fisher's face with a wet sheen. His twitch just wouldn't let up.

"It's true," he said, almost pleading. "One minute there was nobody there and then the . . . the next, there he was. K-killing her."

"Like he stepped out of the wall?"

"I don't *know* where he came from. I swear I don't. And I don't know this man you're asking me about either. Please believe me."

Actually, although he wasn't about to let on, Ryan did believe the little weed. Even Capelli couldn't be stupid enough to be using him. Fisher couldn't lie if his life depended on it.

Ryan took a drag of his cigarette and shrugged.

"I'm going to dig a little deeper," he said, "see just how connected you are. You better hope I don't find anything."

"You won't. I swear."

"And you better not go running to the man about my coming here, because I know where you live—understand?"

Fisher's scared look was verging on terror now. "I . . . I don't even know *who* you are."

Ryan gave one of his beatific smiles. "So let's just keep it that way. Thanks for your time, Mikey-boy."

Fisher was almost visibly wilting with relief as Ryan turned and headed back out to his car.

Okay, Ryan thought as he got in behind the wheel. Maybe there's no connection with the wiseguys. He looked at the Fisher house and tapped the steering wheel, thinking. That only left Papa Jo-el.

Dealing with Papa Jo-el was going to play a little harder, but Ryan didn't foresee any real problems. The only real problem would come up if Papa Jo-el *wasn't* involved, because that meant the killings had nothing to do with Mickey's business. It'd just be some psycho running around, getting his jollies. But that wasn't going to stop Mickey from wanting him to deal with it.

A psycho, he thought. Great.

How the fuck was he supposed to deal with *that*?

The rest of the day seemed to drag on forever, until it was finally time that the detectives could call it quits. Frank left to keep his date while Thomas went home to eat and change into jeans and a checkered flannel shirt. Angie wasn't in when he got back. Reading between the lines of the note she'd left, he knew that she wasn't all that pleased with his going off to the reserve when they'd already had so little time together this past month.

He crumpled the note in his fist and tossed it into the garbage, but by the time he sat down to write her a response, the momentary anger had fled.

It wasn't his fault that he had no time left, but it wasn't hers either. Under normal circumstances, he would simply have foregone the trip to the reserve tonight and spent the time with Angie. She deserved it, and God knew, he missed her as much as she was missing him. But he felt he had no choice. Distanced though he was from the concerns of the reserve, it was still hard for him to ignore a summons from Jack Whiteduck.

Past the outriding suburbs that had grown to encircle Newford in ever-thickening clusters over the years, it was another half hour's drive up Highway 14 to reach the reserve. Thomas was tired when he set out from home, tired and irritated and more than a little frustrated. The Slasher case loomed constantly on his mind. Living with it day in and day out as he had for over a month now was steadily taking its toll.

He couldn't blame Angie for feeling the way she did. The case was crawling in between them—the first time something like this had happened in the year and a half that they'd been married. His hours weren't always great at the best of times, but they'd always worked around them and made plenty of time for just the two of them. The Slasher case wasn't allowing them that luxury.

He frowned as he drove, deep furrows wrinkling in his brow. But as the landscape slowly changed around him—from the crowded city streets to blocks of industrial warehouses, factories, shopping malls, fast-food outlets, the suburbs and finally farmland—he felt the tension begin to ease from his shoulders, his brow smoothing. Once he crossed under the Interstate and headed up into the hills that backed onto the reserve, it was as though a great weight had been lifted from him.

Life on the reserve hadn't been what he wanted, but he still loved the land. Every time he left the city behind, following the curves of Highway 14 as it wound through the granite-backed hills heavy with pine, cedar and hardwoods, was like being reborn. By the time he reached the dirt turnoff that led into the reserve, he was a different man: relaxed, alive, *awake*.

His brother was waiting for him in the parking lot that stood between the Longhouse and the general store. John Morningstar was a tall, dark-skinned man. His face was broad, his long black hair pulled back into a single braid that hung almost to his belt. He wore a sweatband with an eagle's feather in it, hanging low over his right ear, and was dressed in fatigues, flat-heeled boots, a plain white T-shirt, and a bush jacket. He had a hunting knife strapped to his belt; a rifle sat on the rack in the cab of his pickup, behind the seat.

He walked over to Thomas's car, offering his hand once Thomas was standing on the pavement beside him.

"It's good to see you, Tom. Been a while."

"Too long," Thomas replied, clasping his brother's hand. He looked around. "Where's Whiteduck?"

John smiled. "Back in the bush. I'll drive you out to where he's staying."

"Thanks. Do you have any idea what he wants?"

"I think I should leave that for him to explain. A word of advice, though."

Thomas's eyebrows rose questioningly.

"Don't call him Jack Whiteduck. The name he uses is the one he was given when he was born, not the one the white men gave him in school. Call him Naganggabo, or Grandfather."

Naganggabo, Thomas thought. It meant "man leading" in Kickaha.

"I'll remember," he said.

John filled him in on the local news as they followed a road that was just two dirt ruts, with undergrowth pushing against the pickup on either side.

"I didn't tell *Niga* you were coming," he said at one point. "I wasn't sure if you'd have time to come by the house when we're done."

"I appreciate that."

Thomas had hoped to get by to see their mother before he drove back to the city, but he wasn't sure how long this meeting with Whiteduck was going to take. And since he had to get in early tomorrow morning . . .

"How's she doing anyway?" he asked.

John smiled. "Talks about you all the time. She clips out the articles every time you're mentioned in the paper with that big case you're working on. Keeps them in a big folder and shows them to all the aunts when they come by."

Thomas laughed.

They drove on in silence for a while, until what passed for a road finally died out. John shut off the engine and the lights. The only sound for a long time was the tick of the engine cooling. Finally John turned to look at Thomas.

"Do you ever miss the reserve?" he asked.

Thomas nodded. "Every time I come back. But—you know how it is."

"Yeah," John said. There was regret in his voice. "I guess I do."

He opened his door and stepped outside, waited for Thomas to join him.

"It's not far now. *Mico'mis* is camping at that place where we used to take Linda and Gabrielle."

"Jesus," Thomas said, as he followed John into the bush. "I haven't thought of them in years. How're they doing?"

"Did you know Linda got married to that friend of Paul's?"

"Yeah, I think you told me about that."

"Well, she's still living with him, over on the east side of the reserve. They got three kids now."

"And Gabrielle?"

When he replied, John's voice was flat. "She's teaching up north on an Algonquin reserve near Maniwaki."

"What's wrong with that?" Thomas asked.

"We need teachers here, too."

Like if you were going to be a cop, why not join the Tribal Police? Thomas thought.

He and John had only argued about Thomas's decision once. Unlike their father, John was willing to respect the choice that Thomas had made—or rather that he had made it. It didn't mean he agreed. Like the other activists, John believed in keeping the band's resources on the reserve. They both knew that further discussion was a fruitless endeavor if they wanted to keep their friendship. John, at least, realized the importance of family ties, even if their father didn't.

Their conversation lagged as they continued on to their old tryst-ing spot. Thomas found old memories stirring as they finally reached the place.

A campfire burned near the overhang of granite that sheltered the little glade. The same little stream ran nearby, hurrying on its way to join the Kickaha River. The trees were mostly pine here—tall giant white spruce. To one side of the overhang, where they'd spread their blankets in the old days, a small sweat lodge had been built—it was a simple affair, just saplings woven together and covered with hides. Between it and the fire, shadows playing across his features, Jack Whiteduck was waiting for them.

No, Thomas corrected himself. Naganggabo.

The old shaman didn't seem any different from that time Thomas had seen him on the playing field behind the school all those years ago. He still wore his buckskins with their quill and beadwork designs. His hair was perhaps a little grayer, though that might only have been the light. He didn't appear to have aged at all.

John and Thomas sat cross-legged on the other side of the fire from Whiteduck. For a long while no one spoke. Whiteduck looked into the fire. His gaze didn't appear to be focused on the burning wood so much as on something that lay much more deeply hidden within the flames. Finally he looked up.

"Wabinose," he said, using Thomas's Kickaha name by way of greeting.

Thomas nodded respectfully. "Hello, *Mico'mis*," he said.

"Thank you for coming."

Thomas made no reply, only waited.

"Do you remember when we spoke before?" Whiteduck asked.

"Behind the school," Thomas said.

Whiteduck nodded. "I told you then that I knew the war that was waging inside you—do you remember that as well?"

"I do."

"I went to the white man's school once," Whiteduck said then. "I went to the white man's college. I graduated and lived in the white man's world, thinking I was a white man, but I was always searching for something—a thing that would fill a hole I felt inside me. For all my years in the white man's world, what I finally learned was that this"—his arm moved to encompass the dark forest that surrounded them—"is my place. So I set all I had aside and became a student once more. But this time I studied not the white man's books, but the way of the Kickaha.

"My teacher's name was Tabobandung—He Who Sees Far."

Thomas thought he could see where this was leading to now. Frank had been right.

"I'm sorry, *Mico'mis*," he said, "but I'm not coming back to the reserve."

"That is your choice."

Thomas frowned. "We're not here so that you can try to talk me into it?"

Whiteduck shook his head. "We are here to discuss the chieftainship of the band."

"I don't understand."

"We are a people who hold to tradition," Whiteduck said. "A Morningstar has always been our chief."

Thomas shot his brother a glance. "You never said anything about Dad being—"

"There's nothing wrong with *Nos*," John told him.

Whiteduck nodded in agreement. "Times are changing. Your father was a good band chief in his time, but we need a leader today who can make decisions quickly. A man who isn't afraid of offending the white man should the betterment of the band lie in such a direction."

Thomas looked at his brother again. "Someone from the Warrior Lodge," he said.

"Exactly," Whiteduck said.

Thomas shook his head. "I don't understand what this has got to do with me. I thought the aunts picked who would be elected."

Tribal politics weren't quite governed by democratic principles. Candidates for positions of office could only be elected after the Council of Elders had given the individual in question their stamp of approval.

"It's true that the elder mothers make such decisions," Whiteduck said, "but they have still been known to listen to advice given by an old man such as myself."

Whiteduck grinned as he spoke, teeth flashing white in the firelight.

"I still don't understand what it's got to do with me," Thomas said.

"After *Nos*," John said, "you're the eldest male Morningstar."

Now Thomas understood. Both he and John were older than any of their cousins.

"I won't interfere," he said, "if that's what's worrying you. I made my choice years ago."

"Men change their minds," Whiteduck said. "I did—once I learned to see the truth."

Thomas shook his head. "Even if I was to come back to the reserve, I still wouldn't want to be chief. That's probably one of the things that made me leave, the way everybody just assumed that I was going to take over from Dad." He glanced at his brother. "I'd be proud to know that my brother's the band chief."

Though, he had to admit to himself, it gave him cause for worry. The Warrior Lodge was always pressing for more immediate solutions to the problems the band had with the white government. Something Whiteduck had said earlier returned to mind. The band needed . . .

. . . *a man who isn't afraid of offending the white man should the betterment of the band lie in such a direction.*

Jesus, he hoped they weren't planning something crazy.

"You would have made a good chief," Whiteduck said to him.

"Thank you," Thomas said. I think, he added to himself. He turned his attention back to his brother. "What does Dad think of this?"

"He's been wanting to step down for some time," John replied. "He was holding off because he kept hoping that you'd . . ." Rather than finishing the sentence, he just shrugged.

There were things that Thomas could say in response to that. It wasn't his fault that his heart lay elsewhere. He hadn't asked to be the oldest son. He had his own life to lead.

But he kept silent. It had all been said before.

"Thank you for indulging an old man and coming so far out of your way to speak with me," Whiteduck said, breaking the silence.

Thomas smiled. Humility didn't suit Whiteduck, but then Thomas caught the fire in the shaman's eyes and realized that the old man was just being polite. He was also indicating that their meeting was over, but Thomas wasn't ready to go. It surprised him that he even wanted to bring this up in front of John, considering how it was one of the main sources of contention between them, but he realized that he'd never have a better opportunity than the present moment to ask what he wanted to ask now.

"Before I go," he said, "I was wondering, *Mico'mis*, if you could help me with something that's troubling me."

Whiteduck nodded for him to continue.

Thomas cleared his throat. He glanced once at his brother, then fixed his attention on the old man sitting across the fire from him.

"I was wondering," he said. "Do you believe in evil spirits—not as analogies for the evil deeds of which people are capable, but as real things with an existence in their own right?"

The shaman's features sharpened with interest.

"Yes," he said. "I do."

"But—"

"You must understand," Whiteduck went on. "You can carve yourself out a piece of the day and call it your own, but no one owns the dark. It has always been so. The night belongs to the *windigo*—do you know what I mean by this term?"

Thomas nodded. A white man might think of the *windigo* only as the monstrous cannibal said to haunt the forests; Whiteduck was using it to refer to all evil spirits.

"We are people of the day," Whiteduck went on. "A council such as we hold now is rarely held after dusk."

"So evil spirits exist."

"Both evil and good," Whiteduck agreed. "The evil are, unfortunately, usually stronger."

"And ghosts?"

"There are two kinds of spirits who walk back to us from death," Whiteduck said. "The very good and the very evil. It's hard to be very

good, which is why we have so few of such spirits. It's not at all difficult to be evil."

"But what brings them back?" Thomas asked. "Why do the evil
spirits return?"

"Either they have been summoned, or they have unfinished business in the land of the living," Whiteduck replied, echoing what Papa
Jo-el had told Thomas over the phone that afternoon.

None of them spoke for a time then. Thomas took a breath. The
way the darkness pressed toward them from beyond the fire and the
deep silence of the forest, combined with the way Whiteduck dis-
cussed such things so matter-of-factly, had a pronounced effect on
him. Here, now, it was easy to believe. . . .

Finally he cleared his throat and asked, "How do you send them
back?"

"If such a thing were summoned," Whiteduck said, "the one who
called it forth must send it back. But if it returned of its own
accord—then first it must complete its business. When its business is
done, it will leave the land of the living by its own free will."

"But you can't force it?"

Whiteduck shrugged. "You can try. But unless its business is complete, it will only return once again. All creatures—even the spirits of
the dead—are bound to their wheels. The best advice I could give in
such a situation would be to stay out of its way."

Stay out of its way, Thomas thought as he and John drove back to the
parking lot where he'd left his car. Right. I'd love to stay out of its way.

Unfortunately, that wasn't an option.

Growing in him all afternoon, he realized, was a kind of intuition.
Jennifer Wilkes, the medical examiner, had felt it, too. He could
sense it in how uncomfortable her voice sounded as she described
how the Slasher appeared to be growing stronger.

They were both feeling the same thing: Something bad was head-ing their way, like a storm of violence. He could almost taste its com-ing. And if it *did* have a supernatural origin . . . then how the hell was he supposed to stop it?

"What was all that about?" John asked as he pulled the pickup in beside Thomas's car.

"All what?" Thomas replied, but he knew what his brother was referring to.

"All this shit about evil spirits. I know how much you believe in them, Tom, so what gives? Were you just having some fun at White-duck's expense?"

"I wish."

John gave him a concerned look. "Something's happening, isn't it? Something bad?"

"I don't know. I don't even know if it's real. It's just that you learn pretty quickly in my business that there's no such thing as coinci-dence. Things connect *because* they're connected, not because they just happen to be in proximity to each other."

"What are you talking about, Tom?"

So Thomas told him. About the dead end he had on the Slasher case, about what their witness had to say, about Papa Jo-el's call and the autopsy findings.

"I'm sure there's a reasonable explanation for it all," he said as he finished up, "but I can't shake this gut feeling that I've got to take all of this hoodoo seriously."

"You'd better," John said. "You don't fuck around with that kind of an evil spirit."

Thomas's "Aw, c'mon" died in his throat. *He'd* brought this up, after all.

"And you watch your step," John went on. "That spirit's going to sense you're messing around in its business and when it does, it'll be coming after you. That's the way it works."

"What do you mean?"

"It's here for a reason," his brother explained. "Spirits are very single-minded. It's heading in one direction, aiming for who the hell knows what, and God help whatever gets in its way."

Thomas could only shake his head.

"I know I brought this up," he said, "but think about what you're saying. Listen to us. We're talking about this kind of thing as though it's real, but it doesn't fit in the real world. If it did, we'd be hearing about it all the time."

"We do," John said. "It just comes to us from what are basically bullshit sources like supermarket tabloids where it gets tangled up in a lot of other hysteria. But you do hear about it."

Thomas opened his door. "I'll think about it some," he said as he stepped out.

John waited until he'd come around the side of the cab to where his car was parked.

"You be careful," he said then.

"I will."

"And if you need help, call me."

Thomas regarded his brother for a long moment, then slowly nodded.

"I'll do that," he said. "Thanks, John."

As he drove home, Thomas thought about what Frank would have to say about all of this and realized he'd better not tell his partner. Not until he had something more concrete. Hell, he wasn't sure he believed in any of it himself. And until he did—

He'd just tell Frank later.

But the bad feeling that had started up after Papa Jo-el's call this afternoon had just been fueled to a higher flame by his conversations with Whiteduck and his brother, and he found himself wondering if there'd even be a later for him to tell Frank.

THIRTEEN

It was a cool night, for which Jim McGann was grateful. By the time he left Meg's apartment, he needed to clear his head. He and Cindy hadn't recaptured that momentary physical intensity that had crackled between them just before he'd spotted Niki outside Shooters earlier in the evening, but they had shared a growing sense of intimacy all the same.

They sat outside on the apartment's small balcony overlooking Lee Street, sipping coffee and enjoying each other's company without the necessity for conversation. An album by the Irish composer Enya was playing on Meg's stereo inside. From the open window behind them, the soft wash of keyboards and multitracked voices slipped out of the apartment to eddy about them on the balcony, counterpointing their introspective mood. When Jim left a little later, Cindy stopped him in the doorway and gave him a long, lingering kiss before she closed the apartment door.

He paused outside the building to lean against its brick face. Jesus, he thought, savoring the cool air on his face. What a night.

He'd never met a woman like Cindy before. She was about a half-dozen years younger than he was—which was true of most of the women he'd dated or had relationships with, but unlike them, she was so together. So *there*. And when he was with her, enclosed in the aura of her attention, she gave him the feeling that no one else existed for her. It was an odd sensation, but definitely not an unpleasant one.

All they'd done in the end was share a good-night kiss, but he felt closer to her, after knowing her for just these few short hours, than he did to people he'd known for months. He didn't think he could have handled more than that one kiss. Not yet. Not tonight.

He knew he was grinning foolishly, but he didn't care. God, he felt good. It had been a perfect night. Just perfect except—

A pale white face flashed in his mind.

Except for that incident with Niki.

His grin faltered, then slipped away. Remembering the look of terror on her face, he couldn't suppress a shiver. He pushed away from the wall and walked briskly to his car, but once recalled, Niki wasn't so easy to leave behind.

He got into the car and started it up, then left it in neutral, the engine idling. He turned the heater on low to take away the sudden chill that had settled over him.

That look, he thought, remembering Niki's fear. What the hell had she *seen* when she looked at him?

It was as if she'd looked on death. As if she'd just recognized the Slasher and realized she was next up for the knife.

Okay, he told himself. Let's not get carried away.

He started to review what he knew of her. First off, her name wasn't Niki; it was Chelsea. Cindy said she hung out up around the

Tombs, squatting in the deserted buildings there along with who knew how many other runaway kids and homeless people.

Those two bits of information didn't exactly illuminate the situation.

That *look* in her eyes . . .

He took a breath, let it out slowly.

What else did he have? She was connected to the Slasher. How, he didn't know, but her terror and the way she'd been drawn to the crime scenes had to mean something.

Maybe she knew who the Slasher was?

That was possible. It didn't explain her fear when she'd seen him, when he'd called out to her. Niki. The name from the graffiti. She hadn't said a thing when he used it, but her panic had been real. And her fear. So the name meant something to her.

He worried at it for a while longer before finally putting the car into first and pulling away from Meg's building. But instead of heading for home, he drove north, toward the Tombs.

Billy Ryan had patience—he had it in spades. When you rushed into a situation, all you did was make mistakes. In his business, mistakes could be fatal. And all it took was one.

So after his little visit with Mike Fisher, he drove back to the Harbour Ritz, where he went to his room and slept through the rest of the afternoon and well into the evening. He had a feeling sleep was going to be at a premium tonight. When he got up, he showered and shaved, then ordered in a late dinner from room service. He didn't leave the hotel until the clubs were starting to close.

He drove out to Upper Foxville and pulled up across the street from The Good Serpent Club just as things were winding down inside. Staying in the car, he watched the last patrons leave. He waited until the staff left and all the lights in the club went off; then he waited some more, until the only lights in the building came from

Papa Jo-el's offices, up there on the second floor. He was just about to get out of the car and cross over when a door opened near the entrance to the club and his quarry stepped out onto the pavement, flanked by a pair of tall, broad-shouldered bodyguards that, with Papa Jo-el's diminutive size, looked like a pair of giants.

They do grow those niggers big, he thought.

He slid lower in his seat so that they wouldn't spot him. He wasn't looking for a confrontation—just a little discussion. If he stepped out of the car right now, could be one or the other of those big black hardcases might get the wrong impression.

He waited for them to get into their own vehicle, but they just walked down the block, Papa Jo-el in the middle, carrying a little black bag, the bodyguards flanking him on either side. Ryan reached under his seat and pulled out the .38 Special that was stowed there. When the three men got to the end of the block, he disengaged his interior light, then got out of the car. Clipping the .38's small holster to the back of his belt, he set off in pursuit, maintaining a discreet distance.

He wondered about that bag Papa Jo-el was carrying.

Could be a payoff, he thought. A little installment of blood money for victim number four, brought down in Mickey's turf.

The way things were working out, Ryan was quite prepared to put off his discussion with Papa Jo-el—maybe indefinitely. What he learned tonight might well make the whole need to talk debatable.

Right place, right time, he thought. Mrs. Ryan's oldest son always did have Lady Luck looking out for him.

All we look upon is illusion, Papa Jo-el had thought as he waited for the night to grow still. He sat in his office, listening to the music that came up through the floor from the club below, watched the lights of the cars going by on the street outside as they reflected on the walls of his office. The flickering play of light and dark only seemed to add to his introspective mood.

Illusion.

This world held a hidden world where the *loa* dwelt. What we saw here was only what they wished us to see.

Illusions.

And what was the illusion that made up the Friday Slasher? Papa Jo-el wondered. What was the truth that hid behind the killings?

The killer was not his responsibility. He knew that. But he also knew that if he dealt with the Slasher—finally, irrevocably, sending its restless spirit back to *Zilet en Bas de l'Eau*—his influence in this city would become a thing that could be physically weighed and measured, not merely in monetary profit, but in the power that his name would hold.

That power would be an illusion—for it belonged to the *loa*—but they would allow him his use of it. The *loa* required their rites and the respect of their priests and *mambos* and followers. Profits in the physical world, monetary or the widening of one's personal influence, were for the strong man to hold, did he but have the courage to grasp them.

It was different here from how it had been in New Orleans. There he had been but one *houngan* among many, his influence small, his congregants few and of no true importance. He soon saw that the power he sought would take too long to amass there, with all the grand shows that the other priests could present before the people.

Papa Jo-el had a true gift; he was *bocor*—magician—as well as priest, but that gift was not enough to lift him quickly through the ranks of the other *houngan*. Better to leave, he had realized. Better to go to another city, where the competition was not so severe. Better to come to Newford, where there was but one *voudoun* church, its priest old.

Clarvius Jones had not been pleased with Papa Jo-el's arrival, less so when he came to understand how Papa Jo-el mixed racketeering with his priestly duties. But there had been little Jones could do, for unlike Papa Jo-el, he was not a *bocor* as well as a priest. The two *houngan* had quickly come to an understanding that they would share the believers of Newford. The people would decide which of the two they would follow.

Jones's congregation was still large, but that was changing. With what Papa Jo-el meant to accomplish tonight, it would change even more. And his success would make his influence felt beyond the sphere of religion. It would be felt in the criminal community. It would be felt in the halls of justice.

All illusion, of course. All part and parcel of this world. But sweet, nevertheless—and profitable.

So he waited for the night to still—for the nightclubs to close, for the streets to empty, for the arrival of that time of the night that belonged to the spirit world. In the heart of its darkness, he would deal with this restless spirit that fed on the blood of young prostitutes whose hair gleamed like honey in the streetlights of the Zone.

Below him, the music from the club finally stilled. Some time later Marcel and Jean Etienne came to him in his office, where he waited.

"Ah, *mes cheres*," he said. "Is it time?"

Neither of his bodyguards responded; the question was merely rhetorical.

They went outside, out into the night already filled with the murmurs and stirrings of restless spirits. Papa Jo-el could feel them all around, he was so attuned to the spirit world at that moment. He left more worldly concerns to his bodyguards, the Etienne brothers. They had their own finely tuned senses, focused on the physical world and the possibility of a threat arising from one of the many less-than-reputable competitors of Papa Jo-el's business dealings, but they never noticed the man who slipped from the red Camaro at the end of the block and shadowed them as they walked the dark streets on either side of their employer.

Like any native of Newford, Jim knew that you didn't park in the Tombs, day or night. By the time you got back to your car—even if you'd been gone for no more than a few minutes—everything of value would have been stripped from it: hubcaps, wheels, stereo, doors, engine parts. So he parked a few blocks south of Gracie Street, in the middle of a long row of tenements between a '67 Caddy and a Toyota, and hiked back to where the blight of no-man's-land began. He brought his Canon and the 300mm telephoto, along with a collapsible monopod, all of it stashed away in a nondescript canvas bag so as to preclude tempting the denizens of the Tombs.

It wasn't all that great an idea to go walking around in here at night, either. Jim knew that as well, but he didn't feel as though he had any choice. He was driven by the image of Niki's—*Chelsea's*, he corrected himself—face. Something had scared her badly, and he was determined to find out what, even if it meant daring the Tombs at night. She was in here, somewhere, hiding from God knew what. But he was going to find her. He was going to help her. He was going to chase that terror from her face because no one, especially not a kid, deserved to live with such fear.

He paused when he reached Gracie Street and looked across to where the Tombs began.

Though a funereal quiet hung over the dark streets of the rest of the city at this time of night, you always knew that life went on under the cover of darkness. People slept in the buildings, looked after their apartments and postage-stamp yards, parked their cars alongside the curb. There was order, even if it slumbered. There was hope.

The Tombs wasn't like that. Jim had been in there before at night and knew what to expect. Even by day, the place had a desperate air of neglect and desolation about it. Jim could remember what it had been like before half the buildings were razed and, when the developers' money ran out, the street people claimed it for their own. It had always been a slum—for as long as Jim had known it—but now it held a deeper darkness at its heart.

Despair and hopelessness walked hand in hand through its rubble-strewn streets, for all the blissful smiles of the junkies and the parties of the runaways and bikers who made it their home. It was a land of the lost, block upon squalid tumbledown block stolen from the city and changed into a nightmare country where only the despairing and hopeless lived. The laughter and music that spilled from the run-aways' squats always seemed too bright, too brittle. The very air held a kind of need, like a junkie who'd waited too long between fixes.

Jim hated the place. He'd signed God knew how many petitions to have it cleaned up.

"And then where will they live?" Meg had asked him once.

They were standing in line at a checkout counter in a Chinese gro-cery over on Flood Street. Meg had refused to sign the petition.

"What are you talking about?" Jim said. "They'll go back to wher-ever they came from. There's government agencies to look after peo-ple like that."

Meg simply shook her head. "It's too late for them to go back," she said. "For most of them, there's no place to go back to."

Jim sighed, remembering. Meg was right. At least here they had shelter of a kind, their own rules to live by. And company, he supposed.

He squared his shoulders and was about to cross the street when movement a block or so down on his right caused him to step back into the shadowed doorway behind him. He watched as three figures crossed Gracie Street at a diagonal, heading for the Tombs. His eyes widened slightly when he recognized the small black man who walked in between his two enormous companions.

Jim wasn't particularly superstitious, but there was something about the little voodoo priest that gave him the creeps. He'd gone along with Mary Harper to take photos for a feature she was doing for *The Star* on the man's church. Papa Jo-el Pilione had been polite and helpful—even when Mary asked him about his alleged ties to the drug trade and loansharking operations—but looking through his lens at the man, Jim had gotten the feeling that there were snakes crawling around inside his head—hundreds of snakes that fed on the poverty of his congregation and those victimized by his racketeering. They looked back out through his eyes with a thousand hungry gazes.

When he and Mary left the man's offices above The Good Serpent, he felt as though he needed a shower. Souping his negatives later at the paper, and running off some contact sheets, those snake eyes still peered out at him from behind Pilione's bland gaze. He knew from Mary's article that one of *voudoun*'s deities was the serpent god Damballah—from which Pilione's club had gotten its name, he supposed—but when he thought of the man, the serpent that came to his mind was the snake from the Garden of Eden. The one that fed on strife. It was its little cousins he saw in the priest's eyes.

What was Pilione doing here? Jim wondered, but he knew the answer even before he asked himself the question:

Something to do with voodoo.

Not real magic, or anything like that. But something to fuel the hold he had over his congregation. Something else that had come out of Mary's research was the rivalry between Pilione and the more established church headed by an older priest named Clarvius Jones. The only reason Jim could see someone like Pilione in the Tombs at night was profit of some kind, and since he was too high up to be dealing on the street, the profit motivation had to be connected to his church.

Jim hadn't been working for the paper long enough to completely lose the drive that had made him such a successful freelancer. Part of that drive was born of an insatiable curiosity. He couldn't help wanting to know what was going on when something puzzled him. And then there was that competitive need to be first with the best shots, to get the scoop on the rest of the paparazzi, with whom he jostled for placement of his photos.

The same intuitive streak that had gained him any number of stunning on-the-spot shots told him that whatever was happening in the Tombs tonight with a voodoo priest was going to be news-worthy.

He waited until the trio had entered the Tombs before he slipped across the street to follow them.

Papa Jo-el needed to be outside tonight and he needed the city's streets, but he wasn't such a fool to think he could do what must be done where a chance cab or patrol car might happen upon him, con-ducting a ritual in the middle of a cross-street. So he chose a deserted part of the Tombs; a graveyard of buildings seemed a most appropri-ate place for the calling up of the dead.

He paused at a place where streets had once met, running north-south and east-west. This would do. The street signs were long gone, but the name of the intersection wasn't important. What was needed was merely the crossroads, a *barriere*, a natural gate through which he would summon the spirit he sought.

Marcel Etienne touched his arm as he was about to lay his black bag down on the broken pavement underfoot.

"Someone watches," he said.

"Where, *mon cher*?"

Marcel shrugged. "I don't know." He glanced at his brother. "But I feel eyes upon us."

Jean Etienne nodded in agreement.

Papa Jo-el closed his eyes and sifted through the impressions that the night carried as it stalked the city around them. Vaguely, he could sense the presence of people, but no danger. Their thoughts were curious about what they saw as intruders, but he could read no enmity in their minds.

"There are always people in this place," he said finally. "But they are only the lost and the lonely; they will not trouble us."

Marcel nodded, but he still looked uneasy.

"Trust me in this, *mon cher*," Papa Jo-el said.

He regarded the brothers, one at a time, holding each man's gaze for a long heartbeat. His teeth gleamed white in the darkness.

"It is time," he said.

The brothers moved to either side of him once more. Sitting on their heels, they began to rhythmically slap their knees with the palms of their hands. Papa Jo-el closed his eyes, letting the rhythm enter that place deep inside him where the gift of the *loa* that made him a *bocor* slept.

He would have preferred traditional drums, but such a sound would only draw unwanted attention to what they did here tonight. In that sense the work of a *voudoun* and a *bocor* were similar. Whether it was for a religious ceremony, or a calling up of magic, the spirits paid more attention when they employed the three drums—*petit, seconde* and *maman*—each with their own specific, designated beat, as well as the sounds drawn from an *ogan*, a bar of iron, to focus the energies of the ritual.

The difference here was that there was no congregation to impress. Here there was only the magic. Papa Jo-el could have done without a rhythm at all—using only the drumming of his heartbeat, the fire in which his offerings would burn and the *vever* he would draw on the ground for what must be done. But the rhythmic slap of the Etienne brothers' hands on their knees made the focusing easier, and it kept them busy—too busy concentrating on maintaining the complexities of the beat to interrupt him in his work with questions or warnings that were no longer necessary.

This was a spirit matter now; in such, he was the guard.

From his black bag he took small pieces of kindling, which he set up on the pavement in the shape of a small pyramid. Returning to his bag, he took out a handful of dried liverwort and herbs, which he stuffed into the side of the pyramid. He bowed his head over the wood for a long moment of silent meditation before lighting the liverwort. Smoke wreathed upward, heavy with the pungent scent of the herbs that had been sprinkled into the moss earlier that evening in his *hounfour*—the temple up above The Good Serpent.

With maize flour, he drew his *vever* before the fire—a complex, cabella-like design to invoke the *loa*. When it was completed to his satisfaction, he sat on his heels and began to slap his palms against his own knees, playing the third counterpoint to the rhythm that the Etienne brothers were maintaining: *petit* to their *seconde* and *maman*. Once the trinity of the rhythm was established, he began to chant softly.

A smile touched his lips as he felt the spirits that walked this night draw closer.

Here we go, Billy Ryan had thought as he watched Jim enter the Tombs behind Papa Jo-el and his bodyguards. The meet was on. He didn't recognize the guy, but he was white. He figured it had to be one of the wops, though he wasn't dressed right. The Italians did like their suits.

He gave the guy a bit of a head start, waited for a cab to go by on Gracie, then slipped across the street himself. It wasn't until Papa Jo-el and his boys settled down to business in the middle of the abandoned intersection that he revised his earlier impression of the other man following them. The guy hunkered down out of sight and started to take something out of the canvas pack he was carrying.

Shit, Ryan thought as he caught the gleam of metal. It wasn't a meet. It was a hit.

But then he realized the guy wasn't putting together a gun. He was setting up a camera—telephoto attached to a monopod, camera body fixed onto the long lens.

Ryan tried to work out what was going down here. What gave? Who was this guy and just where the fuck did *he* fit in?

About then the Etienne brothers crouched down and started to slap their knees. Ryan worked his way in closer through the rubble, choosing a position from which he could see clearly what was going on in the middle of the intersection, but still keep an eye on the photographer. He watched what Papa Jo-el was doing and shook his head.

Christ, they were really into this crap, weren't they?

He began to get the feeling that what was going down here tonight didn't have anything to do with the Slasher or a payoff. It was just some weird voodoo shit. But he stayed all the same, curious now as to how it would all play out.

Jim watched the proceedings through his telephoto. The 300mm lens brought everything up so close that he almost felt he was right there among the three men.

He'd been afraid, at first, to take any shots, sure that the sound of his shutter would alert the men to his presence. But once the two bigger men began their impromptu drumming, he realized that they wouldn't hear a thing. He shot through a whole roll, motor drive whirring softly. He took long shots of the whole scene, close-ups of the men's faces, then various pictures of what Pilione was doing while his companions continued to slap their knees.

When the roll was done, Jim crouched down behind the rubble where he was hiding and removed his film. He stowed it in the pocket of his jacket and inserted a new roll into the back of his camera. He continued to watch the men in the intersection, going through the whole process by feel alone. At this point in his career, he could change films on automatic.

He snapped the back of the camera closed. When he brought the camera back up, balancing its weight on the monopod, he saw that something was happening. There was more smoke than should have been possible from Papa Jo-el's tiny fire.

Maybe Pilione had put some damp leaves on it, Jim thought.

He focused on the smoke, twisting the zoom on the lens to bring it in as close as he could. And then his whole body started to feel numb.

"Jesus H. Christ," he said in a hoarse whisper, the words almost choking in his throat.

This place was more like a graveyard than he had thought, Papa Jo-el realized. The night was thick with spirits, invisible presences drawn by his summoning. Many were errant souls, temporarily cast adrift by the stasis that held their bodies as they slept in the nearby buildings. They were hovering now like moths around the crossroads, curious and uncertain, fear clouding their minds. When they woke in the morning, they would remember nightmares.

The *loa* were there, as well; their drumming presence counter-pointed the rhythm that woke from palms slapped against knees. They, too, were curious, but they had no fear.

And then there were the dead.

There were many who had died in this no-man's-land—lost, rest-less spirits still bound by the trauma that had filled their unhappy lives and the unfortunate circumstances of their deaths.

Not you, not you, not you, he would tell them as he studied them one by one. *The one I seek has fresh blood upon his soul.*

Each spirit he addressed so faded back into the night, freed from his power to wander restlessly through the desolate blocks of the Tombs once more.

His eyes were open, but he looked beyond the littered streets, into the hidden world of the *loa*, searching, searching. But the spirit he sought found him first.

Smoke billowed on the pavement, rising from its cracks in a dark cloud that took shape, then a physical presence, with alarming speed. Its body was a massive corpulent thing, a white mountain of dead flesh dwarfing the bulky shapes of the Etienne brothers, who continued to slap palms to knees on either side of Papa Jo-el. Its features were unremarkable; its face was wide and fat, a bland, common face, save for the eyes, which burned from fleshy sockets like a pair of smoldering coals. Hunger raged in their fire; they existed only to invoke terror, to freeze the prey before it was slain.

But Papa Jo-el had no fear of the spirit. No matter its monstrous presence, or the speed with which it had gained a physical shape, he had still been prepared for its appearance.

"You have been summoned by my power," he said. He spoke in Creole, using the words of magic that would mean nothing to his hidden watchers but which all spirits understood. "I command you."

Its voice, when it replied, was a sound one could only imagine issuing from a grave.

"Bull*shit*!" the creature roared.

From its side, it lifted a hand holding a hunting knife with a twelve-inch blade. It brought the knife up, plunging it into Papa Jo-el's chest with such force that the *voudoun* was lifted up, from a crouch to his tiptoes, until he was right off his feet. He hung, impaled on the blade, calm words of power swallowed by a scream of pain.

For long moments the Etienne brothers were frozen where they sat, staring at the terrible, impossible tableau. Then, like mirror images, they rose liquidly to their feet and charged the creature. It flung Papa Jo-el's dying body from the end of its blade with such force that it landed a half-dozen yards from where they stood. Blood sprayed from its knife as it brought the blade around in a long sweeping arc to meet the brothers' attack.

It cut through Marcel's throat, through windpipe, jugular veins and carotid arteries, until it severed his spinal cord. Marcel staggered back, eyes wide with fear and pain, body collapsing, blood spewing from between his fingers when he reached up to hold his throat together. It was a useless gesture. He died before he hit the ground.

The blade emerged from Marcel's flesh in another long bloody arc as Jean threw himself upon the creature. The force of his attack should have knocked the killer to the ground, but the monster held firm. Its left hand caught one of Jean's arms, snapping the bone as it threw the bodyguard away. Jean tumbled to the ground. Before he could rise, the creature had him by the throat in a grip that couldn't be broken.

The blade plunged into his chest, was pulled out, thrust in again. The creature stabbed him, over and over again, until it seemed that all he held at the length of his left arm was a slab of sloppily butchered meat.

The creature let Jean's corpse fall to the pavement. It lifted the blade to its mouth and licked the blood from it; then its head went even farther back, and it howled at the night skies—howled and howled as its body dissolved back into smoke and then was gone.

Ryan hadn't seen the inside of a church in years, but he made the sign of the cross all the same as he stared upon the carnage left in the creature's wake. Everything that had brought him here was forgotten—Papa Jo-el, profit, the photographer. For the first time in his life, panic rose inside him with the force of a tidal wave, and he simply fled.

It wasn't just the brutality of the killings. He'd seen worse in his time, been involved in worse in his time. But there was something about that . . . that *thing* that had killed the niggers. It was like the creature had left a finger in his head—like it had left a piece of itself inside him. An echo. A voice. A cold voice carried on a midnight wind. He could hear it whispering, whispering. . . .

All he could do was try to get away from it.

How long he ran, he didn't know, but by the time he finally fell against the side of a building, his lungs dragging in painful breaths, he was blocks away. He let himself slide to the pavement and sat there with his head bowed, his back against the wall. A litany ran through his head.

Jesus, Jesus, Jesus, Jesus. . . .

And under it, that cold whisper. No words, nothing intelligible, just a voice, an awful voice.

Jesus.

It wasn't for comfort that he called on the son of a God he'd long since stopped worshiping. It was just the only word that seemed able to move across the terrorized field of his mind. The litany helped push the cold whispering back, away, until he could almost ignore it.

Slowly his breathing steadied and his ability to think returned to some semblance of normality, although after what he'd just seen, he didn't know what was normal anymore.

No wonder the cops couldn't track down the Slasher, he thought. Fucking guy was a monster from one of those B horror flicks.

He shook his head. What the hell was he thinking? No matter what he thought he'd seen go down in the Tombs, there had to be a rational explanation.

Oh yeah? a part of him asked. Then why were you so scared you almost crapped your pants getting out of there so fast?

Billy Ryan knew he was a lot of things, but a coward wasn't one of them. He'd never panicked before. He didn't even understand the mindless fear that had overtaken him. He'd seen it before, trapped in the eyes of men just before he killed them, when they *knew* they were going to die, but he'd never understood it before.

But now . . .

The midnight voice stirred deep in his mind.

Cold sweat still beaded his face. His shirt clung wetly to his back. He wiped his face with the sleeve of his jacket and looked northward, up the block, back the way he'd run. Slowly he got to his feet. He pulled his .38 from the holster at the small of his back, checked its load, then replaced it.

Fuck this, he thought.

He was going back. He had to see just exactly what had gone down. If he didn't go, he didn't think he could live with himself. He couldn't live with what not going would prove him to be. He'd be just another chickenshit small-time hood without the balls to stand up and be counted when the chips came down. He'd be jumping at shadows, questioning everything for its risk, whether it was dealing with one of Mickey's "problems" or just taking a piss.

But when he got back to that intersection in the Tombs, the creature was gone. As was the guy with the camera. All that remained were the corpses of the three men he'd seen butchered by something that couldn't possibly exist, and the echoing whisper that was going to drive him insane, if he hadn't already gone straight around the bend.

Looking down on the creature's handiwork, he felt the cold voice growing stronger. The midnight wind carried its whisper through the emptiness inside him. All he had to fight that voice was his fear.

Jim hadn't bolted, not right away, though his every sense screamed for him to just get—out of—here.

But he couldn't move. He leaned against the rubble he'd been hiding behind, using it for support to keep him from just falling flat on the ground, and stared out at the intersection. It was deserted now—except for the bodies. And something else: a whispering sound

that seemed to be more in his head than originating from any exter-
nal source.

Slowly he got to his feet. He shuffled forward, holding the monopod
in both hands, ready to wield his camera like a club if anything jumped
out at him, but the night was preternaturally still in the wake of the
sudden violence he'd seen enacted before him just moments ago. He
had the disquieting feeling that the whole world had died; everybody
in it had just gone away, and he was left to wander alone in its ruins.

When he got to where the bodies lay, his nostrils filled with the
sharp metallic smell of the blood that seemed to be everywhere. He
hated that smell. It was something he never got used to, no matter
how many accidents he'd covered.

His stomach did a quick flip as he looked on the corpse that the
killer had finished last.

"Jesus," he said softly.

His voice sounded flat to his ears, distanced, empty. He felt as
though he were in some surrealistic wasteland—a painting, a photograph, not a real place. All that peopled it was his fear and the soft whis-
pery sound that he still couldn't place. It was like a name being called
over and over again—not his, not recognizable, just repeated endlessly.

Get out of here, he told himself. Now, before the thing that did
this comes back.

But he couldn't seem to move. All he could do was look upon the
carnage and shiver.

It wasn't always possible, but most times he was able to use his
camera to distance himself from a situation such as this. The lens
provided a buffer against reality. Tonight he couldn't even think of
setting it up and taking another shot.

A rustling in the weeds at the far side of the intersection had him
turning around, camera raised defensively. He shuddered when he
saw the rat that froze at his movement. It scurried back into the

weeds, and he started to back up himself. He took one step, then another. He stumbled over a buckling piece of pavement, caught his balance, but he still couldn't turn away to watch where he was going. He had the sure sense that if he did, the killer would reappear and kill him as well.

He didn't turn until the rubble finally hid the bodies from his sight; then he fled, running back to where he'd parked his car, as though all the fiends of his childhood nightmares were on his trail. When he reached the car, he tossed the camera into the backseat, never considering the possible damage the rough treatment might do to it, and quickly slipped behind the wheel.

He locked the door and put the key in the ignition, but then he got the shakes so bad that he couldn't seem to start the car up.

Now he knew where the look of terror on Niki's face had come from.

But what did any of it have to do with him?

The graffiti flashed in his mind. Red lips, blackly outlined. The dyslexically spelled name. NIKI.

He put his hands in his face and leaned his brow against the top of the steering wheel.

What he had seen was impossible. That . . . that *thing* . . . just appearing out of the smoke—called up by some makeshift voodoo ritual. What did the priest have to do with the killings? Why would he have called up that *thing* to kill those girls? Why had the monster turned on him?

He could see its face again as though he still had the camera to his eye, the telephoto bringing its monstrous features into an awful close-up. It was almost familiar, that face, but he couldn't place it.

He shivered—nightmare tremors still crawling up and down his spine whenever he thought of what he'd seen. The whisper in his head wouldn't go away.

That monstrous *thing* . . .

What did it have to do with Chelsea—the girl he called Niki?

He remembered the look on her face when he'd called out to her earlier. Her terror . . .

What did it have to do with *him*?

It was a long while before he could finally start the car and drive. He didn't go home. Instead, he drove as though in a daze, straight to *The Star*'s offices on Perry Street. The security guard had to call him back to sign in and looked at him with concern as he scrawled his name and the time on the appropriate piece of paper, held in a clipboard.

"Are you feeling okay, Mr. McGann?" he asked.

Jim hardly heard the man. He just nodded and muttered something as he headed for the bank of elevators at the far side of the lobby. He got up to the lab without running into anyone else, and souped his two films. Being busy helped keep the memories at bay, but he started to shake again while he was waiting for the negatives to dry—violent tremors that rattled his teeth against each other. The sound in his head grew stronger. It was like the buzzing of hundreds of flies, or like a dark, cold slithering that uncoiled and threatened to fill his head with its insidious presence. It was all he could do not to lie down on the floor and let it all just take him away. He hugged himself, waiting numbly for the feeling to pass, for the sound to die down.

When the shaking finally eased, he went into the washroom and washed his face with hot water. The heat helped, but only momentarily. The chill inside him just wouldn't go away. The whisper—that awful voice—remained as well, but it was quiet now, almost silent.

He ran off contact sheets once the negatives were dry and sat down at Grant's desk to pore over them. He was ready to call the cops, to hand over what he had, but first he wanted to look at that monstrous face once more, to find out why it seemed familiar. The magnifying glass began to shake in his hand as he realized what he was looking at.

The three black men were there—Pilione and his two big companions—but the monster wasn't in any of the pictures. There was a blurry one of Pilione, suspended in the air, but nothing was holding him up. Another one—very blurry, this time—showed Pilione's two big companions rushing . . . nothing.

The photos he'd taken of the killings showed only the three victims—moving around as though fighting an invisible foe. Their killer wasn't in a single one of them.

Jim broke into a cold sweat.

It was impossible. He'd *seen* that monster. It had appeared in a cloud of smoke, killed the three men, then vanished again. It had been real—Jim had no doubts about that whatsoever. But according to his pictures, the thing had never existed. It just wasn't *there*.

The camera doesn't lie, he thought.

He shivered again.

Okay. The camera doesn't lie. The monster he'd seen tonight didn't exist, because it didn't appear in any of the photos. He had to have hallucinated it. Except . . .

He stared down at the contact sheets.

Then what the hell killed those men?

The whispering grew stronger in his mind as though it knew the answer, as though the name it repeated was a talisman that would explain all if he could only make it out. But listening to that voice in his head was too much like eavesdropping. He could hear the sound of it, but the sense wasn't intelligible.

Jim had the uneasy feeling that if he ever did decipher its message, he wouldn't live long enough to regret it. As it was, it was making him feel crazy. It made him want to strike out at it, at something, at *any*thing.

FOURTEEN

He was trapped again in the cold place, lost in its dark and its silence, his enormous body folded in upon itself in a fetal position as he attempted to conserve what little warmth it still held. But the cold lay within as well as without—there was no escaping it—and the darkness was thick and constant. The silence was absolute.

There were few distractions.

Mostly he lived in his memories, which formed an endless stream-of-consciousness parade that wasn't always pleasing.

He didn't like remembering his childhood and the basement where his brother took him and made him pull down his pants so that his brother could press his hard sex up into him.

He didn't like to see the teenager he'd been, already so obese and unwanted, always in the shadows, playing with himself as he peeped in windows, getting beaten up when he got caught.

He didn't like it when his wife was there, screaming at him

because she'd discovered what he was doing with their daughter. Why couldn't his wife believe him when he told her how much their daughter loved it? They all loved it. All the little children loved it. They all loved him.

The little children.

He liked thinking of them best. He liked the memories where he stood, towering over them, love in his eyes as he smiled at their pale little faces, with eyes squeezed shut and wet with happy tears, little bodies trembling with eagerness as he showed them what he wanted from them, showed them what he liked to have them do—with each other, but mostly, oh, mostly with him. He would rearrange them in his mind—their little faces, their little limbs, their little torsos, their little sexes—just as he used to do before the cold dark claimed him.

He liked doing it better here. It wasn't so messy. There wasn't all the blood. Their precious little hearts didn't stop beating. Instead they lived on and on and on, no matter what he did to them.

But mostly there was only the dark and the cold, and the memory of the harridan-sharp blade of his wife's anger cutting at him while his daughter, his precious little daughter, stood there staring, so frightened of him—frightened of *him*, of all people—when he loved her with all his heart and soul.

When she came to mind, he'd call out to her. He'd call and call and call. He could hear his voice escape from the cold dark, carried on the back of a midnight wind, looking, looking, always looking for her, because, of all the little children, he'd loved her the best.

She'd been bad, though. She'd told secrets she'd promised to keep, so she had to be punished. But he still loved her—that was why he had to punish her. She had to learn her lessons, she had to learn never to tell, so that they could be together again.

Surely, she could understand that? Surely, she could see that it would only hurt for a little while and then they'd be together again and she'd love him even more because she'd know then how he'd been right, how they were always meant to be together.

But she never answered. Whenever he thought he'd found her, she'd just run away. Or she'd pretend she didn't know who he was. Like he wasn't her father. Like he couldn't recognize his daughter now that she'd grown up. But he knew her by her blonde hair and the clothes she wore. She always looked just the way he'd have dressed her if her mother hadn't taken her away from him.

It was no good her denying who she was. He always *knew*. But it made him angry, her denials. So angry. He wouldn't mean to cut her so deeply that all the blood came spilling out and she hung there empty in his hand, just this dead thing that wasn't his daughter. He knew she wasn't, because he could still *feel* her out there, someplace else, still hiding from him when he dropped the bodies on the pavement and the cold dark place called him back.

He didn't remember how he'd first escaped. He'd been calling and calling for her, so desperate, so *needful*. And suddenly the dark and the cold lost its hold on him. It was just for a moment, but the dark cold place was gone, and he was walking down a half-familiar street, breathing air, nostrils filled with smells, ears ringing with sound, eyes sucking in a hundred thousand images. . . .

Just a moment, and then he was back again.

But he didn't forget—how could he forget the rush of sensation that had flooded him? He worked harder after that, pushing at the dark, trying to ignore the cold, reaching, reaching, calling out for her.

And sometimes he escaped again.

Sometimes all he managed to do was send his dreams out into the city, where they scurried through its night streets, remembering, searching for what was lost, but never finding it. They touched mostly the weak-minded, or children, leaving slight residues of unreasoning fear in their wake.

But sometimes he escaped again. And it started to get easier, each time he did it. He started to feel stronger. It was good, it was so good, even if it was never for long. With black blood he wrote her name on walls—

NIKI, NIKI, NIKI

—because he'd heard somewhere once that names were magic, and everybody knows blood holds power. Writing her name would bind him to her again, he believed. But she never came.

He'd imagine her tiny lips, down there on his sex, so he'd draw them—red, red, oh red—beside her name so that she'd see them and remember how good it had been for them—good for them both. She'd remember how much he loved her and she'd come back to him. But she never came. He always had to go looking for her.

And when he found her, when he tried to embrace the hot fire of life that pulsed in her breast, everything always seemed to go wrong. She'd try to fight him. She'd deny him. The fire would quicken sweetly with her fear, but suddenly he'd have the knife again, and all too soon there'd be blood everywhere, her blood; the heat would flare and be gone, and he'd sense that she was somewhere else. She was no longer in the body that he'd drop on the pavement at his feet, but somewhere else, laughing at him, denying him, hiding, always hiding.

He thought it would be an endless circle: He'd call; she'd come. He'd try to hold her, she'd deny him. He'd have the knife; she'd suddenly be somewhere else, leaving him to hold some dead thing in his bands.

It didn't matter if he was getting stronger, if it was getting easier to escape, if only for such a short time. She was always out of reach, always hiding. Don't hide from Daddy, I won't hurt you, I won't hurt you for long. Daddy loves you, remember always, Daddy loves when you hold him so, and touch him so, and put your sweet mouth . . . so. . . .

But then he heard the call. It rang like a clarion through the endless silence of the cold dark place, summoning him to her. Except when he got there, it wasn't his little girl waiting for him, but some witchy black man.

You have been summoned by my power, the witchy man said, like someone had put him in charge.

But all he wanted to know was: Where was his little girl?

I command you.

The knife had done its work, and he was back again, in the cold, in the dark, in the silence. But this time it was different. He could feel that something had been broken. The dark wasn't so black; the cold didn't cut all the way to the marrow of his bones. There was a whisper of a midnight wind in the silence.

Soon he'd be able to escape again. Soon the cold dark wouldn't be able to draw him back again. Soon he'd find his little girl, and they'd live happily ever after again, just like in a fairy tale, because she was his princess and he loved her with all his heart, loved her better than all the other little children he'd ever played with.

Soon . . . soon. . . .

But first he had to rest. Because somewhere out there, where the cold dark couldn't touch it, the sun was rising, the day was coming, coming to steal away his strength, but he needed to be strong, because only a strong man could hold onto what was his, and she was his.

NIKI.

The wind caught her name, and it echoed through the cold reaches around him. He smiled in the dark, hugged himself more tightly.

Daddy's coming, he said, and the wind took those words away with it as well, through the cold dark and into the day beyond.

Daddy's coming for you, Niki, coming for you and for the son of a bitch who thought shooting a father would keep him from being with his precious little girl. God help him and anybody who thought they could own a piece of his Niki, anybody who thought they could protect her, because that was his job and he was going to show them just how good he was at his work. He was going to show them all.

NIKI.

The midnight wind took her name and chased it out to where the morning sun was creeping through the city's streets.

Daddy's coming for you, sweet thing. He's missed you so bad, he's never going away again. We're going to have such fun again, you and me, just you and me, playing in the dark like we always did, all those games you like so much, going to put your face right down there where it feels so good. . . .

He fell asleep, dreaming of his little children, only this time they all had his daughter's face.

NIKI.

A dozen little girls, all the same, smiling up at him, trembling, happy.

He smiled in that cold dark place, heat rising up from his groin to spread throughout his corpulent body. The silence was broken now by the sound of his rhythmic grunting as his hands went down under the massive fatty slab that was his belly, moving up and down, up and down.

NIKI.

FIFTEEN

The fire was burning low by the time John Morningstar returned from dropping his brother off at his car by the Longhouse. He walked silently out of the bush and into the clearing and sat down cross-legged by the fire, directly across from the shaman. An owl called, deep in the forest. Whiteduck nodded, but whether in response to the hoot of the owl or his own return, John couldn't tell.

Whiteduck's features were hidden in shadow, but the dull glow of the coals made his gray braids look like the white clay streaks daubed on a Ghost Dancer's chest and cheeks. There was always a stillness about him, even when he was moving, but at the moment, John thought that Whiteduck seemed more closely related to the granite outcrops that pushed up through the cedar and pine roots around them, than to any living being.

"Your brother's spirit is troubled," Whiteduck said finally.

John nodded in agreement. "He should never have left the reserve. We need him here."

Whiteduck shrugged. "It is in each man and woman to do what they must do with their life; we can advise, but we cannot command."

"I know."

"We must also learn to respect the choices they make."

By "we," John knew the shaman was referring to John himself.

"I try," he said. "But when I see all of our resources draining away . . ."

Whiteduck smiled, his teeth flashing briefly in the dark.

"It is true," he said, "that our brothers and sisters are our greatest natural resource, Kitchi-noka, but it is also true that the more you try to force them to help you, the quicker you drive them away."

Kitchi-noka was John's birth name; it meant Great Bear. It was an auspicious name, for the Kickaha considered bears to be the animals most closely related to human beings. Their totem spirits were renowned not simply for the wisdom they could impart, but for the strength as well.

"My brother told me something strange before he left," John said after a moment.

"To do with the spirit that haunts him?" Whiteduck asked.

John didn't show any surprise. It would have surprised him if Whiteduck hadn't known. So he simply nodded in response to the shaman's question and went on to relate the conversation that had passed between Thomas and himself in the parking lot by the Longhouse.

"Did he ask you for your help?" Whiteduck asked when John was done.

John shook his head. "I don't think he truly believes the spirit is real."

"Perhaps this is something he must face on his own," Whiteduck said. "Perhaps it will define the man he is to be."

"I don't understand."

"When he confronts this evil spirit," Whiteduck said, "it will have to be either as a white man or a Kickaha."

John made no reply, but he poked at the coals with a stick, obviously uncomfortable.

"You believe you should help him," Whiteduck said.

John nodded. "He doesn't really know what he's facing. He doesn't even *believe* in it. Going into battle without understanding his enemy . . . how can he hope to survive?"

Whiteduck said nothing for a time.

"Am I wrong?" John asked.

Whiteduck shrugged. "It is a good thing to understand the ties that bind one to one's family."

"But?" John asked, voicing the unspoken conjunction.

"What if I told you that your brother must face this on his own?" Whiteduck said.

"I wouldn't believe you. You've always taught me that the most important thing is to give support to one's family and tribe."

Whiteduck nodded. "And if I told you that as chief of our band, it would be far too much a risk to our purposes for you to endanger yourself in such a way? As chief, your first duty is to the band, not to your family."

"I have to choose?" John asked. "Between the band and my brother?"

Whiteduck nodded again. "The lot of a chief is a difficult trail to follow."

"You believe that helping my brother puts me at too much risk? That the band could suffer for it?"

Whiteduck nodded. "You are this generation's hope, Kitchi-noka. The time has come when we must stop speaking, but act. Who else do you know who is as spiritually and physically prepared to lead our people? Who else will the aunts accept without question?"

There was a tightness in John's chest as he carefully thought things through. Like his brother, he had never wanted to follow in his father's footsteps and be the band chief; but unlike Thomas, when Whiteduck first approached him, he had known that if his dreams for the tribe's sovereignty were to be realized, he would have to do his part. He knew it would require sacrifices. The cost to him was to set his private life aside and live for the band and the cause that would win them a treaty with the white men that could never be broken— not because of the white men's goodwill or integrity but because the tribe had become so strong that the white men had no choice but to listen to them.

I'm not doing this for me, he told himself. I'm not doing this because I don't care about Tom. I'm doing this because if I don't, everything we've been working for will mean nothing. Grandfather Whiteduck would have to start all over again and he is already so old. . . .

"I will do as you advise," he said. "I won't put my brother's life above the good of the band."

Whiteduck's teeth flashed in a quick grin. "Spoken like a true chief."

Then why did he feel like such a shit? John wondered.

"I know how hard a decision that was to make," Whiteduck said. "You will find, when you become chief and we begin our struggle to regain our land, that you will face such decisions time and time again. They will never come any easier. If they do, then there will be something wrong inside you and you won't be fit to be our chief."

John swallowed thickly. "I know," he said.

"What we do is important for the good of our people as a whole. We cannot let the fate of an individual sway us from our purpose."

A vision of Tom being rent by some monstrous thing flashed in John's head. He swallowed again. His throat and chest felt so tight he couldn't seem to breathe. But he kept a stoic face. He just hoped that when they met again in *Epanggishimuk*, the Land of the Souls, his brother and their mother would forgive him.

"I . . . I know," he repeated.

Whiteduck smiled sympathetically. "But you are not chief yet," he said.

John regarded him steadily for a long moment.

"What are you saying, *Mico'mis*?" he asked finally.

"Go and help your brother."

SIXTEEN

Cindy woke up in Meg's spare bedroom and simply lay there for a long while, enjoying the sensation of not being in some cheap hotel or a room at the Y. The bedroom wasn't luxurious, but it certainly didn't have that feel of transience, as though a different person stayed there every night, week after week, twelve months a year.

The centerpiece of the room was the three-quarter-sized iron bed, painted white with brass knobs on each post and a Laura Ashley comforter spread over its mattress. Against one wall stood a dresser, also white, with a painted border of straw wreaths around the mirror, bunches of flowers and geese that were repeated along the top of the room's window and door frames. Lace curtains with a cottage design kept the next-door neighbor from peering in. A hooked throw rug lay beside the bed, and on the walls were two watercolors depicting vibrant country scenes.

The end result was a room that was pretty, without being cloying. A comfortable space to wake up in.

There was something to be said for settling down in one place, Cindy thought when she finally arose.

She got dressed and tiptoed to the washroom, not wanting to wake Meg, who must have got in late last night, because she still wasn't home by the time Cindy had gone to bed herself.

She had to search a bit in the kitchen to find coffee filters and ground coffee, but soon she had boiling water dripping through a Melitta filter. The resulting dark liquid filled the apartment with that unmistakable aroma of freshly made coffee. Cindy found a copy of *The Star*'s Sunday edition in the hall outside the apartment door and took it and her coffee out onto the balcony. She laughed when she reached the paper's Living section and found a color photo of herself and her sax. Jim was credited for the photo.

He's not a bad photographer, she thought. Not bad at all. He certainly made her look good, at any rate.

Her smile broadened as she read the caption: "Saxy and free, street musician Cindy Draper supports a cross-country trip by playing her own brand of jazz on street corners and in parks."

Unfortunately, while thinking of Jim gave her a good feeling, it also brought back to mind that look of terror that had crossed Chelsea's face when he'd tried to talk to her outside of Shooters last night. Cindy didn't want to think that he was responsible for that terror—he'd said he wasn't and she wanted to believe him. But if Chelsea wasn't scared of Jim, then what *had* terrified her so?

With an effort, Cindy tried to put the question out of her mind. She leafed through the rest of the paper until she finished her coffee. When she went back inside, Meg came wandering up the short hall from her bedroom, wrapped in a pink terry cloth bathrobe, her eyes heavy with sleep. She muttered something that sounded vaguely like the last half of "Good morning"—making of it a statement, rather than a greeting—before dropping down on the sofa. Laying her head on the backrest, she drew her legs up under her.

Cindy brought her a coffee, which she accepted with another mumble, which might have been "Thanks." While Meg sipped at the coffee, Cindy started making breakfast—eggs, bacon, home fries, and toast—and had it all ready by the time Meg started to wake up.

"I could get used to this," Meg said as she sat down at the table and looked over the spread of food. "Did you ever consider hiring yourself out as a live-in cook?"

"I do breakfast and that's about it," Cindy replied. "Actually, I'm not all that great a cook."

"Ditto," Meg said. "I admit to being a fast-food junkie."

Cindy regarded Meg's trim figure and clear complexion.

"You'd never know it," she said.

"It's a deep, dark secret—don't tell anybody." Meg dipped her toast into the yolk of her egg and took a bite. "So," she added, speaking around her mouthful, "how was your night?"

"Kind of scary." At Meg's raised eyebrows, Cindy went on to explain. "I just don't trust it when things get this intense, this fast."

Meg shook her head. "Jeez, maybe I should revise my opinion of Jim. I always thought he'd be kind of sweet and just a little diffident on a first date."

"You never dated him?"

"Not boy-girl dating—just as friends."

"Why not?"

Meg shrugged. "We were both involved with other people when we first met and that sort of defined our relationship. Since then, there's never seemed to be any need to change it. I think we both like being friends rather than complicating things."

"Well, it wasn't what you were thinking," Cindy said. "He was pretty sweet, actually. It's just that . . ." She could feel a blush creeping up her neck. "The attraction level between us got revved up pretty high—and that was just in the restaurant."

"Sounds like fun."

"I guess. It just seems to be happening too fast."

"Well, Jim can get a little intense," Meg said. "Especially when he's keen on something. And sometimes he gets these weird leaps of intuition. . . ."

"Like what?" Cindy asked when Meg's voice just trailed off.

"Oh, you know. Where to be when something's going down that would make a good photo—that kind of a thing."

They concentrated on eating for a while then. When Meg had finished mopping up the last of the yolk on her plate with another piece of toast, Cindy spoke up again.

"So what's Jim really like?"

"He's good people," Meg said. "Really."

"What do you think about him and Chelsea?"

"Who's Chelsea?"

"The girl he calls Niki—her real name's Chelsea."

"He told you about that?"

Cindy nodded.

"Well, I don't see the connection between her and the Slasher," Meg said. "Not the way he does, if that's what you're getting at."

"No, it's not that. It's just . . ."

Cindy hesitated for a moment, then told Meg about what had happened outside the restaurant the previous night.

"What worries me," she added as she finished, "is that there's something going on there. The way she looked at him—she was terrified."

"What exactly are you saying?"

Cindy studied her for a moment, then realized it wasn't Meg's protective instinct cutting in; she was just curious.

"I don't know," Cindy said. "I like Jim—probably more than I should, considering how short a time I've known him. But liking's one thing. I can see he's got depths, but so far all I know is the surface. I don't really *know* him—not like I guess you do."

"I'll tell you this," Meg said. "There's no way he'd hurt anybody— at least not deliberately. He may think more with his dick than his head from time to time, but then what guy doesn't? When it comes down to basics, he really is a good person." She paused, thinking for a moment. "Maybe what I'm trying to say is he's a very moral sort of person. You can count on him to do what he says he's going to do, and what he tries to do is the right thing."

Cindy nodded. "I guess I was hoping you'd say something like that."

"I'm not just saying it," Meg told her. "I mean it."

"That's good."

The conversation lagged again then, though not uncomfortably so. Cindy didn't know what Meg was thinking about, but she knew what was running through her mind. If she really wanted to find out what was going on between Chelsea and Jim—what that terrified *look* had meant—she'd have to talk to Chelsea herself.

"I think I'll go out for a while," she said. "If Jim calls, or comes by, tell him I'll be back later."

Meg gave her a thoughtful look. "Sure."

"And Meg—thanks for putting me up. I don't see a whole lot of kindness, being on the road the way I am. At least not without it costing something."

What troubled her most about staying over here, she realized, was how it allowed her to let down her guard. Meg and Jim were both so easygoing that she couldn't help but relax around them. But out on the road, it was a different story. Out on the road, everybody wanted a piece of you.

She'd left home because her father was an alcoholic, and when he wasn't trying to knock her lights out in a drunken rage, he expected her to baby him like she was his mother. No wonder her own mother had left him. Only why, Cindy had wondered ever since her mother walked out, hadn't Mom taken her along?

Things went from bad to worse, living with her dad, until not even her guilt was strong enough to keep her there anymore. Like her mother, one day she just walked out. She took her sax and a knapsack full of clothes, cleaned out her bank account, and took the first bus away. Where was she going? She didn't know. Away. To the coast. And when she got there, she'd probably turn right around and head back, because whatever she was looking for couldn't be found busking on a street corner or aimlessly wandering the country. She'd realized that her first couple of months on the road.

What she was looking for, she was never going to find: a family. Stability.

Because every time she met someone who seemed nice, either it got weird and she'd run, or she'd panic. And then run. Like she wanted to do now. But this time she thought she'd stick it out. She had to try again, because if she didn't, she knew how she was going to end up: She'd be one of those bag ladies, begging for handouts down on the Pier. Or she'd be buried in a shallow roadside grave along some highway to nowhere, because she'd made the mistake of thinking the guy sitting next to her on the bus was okay. . . .

"You all right?" Meg asked.

Cindy gave a quick, embarrassed laugh when she realized that she'd just been standing by the table, lost in a brain ramble.

"Sure," she said.

She went back to the bedroom and changed. Remembering what it had been like in the Tombs, she went for practical gear: jeans, sturdy walking shoes, and a T-shirt with a flannel shirt over top. She put her ID and some money in the front pocket of her jeans, not wanting to bring a purse. She left her sax behind as well, since it would only be a cumbersome burden for what she had planned. The last thing she did was take her jean jacket from her pack. She carried it with her as she returned to the apartment's main living area.

Meg gave her a critical look, then got up and went to the hall closet. She rummaged around on its top shelf for a bit, then tossed Cindy a beret.

"Put your hair up under this," she said. "It might help you look a little less pretty, though I doubt it. Maybe you could try smudging a little dirt on your cheeks. The more you look like some scruffy down-and-outer, the less likely you'll have someone hassling you."

Cindy regarded her with confusion. "What are you talking about?" she asked.

"You're going to the Tombs, aren't you?"

"How did you know?"

"I get a feel for this kind of a thing—Jim's not the only one with intuition around here. You're going to look for that girl."

Cindy nodded. "Yeah. I feel like I have to."

"You and Jim," Meg said, shaking her head. "What is it with this girl that she gets people all fired up and hot to find her?"

"I don't know. It's just . . ." Cindy sighed. "I don't know," she repeated.

"Do you know her?" Meg asked.

"Not really. I ran into her two nights ago, in a squat in the Tombs. She was acting a little strange—I remember thinking she was messed up on drugs, but now . . . after last night . . . I know she was just scared."

"Of what?"

"That's what I guess I'm going to find out."

Meg studied her for a long, quiet moment.

"Do you want some company?" she asked finally.

"No. This is something—"

"You've got to do on your own. I thought you'd say something like that."

"I'll be back," Cindy said.

Meg studied her again. For a moment Cindy was sure she was going to try to talk her out of going off on her own, but then Meg just shook her head.

"Just be careful," was all she said.

Jim felt as if he had a hangover when he woke up. He had a sharp pain behind his left eye, and as soon as he got up, the vaguely queasy feeling in his stomach intensified so that he had to stumble into the bathroom, where he vomited into the toilet bowl. Leaning weakly against the white porcelain, the smell of bile rearing up at him out of the bowl, he actually felt worse than he had before he'd thrown up. Usually the release made him feel better.

It took him a while to realize what it was. Behind the ache in his head, the source of it was that alien murmur, that whispering voice.

He flushed, but stayed on the floor, sitting with his back against the tub, his chin on his chest. Slowly the nausea ebbed. The headache took longer, but by the time he'd managed to shave and take a shower, it had left the area behind his eye and was just a vague ache at the back of his head. His memories of the previous night were harder to ignore. The whisper didn't go away at all. It took a constant vigilance to keep it at bay, to stop himself from just wanting to strike out at something.

He drank a cup of coffee, but couldn't face having breakfast. Back in his living room, he took out the photos he'd printed up last night at *The Star*. They hadn't changed. In them, Papa Jo-el Pilione and his two men were still being butchered; there was still no evidence of the creature responsible for the carnage.

I can't handle this, Jim thought.

He stared at the photos, willing the creature to reappear. It had to be there. He'd *seen* the damn thing—hadn't he? It just wasn't fucking possible that it shouldn't show up in the photos. But then, what about last night was possible?

Voodoo ceremonies and murderous spirits—it was the stuff of late night B movies, plain and simple. It wasn't real.

But he'd seen it all the same. And in his head whispered a constant reminder.

After a while he shuffled the photos together again and slipped them back into their folder. He thought about the photo shoot he'd gone on with Mary, but he couldn't remember a damn thing about voodoo, Pilione, or anything useful at all from that day. All he'd taken away with him, on film and in his memories, were the impressions that Pilione's temple was just a seedy loft filled with candles and icons, Pilione himself was nothing more than a con man, and the whole voodoo thing was just so much bullshit.

He rubbed his face with the palm of his hand. Well, he knew better now, didn't he? He didn't know what exactly it was that he'd seen last night, but he'd sure as hell seen *something* for which there was no rational explanation.

So what did he do about it?

He could just let it go. No one had seen him there, no one knew. He could just forget about Niki and the Slasher—just take the assignments that Grant handed him and forget about playing hero. Except—

Niki's terrified features flashed across his mind. He closed his eyes, but that just made her come into tighter focus. He could see the

Slasher . . . that *thing* from last night . . . bringing his knife down on her. . . .

The whispering behind his headache grew stronger, almost like laughter—a dark, cold, *soft* laughter that was all the more insidious for its faintness.

Sweat stood out on his brow. The vague throb behind his left eye sharpened into a pulsing ache. He got up and walked out onto the small balcony off his living room. The morning air was still cool. It helped calm him, but not much.

He had to see it through, he realized. It scared the shit out of him, but he had to see it through. Not just to help some street kid he didn't know, but for his own sanity. Because if what he'd seen last night *wasn't* real, if the whispering inside him, and the urge to commit his own acts of violence, had their source in his own psyche . . .

Don't even think about it, he told himself.

He went back into the apartment and flicked on the TV, switching channels until he got to the all-news cable network. He had to wait about fifteen minutes before they reran the story: Three men dead in the Tombs, brutally murdered, the police had no suspects, they were making no statement beyond "No comment." Pilione's alleged criminal connections were mentioned, as was his voodoo church, and that was it. More news would be forthcoming as it broke.

So far they hadn't even made the connection to the Friday Slasher. But why should they? So far as they were concerned, this was a gangland killing; it had no connection to the deaths of blonde hookers. But then the newspeople and cops hadn't been there last night. They hadn't seen it go down the way he had.

More news forthcoming. . . .

Jim picked up his remote control and turned off the TV.

I could give you some forthcoming news, he thought, then just shook his head. Who'd believe him? He wasn't sure he even believed it himself. If he went to the police with his story, they'd probably arrest him. And there was no one else he could go to. The paper? Grant would just make him take some vacation time. And he sure as hell wasn't going to involve either Meg or Cindy in this. It wasn't their concern, and the way he was feeling right now—

No, he'd never hurt them, he told himself. But he had to get rid of that sound in his head before something snapped.

He had to deal with this on his own. It was nobody's concern except for his. Who else would even care . . . ?

A memory came to him, cutting through his confusion as dramatically as the Slasher's blade had cut those men last night. In his mind's eye he was back at Pilione's temple with Mary. He was taking some shots of the candle- and icon-covered altar, only half-listening to Mary and Pilione discussing the various roles he and the other members of his church played in their ceremonies. What came back to Jim now was that Pilione didn't run the show on his own. He had drummers and a priestess helping him.

He nodded to himself. The priestess. If what happened last night was anybody's concern, then it was going to be hers. And she'd at least believe him.

He tried to remember if he'd seen her that day of the photo shoot, but he couldn't call her features up in his mind. There'd been some women around, but he couldn't remember being introduced to any of them, and Pilione hadn't indicated that any of them were involved in his temple except as part of the congregation. He supposed he could give Mary a call to find out who the priestess was, but with Pilione all over the news, it wouldn't take Mary long to figure he was on to something, and this was something he couldn't share.

He went into his spare bedroom, which served as a storage area except for those few times when he had friends from out of town staying. He dug through an old stack of *Star* clippings until he found Mary's article. Looking at photos of Pilione gave him the creeps, but he persevered, reading through the whole article until he came upon a name: Isabeau.

Isabeau Fontenot was the name of the woman Pilione said assisted him in his services.

Jim dug his phone book out from under a stack of photography magazines, then paused for a moment. He couldn't very well look up voodoo churches to get the number, but then he realized he didn't have to. He turned to the F's and found a listing for Fontenot, I., with an address in Upper Foxville, just a few blocks from The Good Serpent Club.

He dialed the number and was surprised when it was answered halfway through the first ring.

"Yes?"

"I'd like to speak to Isabeau Fontenot," Jim said.

"This is she."

The husky voice with its slight singsong trace of a Caribbean accent immediately delivered a picture into Jim's mind that was put together from the voodoo priestesses of a half-dozen bad horror movies.

"My name's Jim McGann and I was—"

"Are you a reporter?"

"Yes—I mean, no. That is, I work for *The Star* as a photographer, but this is personal."

There was a moment's pause as the woman on the other end of the line considered that.

Shit, Jim thought. She's probably got media crawling all over her. The last thing she's going to want to do is talk to me.

"I remember you," she said finally.

Was that good or bad? Jim wondered.

"This is about . . . last night?" she added.

"Yes. I . . . ." There was no point in beating around the bush, Jim realized. "I was there."

"I see."

Jim read volumes of meaning into those two simple words.

"I had nothing to do with what . . . happened," he said quickly. "But I saw it."

"Yes."

God, she was a cool customer, Jim thought. She wasn't giving him back a thing.

"I need to talk to someone about it," he said.

"Why me?"

Jim took a deep breath and plunged right in. "Because what I saw . . . I'm not sure it was real."

There was another considering pause from the other end of the line. Jim decided to wait her out.

"Perhaps we should talk," the woman said finally. "Do you have my address?"

No way, Jim thought. If this voodoo shit was real, there was no way he was going to head out to her own turf, where he might get whammied with some curse.

"Ah, could we maybe meet somewhere else?" he tried.

She gave a deep-throated laugh that held no humor. "Somewhere public?" she asked.

"Something like that."

"Or I could meet you at your own home—unless you believe that to be . . . unsafe as well."

Put like that, it made Jim feel like a jerk.

"No," he said. "My place would be fine." He gave her the address.

"I will be half an hour," the woman said. "No longer."

She hung up before Jim could reply.

He cradled the receiver thoughtfully and wondered just what he'd gotten himself into. What, he asked himself, makes this place feel any more safe? Nothing did. She'd just shamed him into agreeing.

Great way to start things off, he thought.

Then he scanned the room and saw what a mess the place was. Jesus, he had less than a half hour to make it look at least vaguely presentable.

He started off by gathering up an armload of magazines from the floor by the sofa and carting them into the spare bedroom. And all the while a midnight wind carried its cold whisper through his mind.

Cindy had thought it would be better prowling through the Tombs during the day than it had been the night she'd come looking for a squat, but she was wrong. It was no less unpleasant, just different.

The other night she'd gotten into town too late to look for a good busking spot and been too broke to afford a hotel room. A girl she stopped by the Pier had told her about the deserted tenements in the Tombs, so she'd gone.

The whole place was scarier than she'd expected, but by that time, at that late hour, she just wanted to get off the streets. She hadn't slept well in that little room she laid claim to in the old abandoned tenement where she spent the night. Every noise had her imagining that some old rubbie—or worse, one of the bikers she'd spotted hanging around in a couple of the doorways—was edging into her room. She'd slept fully dressed on top of her bedroll, holding her sax tightly against her like it was the lover she'd long since given up on finding.

By day, the Tombs wasn't quite so scary. She still felt nervous, but it was the way it all looked so depressing that wore on her the most. She wondered why the city had let it get like this. It was just a warren of abandoned buildings, junked vehicles, and litter-covered lots. Except for a couple of the city's main arteries that had to cut through the area—Yoors Street and Williamson—the streets were in terrible condition. Pavement buckled, weeds grew up through inch-wide cracks, and there was refuse everywhere.

The people she saw just looked lost. It was too early in the day for many of the kids to be up and about—though she'd already had to make a wide berth around a couple of bikers in greasy jeans and T-shirts who were working on a chopper in front of what must once have been a classy office building. There was no sense in pushing her luck, she'd thought when she first spotted them.

Mostly she saw derelicts and the homeless, picking through the refuse in the empty lots as though there were something there to find. They looked like they were at the end of their lives, and some of them, she realized, weren't all that much older than she was. She was glad she'd dressed down and taken Meg's advice and rubbed some dirt on her hands and face before entering the Tombs; none of the derelicts approached her for a handout.

She wandered aimlessly around for a half hour or so, shocked again at the sheer size of the area and wondering where she was ever going to find Chelsea. There was just too much space. Too many lots, too many buildings, block upon block of them.

If a person wanted to hide, she realized, this was definitely the place.

Finally she tried to find the building she'd stayed in on her first night in town. That took her the better part of another half hour because to her untrained eye, everything looked the same. But then she recognized some graffiti on the side of a building. There was an enormous peace sign painted on the flaking stone, with the legend "War sucks" written under it. Someone had added "So does life" with red spray paint.

Taking a deep breath, Cindy went inside. There were almost a dozen sleeping figures in the foyer—runaways, she decided by their ages. Most of them had dirty faces, and ragged and frayed clothes, though here and there newcomers stood out because what they wore wasn't quite so threadbare—yet.

Under a sweet smell of refuse, the air held an unpleasant hint of urine and body odor that she hadn't noticed the other night. Did sleeping one night in a clean bed do that to you? she wondered. She'd smelled worse—slept in places that smelled worse when it came right down to it—so she wasn't all that surprised that she hadn't noticed the odor yesterday morning when she left; by then, she knew, she'd gotten used to it.

A guy with skin so transparent he looked like a walking corpse was sitting up against the wall near the elevator, which no longer worked. He had earphones on, but they weren't connected to a radio or tape machine. He just played with their jack, rolling it back and forth between his thumb and forefinger, one foot tapping to a rhythm only he could hear. He watched Cindy as she looked over the faces of his sleeping companions.

"Whatcha lookin' for?" he asked finally.

"A friend."

"Yeah? Your friend got a name?"

"Chelsea." Cindy gave a brief description of the girl.

"Maybe I know her," the boy said. "Whatcha want her for?"

Cindy had thought out the story she'd use on her walk up to the Tombs from Meg's apartment.

"She owes me," she told the boy.

"Money or dope?"

"Dope."

The boy's grin went wide. "Well, hey. You want dope, I got dope."

"Yeah," Cindy said. "But I already paid Chelsea."

"I'm reliable," the boy said. "I only carry good shit. Primo quality."

Right, Cindy thought. That's why you're sitting here in a squat, buzzed out on who knew what.

"I told you," she began.

"Yeah, yeah—you already put out the bread. But next time you got a hurt on, you think about comin' to me why dontcha? Name's Bobby Brown—like the singer, y'know, only I ain't got his color."

You can say that again, Cindy thought.

"Or his moves," Bobby added after a moment. "But I got connections that'll get you the best shit you ever put in your needle, babe."

"I'll remember that," Cindy said.

"The name's Bobby Brown, you just ask around; everybody knows me, where I be found."

His foot tapped in time to his short impromptu rap, the earphone jack twirling between his fingers. He grinned again, and this time Cindy found herself smiling back at him. He was a junkie pusher and looked half-dead, but she couldn't deny that he still had charm. She wondered what he'd been like before he came down so far in the world.

"Chelsea's got herself a squat up on the second floor," he said, indicating the stairwell with a jerk of his thumb. "Just take a right and it's a few doors down. I saw her come in right around dawn and I'll tell you this, babe, she looked fucked up but good. I'm talkin' *wired*. You ask me, she stiffed you and took serious possession of your delivery. You'll be wantin' to talk to me about a deal when you get back."

"Thanks," Cindy said.

Before she could leave, Bobby added, "Do your friend a favor, why dontcha. I didn't know she was dealin', but if she is, she's goin' to want to find herself another building, 'cause all the business in this one belongs to me."

"I . . . I met her downtown," Cindy said.

"Don't mean shit to me. You're here now, aren't you?"

"I'll tell her."

When she started for the stairs, Bobby's gaze had already taken on a faraway look once more. He tapped his foot, fingered the earphone jack. Cindy realized that so far as he was concerned, she no longer existed—at least until she walked up to him with some cash in hand.

She felt even more depressed as she went up the stairs. Bobby wasn't much more than sixteen years old, she thought. She wondered if he'd even live to turn seventeen.

The kids had taken to using the back of the stairs on the ground floor of the stairwell as a toilet she realized as the stench of urine and feces followed her up. The air was a little cleaner when she stepped onto the second floor and turned right.

She walked slowly down the hall, looking in the doorways, but the rooms were empty. She thought about calling out Chelsea's name, but then she found her, almost at the end of the hall. Chelsea had her back to her, but Cindy recognized the spiked hair. The girl appeared to be stuffing a backpack with clothes.

"Chelsea?" Cindy called, pitching her voice low.

The girl turned with a snarl. Her hand dipped into her pocket and came up with a switchblade. The *snick* of the blade leaving its handle hung in the air with a sure promise of violence.

"E-easy," Cindy said.

"Who the fuck are you?"

"I'm just a friend. We ran into each other a couple of nights ago—remember? Here, in the building."

It was like trying to calm down a cornered animal, Cindy thought. Fear lay thick in Chelsea's eyes. She looked over Cindy's shoulder, then focused on her again. The knife trembled in her hand.

"Did . . . did *he* send you?" she demanded.

"He? You mean . . . Jim?"

"Who's Jim?"

"Last night," Cindy said. "Jim's the guy who scared you outside the restaurant. He didn't mean to do it."

Chelsea regarded her with an expression Cindy couldn't read. The fear was still there, stretching the skin tightly across her cheekbones and brow and flaring in her eyes. Cindy could also see that Chelsea

remembered Jim calling out to her last night, but there was something else warring with her memories: a kind of confusion that
seemed to paralyze her. The young dealer's words returned to her—

She looked fucked up but good. I'm talkin' wired.

—and Cindy realized where she'd seen that kind of look before.

"What did you take?" she asked. "And how much of it?"

Chelsea blinked. "You think I'm on drugs?"

"Look," Cindy said. "We've all had bad trips. You'll get through it."
She kept her voice pitched low and comforting. "We can just stay here
and wait till you come down—I won't leave you alone—or we can go to
a hospital. I've got some money to cover the expenses, so you don't—"

Chelsea gave a short, bitter laugh, cutting her off.

"Jesus," she said. "I wish this was a bad trip."

"You're not—"

"I don't do drugs anymore," Chelsea said, "but maybe I should
take them up again. I never heard him in those days."

"Heard who?"

"Him. My father. He's here"—Chelsea tapped the forefinger of
her free hand against her temple—"in my head. He never shuts up."

Listening to Chelsea's denial, all Cindy could think of was her own
father, plastered out of his mind and trying to tell her that he hadn't
had a drink, not even a beer, all day.

"Listen," she tried.

"Oh, I know what it sounds like," Chelsea said, "Don't think I
don't. The fucker's supposed to be dead, except I can *hear* him in my
head. And he goes around killing all those people when all . . . when
all he really wants . . ." Chelsea's voice broke and tears filled her eyes.
"All he really wants to do . . . is kill . . . me. . . ."

Cindy's heart went out to her. Maybe Chelsea was messed up on
some drug and denying it, but that didn't mean she had to face it by
herself.

"You don't have to be alone," she said, taking a step forward. "I can—"

She stopped in her tracks as Chelsea waved the switchblade menacingly at her. Chelsea wiped at her eyes with her sleeve.

"Who are you?" she asked, returning to what she'd wanted to know when Cindy first appeared in the doorway. "What the fuck do you want from me?"

"I just want to help you."

"Why?"

"I . . . I don't really know. I guess it's because you're scared and you look like you need a friend, and I know what it's like to be alone and have no one be there for me. I guess I'm trying to be the friend to you that I wish I'd had."

"Even though you don't know shit about me?"

"Maybe because I don't know you," Cindy replied honestly. "It seems to me that it's always the people who are supposed to be closest to us who hurt us the most."

She thought of her mother, running off and leaving her. She thought of her father, drunk and abusive. She thought of her aunt, who wouldn't believe her stories of how her father—her aunt's own brother—beat her. She thought of her neighbors, who didn't want to get involved even though they knew the noises they heard next door were those of a grown man beating his child.

Something of what she was thinking must have shown on her face, because Chelsea was nodding as though in agreement to something unspoken that had passed between them. She folded the knife's blade back into its handle and stowed it in her pocket.

"Your dad used to . . . fuck you?" Chelsea asked.

Cindy shook her head. "He was an alcoholic. He used to beat me when he got drunk."

Chelsea shrugged. "Same difference. It's all a power trip, isn't it?"

"I guess."

"You don't look too fucked up," Chelsea said after a moment.

Cindy hesitated for a moment, then slowly pulled her shirt out of her jeans and bared her midriff. The scars of a dozen or more cigarette burns pocked her pink skin.

"Jesus," Chelsea said.

She sat down on the floor and leaned against the windowsill as Cindy silently tucked her shirt back into her jeans. She looked out at the empty lot that lay beside the building, where weeds, trash and rubble vied for ownership. Cindy took what the change in Chelsea's mood offered and came all the way into the room. She sat cross-legged on the floor, close enough to touch the other girl, but kept her hands on her knees.

"That guy last night," Chelsea said. "He's a friend of yours?"

Cindy nodded.

"Where'd he get my name?"

"Niki's your real name?" Cindy asked.

The girl nodded. "So's Chelsea. My first name's Nicola."

"He didn't really know it was your name. It's . . . He saw you at those places where those girls got killed and thought there was some connection with your being there."

Niki turned to look at her. "But where'd he get the name?"

"From—this is going to sound crazy—but he got it from the graffiti."

"Doesn't sound crazy to me," Niki said. "Nothing sounds crazy anymore."

"What do you mean? What is it that you're so scared of?"

Niki turned to look out the window again.

"My father started abusing me when I was still in my cradle," she said. She spoke without turning; her voice was flat, empty of emotion. "I don't remember that, but I can remember how it was when I got a little older. My old lady finally got the guts to leave him when I turned seven. We moved away—right across the country. Things weren't great, but they were okay, you know?

"But then when I turned thirteen, her latest beau put the make on me and I just had to go. I've lived on the streets for the last five years. I'm not saying everything I did was right, but I got by. I survived."

She paused, the pause lengthening until Cindy said, "I think I get the picture."

Niki'd probably started turning tricks. It was an easy life to fall into; it had almost happened to Cindy herself, but she'd been lucky. She hit the road when she was older, and all the bullshit pickup lines from the pimps never cut it with her. But for a young thirteen-year-old with no place to go . . .

"Maybe you do," Niki said. "It doesn't matter."

"It does matter," Cindy said.

Niki turned to look at her. She studied her for a long moment, then slowly shook her head.

"You really do give a shit, don't you?" she said.

When she spoke, her voice cracked—just a touch. Cindy found her throat going thick. There was a tight feeling in her chest, like her skin had suddenly become a couple of sizes too small. She reached out a hand and Niki took it. It was all the response Cindy could give right then; she didn't trust her own voice.

Niki looked away again, but she held onto Cindy's hand. Her voice regained its flat tone.

"But the way things went," she said, "I could see my whole life was going downhill. I was in a dead-end situation and no one was going to help me unless I helped myself. I didn't know what to do until I was reading this old magazine at a Welfare office. There was an article in it about serial killers and that was where I found out that the old man was finally dead."

"Your father . . . he was . . . killed by one of those people?" Cindy asked.

Niki gave another of her short, bitter laughs. "Fuck no. He was one of them. After my old lady took us away, he started getting his jollies out of killing the kids he fucked."

"Oh my God. . . ."

"Yeah, right. Anyway he finally got his own. He—get this—he got caught because there just happened to be a cop driving behind him and he got nervous so he jumped a red light. He ended up trying to shoot the cop, only he got killed instead. They found a bunch of dead kids in the trunk of his car."

With every word Niki spoke, the numb feeling inside Cindy deepened.

"Anyway, when I heard he was dead, I figured maybe I'd come back and try to make a new start here. You know, finish high school, try to get a real life instead of living in the shadows. I thought I could feel my old hometown calling me back. It was like it was saying, some bad shit went down here, but now everything's okay. Now there's a chance to do it right.

"So I came back, except I found out that it was his voice I heard in my head. He was calling me back."

"He . . . ?" Cindy asked, dreading the answer.

"My old man."

Niki turned back from the window. She looked straight at Cindy; her bright blue eyes were clear and sane.

"He's not dead anymore, you see," she said. "He's come back and he's looking for me."

"But—"

"All those girls he's killed—that's me he's killing. And he's going to keep doing it over and over again until he gets it right."

Cindy started to shake her head. "That's imposs—"

"I *know* it's fucking impossible," Niki said. "What do you think I am, stupid? But it's happening all the same."

Cindy didn't know what to say or do. Did she play along with the story—weren't you supposed to humor crazy people?—or did she try to get Niki to see the truth?

"I thought maybe I could do something," Niki went on. "I thought maybe I could stop him—make a difference. But I know now I can't. He's just too strong. And besides, how do you kill something that's already dead?"

"You can't."

"Exactly my point."

"You can't," Cindy said, "because people don't come back from the dead."

Niki freed her hand. Reaching up, she pulled off Cindy's beret so that the honey-blonde hair that had been hidden under it fell free.

"This is a dye job," she said, lifting a hand to her own hair. "I'm blond, just like you."

"What does that have to—"

"All those girls he's killed are blonde, too. So if you're so sure of yourself, why don't you leave your hat off and go walking around in the Zone next Friday night?" Niki paused, then added, "Or maybe any night. I got a feeling he's about to start changing his habits."

"I didn't say there wasn't a killer," Cindy said.

"You're just saying he's not my old man."

"Not if your father's dead."

"Oh, he's dead all right."

Niki cocked her head as though listening. Cindy tried, but she couldn't hear a thing.

"The way I see it," Niki said, "is either I'm crazy and it's all in my head . . ."

She looked too sane, Cindy thought. That was the scariest thing.

". . . or I'm not and he's really out there. Either way, you're better off not hanging around me."

"I . . . I don't know what to do," Cindy said.

"Yeah, well I do. I'm getting my ass out of here. Maybe he'll follow me and maybe he won't. All I know is that if I *do* stay here, I'm dead meat. I think I'll take my chances and just hit the road."

This time she was the one to reach out and offer comfort.

"I know what it all sounds like," she said. "Honestly I do. If I were you, I'd get away from me just about as fast as I could. But I want to thank you for trying to help. Nobody's ever done that before—not without wanting something I didn't want to give them in return."

Niki's words echoed what Cindy had been thinking earlier this morning in Meg's apartment: Out on the road, everybody wants a piece of you. That's what was going to happen to Niki if Cindy let her go now.

"I still want to help," she said. "I just don't know how."

"Tell me about it."

Niki gave her hand a squeeze. Handing Cindy back her beret, she got up and returned to stuffing her clothes in her backpack.

Cindy moved closer to the window. She looked out over the wasteland of empty lots and abandoned buildings. It seemed to reflect what lay inside her right at that moment. When she turned back, Niki had her gear all packed. She was standing in the middle of the room, holding her backpack by its straps.

"Come with me," Cindy said. "Talk to my friend Jim."

"What can he do?"

"I don't know. But he knows the city. He works for a paper. He's got lots of connections. Maybe he knows somebody that can help us."

"Like who?" Niki asked. "I'm not going to see a shrink."

"Maybe there's someone who can . . . I don't know . . . exorcise your ghost."

Niki gave her a sad smile. "What? You're offering me a—what do you call them?—a placebo? Niki thinks the ghost's been chased away, so Niki'll become sane again?"

"No."

"Come on. *You* don't believe and I figure you're at least sympathetic. What are my chances anyone else will?"

"At least talk to him."

"I . . ."

"Please."

Niki shook her head. "I just don't get it. Why are you so concerned?"

"Because I don't want to see you throw your life away, that's why. You came here to start over; all you're going to find on the road is the same dead end you were trying to escape."

"No shit," Niki said, but then she sighed. "Okay. We'll see your friend. But then I'm out of here and you don't try to stop me—is that a deal?"

"It's a deal."

"Describe to me again the events as you saw them," Isabeau Fontenot asked Jim after he'd related a disjointed account of what had happened in the Tombs last night.

At the door earlier she hadn't been anything like what Jim had expected, not at all the voluptuous caricature from a B movie. Instead she was a thin mulatto in her midtwenties. Although she was rather plain, she had a presence that immediately commanded one's attention. She was dressed in a bright red, yellow, and green flower-print dress, and her hair was done up in what looked like hundreds of cornrow braids. In one hand she carried a large brown leather bag. She seemed all sharp angles, but her large, dark brown eyes promised warmth if they could be made to smile.

"Ah . . . Ms. Fontenot," he'd begun, suddenly feeling awkward.

"Call me Ti Beau," she said. "It's the name I am known by in my . . . work."

"Right. Ti Beau it is. Listen, thanks for coming, I—"

She walked past him and sat down on the sofa, setting her bag at her feet. Before Jim could offer her coffee or tea, she got right down to business.

"Tell me what you saw," she said.

So Jim went through it, and now he repeated the story when she asked him to. This time he managed a more coherent version. She looked through the photographs as he spoke, nodding to herself when he was done.

"It was not a *voudoun* ceremony you saw," she said.

"Well, it sure as hell *looked* like—"

"Papa Jo-el was a *bocor*—a sorcerer—as well as a *houngan*," she said. "What you saw bears no relationship to the worship of the *loa*."

"Then what *was* he doing?"

"Raising a *guédé*, I would imagine. A spirit of the dead," she added at his blank look.

"So . . . what I saw . . . it was real?"

Ti Beau nodded.

"Jesus," Jim said softly.

The woman's composed presence helped stem the panic that Jim could feel rising up in him. He took a couple of steadying breaths. They helped as well. Now if he could just get rid of that damned *sound* in his head. . . .

He found Ti Beau studying him.

"There is something about you," she said when he caught her glance. "Are you in pain?"

Jim nodded. "Ever since I saw that thing last night, I've had this . . . sound in my head. It's like a kind of whispering—a voice, but I can't make out what it's saying. I think it's a name."

"And it troubles you?"

Jim looked at her as if she was crazy. Just talking about the damned sound had it clamoring in his head, overriding all his efforts to keep it at bay. He felt himself wanting just to hit Ti Beau, take a baseball bat, or maybe a bread knife from the kitchen, and just—

She reached forward suddenly and laid a cool hand on his brow. Her fingers traced a design upon his temple and the fever seemed to pass. The whispering was still there, but it was more distant now. Just like that, he could handle it again.

"The curse of a *guédé,*" Ti Beau said thoughtfully.

"What are you talking about?"

"This spirit is very strong," she said by way of reply. "It has left a sliver of itself in you."

Jim's stomach did a slow, queasy flip.

"In . . . me . . . ," he managed.

Ti Beau nodded. "It can happen—when the *guédé* is very strong."

"It makes me feel . . . crazy, you know? Like I just want to break something."

Ti Beau nodded again. She undid the fastening of the leather bag at her feet and rummaged about in it until her hand came up with a small leather pouch attached to a leather thong. Before Jim could protest, she slipped the thong over his head and let the pouch fall against his chest.

The change was instantaneous. One moment the whispering ran though his head, cold and murderous, the next it was gone.

Jim lifted a wondering hand to the pouch. "Jesus," he said as he prodded it gingerly with a finger. "What . . . what is this?"

"*Gris-gris,*" Ti Beau said. "A small charm to keep unfriendly spirits at bay."

"It . . . it really works."

She gave him a brief smile. "I would have been gravely disappointed if it had not."

"I didn't mean any disrespect. It's just—"

"That you are not a believer."

Jim nodded. His fingers closed around the pouch, and he savored the blessed silence in his head.

"Thank you," he said.

"You are welcome. I'm glad to have been able to help you in such a small thing." He got another brief smile from her; then she was all business again. "Why exactly did you wish to see me?"

Christ, Jim thought. Like shutting off that damned sound in his head wasn't worth the price of admission?

He let go of the *gris-gris* pouch and tried to put his train of thought back together again.

"Okay," he said. "So your boss—"

"He was the *houngan* of the temple in which I am *mambo*," Ti Beau corrected him. "I have no 'boss,' save *les invisibles*."

"Right." Jim rephrased his question. "Why was he raising a spirit of the dead?"

Ti Beau regarded the photos again—both the ones Jim had taken the night before and those of Niki and the graffiti.

"If the *guédé* that killed Papa Jo-el is the same one that is murdering all those girls," she said, "then I believe he was trying to drive it away from the city. Had he succeeded, it would have counted as a great coup in his rivalry with Clarvius, for it would have shown that *les invisibles* looked more favorably upon him."

"Clarvius Jones?" Jim asked.

Ti Bean nodded.

Jim went back to what she'd been saying before he interrupted her. "So you think this . . . uh, ghost . . . is the Slasher?"

Ti Beau nodded. "I sense the same connection as you do," she said. "The *guédé*, this girl, the graffiti. I wonder what her relationship to the dead man is."

"Why would there be a relationship?"

"*Guédé* such as this one are spirits who remain in the Place Between—in Limbo. They seek to regain the flesh they lost so that they can walk in the world of men once more as *les damnés*."

"The damned," Jim said, finding that term, at least, easy to translate.

Ti Beau nodded. "The undead," she said. "There are many ways for them to regain flesh, but the most effective method is to impregnate the body of a female blood relation and be 'born' once more. Could she be its daughter, or a niece?"

"I don't know. I don't know the girl. I don't even know for sure if there *is* a connection. Cindy said her name was Chelsea."

"Names can be changed." Ti Beau fingered Niki's photo. "I sense secrets here."

"But—"

"The terror you tell me that came over her when you called out to her—that is the terror of facing a *guédé*, would you not think?"

"I suppose. But what does it need to regain a body for? That creature was physically *there* last night. It was wielding a knife and tossing those guys around."

"The dead can manifest in physical form," Ti Beau explained, "but such an effect is only temporary."

They both fell silent then. As Jim considered what they'd been talking about, he began again to question his own sanity. What was he doing, talking about all this hoodoo stuff as though it were real?

Because he *saw* it last night. He saw that thing just take shape out of a mist, kill three men, and then disappear.

"So what do we do?" he asked.

Ti Beau regarded him with raised eyebrows. "Do?"

"About this . . . this *guédé*."

"Are you so sure you wish to involve yourself further?"

"Are you kidding? I feel like just packing up and leaving the city."

"Then why don't you?"

"I can't," Jim said. "I've thought about it, but I can't do it."

"There is no shame in fearing such a malevolent *guédé*," Ti Beau said. "Or in fleeing its haunts."

Jim shook his head. "But I *know* now," he said. "If I don't try to do something and somebody else dies, their deaths are going to be on my conscience. I'd go to the cops like a shot if I thought they'd listen, but there's no way they'd take any of this seriously. Christ, sometimes I can't believe *I'm* taking it seriously."

Ti Beau studied him for a moment, a hint of a smile touching her eyes as his hand rose to finger the *gris-gris* pouch that dangled against his chest. The smile immediately softened the sharp angles of her features.

"You are a good man," she said.

The compliment made Jim blush. "Yeah, well . . ."

"And I know exactly what you mean, but I'm not so sure either of us can do a thing."

"What do you mean? Can't you just do whatever it is you guys do and . . ."

His voice trailed off at her weary smile.

"I am merely a *mambo*," she said. "I am a healer, a guide to the Mysteries, not a sorcerer. What little power I have is loaned to me by my *loa*, Zaka. He is the Spirit of the Land, the Tender of the Fields. His power is in healing and growth. What magics I have are just small *gris-gris*—charms, little spells, like the one you now wear about your neck. This *guédé* seems too strong for what I can do. If I knew more, if I knew for sure that the girl is to be his conduit to this world . . ." She shrugged. "One would need to be possessed by the power of Baron Samedi or Chango to deal with such a spirit without more knowledge."

"These are all . . . *loa*?"

Ti Beau nodded.

"And everybody's got a different one?"

"No," she said. "You have only the *loa* who comes to you, but the *loa* have more than one channel for their powers. Is the Christian God perceived by only one priest?"

"Well, how do you get a *loa*?" Jim asked.

"You do not *get* one," Ti Beau said with just a slight irritation in her voice. "There are ceremonies and initiations to undergo before you *invite* a *loa* to possess you."

"Yeah, but—"

"I know what you are driving at," she said, "but we have neither the time nor do you have the proper respect for you to invite a *loa* to come to you. Such a possession isn't like a suit of clothes that you may take on or off, or experiment with in various styles."

"Still," Jim began, but then the doorbell rang, interrupting them.

At the door Jim found Cindy standing in the hallway.

"Hi, Jim," she said. "I hope we're not bothering you. It's just . . ."

Her voice trailed off when she saw Ti Beau sitting on the sofa.

"It's not what you think," Jim said at the quick flash of disappointment he saw in her eyes. "Her name's Ti Beau and she's just helping me with . . ."

His own voice trailed off as he noticed Cindy's companion. Ti Beau was also looking at the girl with the spiked black hair who stood behind Cindy.

"This changes everything," the *mambo* said softly.

SEVENTEEN

Angie still wasn't home by the time Thomas returned to their apartment. He stood in the center of the living room, jacket in hand, and looked around himself as though seeing the familiar room for the first time. The apartment was a far cry from the reserve. The room's lines were clean, the furnishings uncluttered. It held a mixture of old and new, glass and wood, leather sofa and a morris chair, high-end stereo and Angie's old acoustic guitar, contemporary prints and native art.

It was a far cry as well from most cops' apartments he'd been in, and he wondered, not for the first time, how he'd come to be here. For all its seeming contradictions, the room exuded calm. But the weight of the Slasher case and the unspoken reproach in his brother's eyes, combined with the drive back into the city, had brought all his tension back. He felt as if he were sleepwalking—stretched tight as a drawn bowstring and so beat he could barely keep to his feet. Did he even belong in a place like this?

It was getting to be too much, he realized. The case, his brother's need, the city. And Angie. It was so late. Where could she be at this time of night?

Don't think about it, he told himself. You'll just make yourself more crazy.

But it was hard.

He didn't think he'd get to sleep, but no sooner did his head hit the pillow than he was gone.

When the alarm woke him next morning, Angie was lying next to him. He tried to get out of bed without waking her, but she turned to look at him with a sleepy gaze as soon as he shifted his weight.

"Do you have to go?" she asked.

Thomas nodded.

She didn't say anything, but then she didn't have to. Normally they made time for each other—not because they felt they had to, but because they wanted to. It was what made the marriage work. They were friends as much as lovers.

"I . . . I'm thinking of quitting," Thomas said.

Angie sat up against the headboard, pulling the sheets up around her. She still looked half-asleep.

"The case?" she asked.

Thomas shook his head. "No, the job."

That brought her completely awake. The surprise in her features mirrored Thomas's own. He hadn't known he was going to say that himself until the words came out—seemingly of their own accord.

Angie put a hand on his arm. "Listen," she said. "I'm sorry about yesterday. I stayed late at Brenda's because I was upset, but I should have come home and talked it out with you. I know what kind of pressure this case has been putting on you. It's just—"

"It's not only because of us," Thomas said.

God knew he loved his job, but the more he thought of quitting, the more right it felt.

"Though I think that's a large part of it," he went on. "I won't deny it. It's . . ." He sighed. "I don't think I'm making the difference I thought I would. I thought that when I made detective it would change things, but it just seems to get worse. People are still dying out there. I see things on the job that I can't believe people are capable of doing to each other, but it goes on, every day, day after day."

"But you and Frank . . ."

"I know," Thomas said. "We've got a damn good conviction record, but we're not even scratching the surface."

"And if you weren't there?" Angie asked.

Thomas just shrugged. Did they really make that much of a difference? How much could just two cops, no matter how well-intentioned, really do?

He rubbed his face. His skin felt too tight—swollen from sleep—but he could've slept straight through the day and still not gotten enough.

Angie was still regarding him, the worry plain in her eyes.

"What happened last night?" she asked. "What did your brother say to you?"

"It's nothing John did or said."

He told her about his meeting with Whiteduck and his brother.

"Then what is it?" Angie asked. "Did you change your mind?"

"About being band chief? No. It's just . . . I can't put it into words, Angie. It's like I've caught a kind of . . . of malaise." It was an odd choice of a word for him, but it summed things up totally. "And now that it's got hold of me, it won't go away."

Angie started to say something, but then the phone rang. Thomas picked it up. His chest felt even tighter than before, as though subconsciously, he already knew it wasn't going to be good.

"We've got a problem," his partner told him over the line. "The Slasher was out again last night."

"But that's—"

Impossible, Thomas had been about to say. Because the spirit could only manifest in this world on his death night.

Jesus, he thought. Was he that wired into the things Papa Jo-el and his brother had been telling him?

"That's what?" Frank asked.

"Nothing. Has the victim been IDed yet?"

"Try victims," Frank replied. "As in more than one. He killed three blacks in the Tombs last night: Papa Jo-el and a couple of his bodyguards— the Etienne brothers. Seems the Slasher caught them in the middle of some kind of ritual."

"How do they know it was the Slasher?"

"Same MO. That woman in the ME's office—what's her name?"

"Wilkes."

"Yeah. Wilkes said you'd know what she's talking about. This has got to do with the perp getting stronger each time he kills, right?"

"That's what she says."

Frank made an affirmative grunt. "Looking at the body of the Wilson girl, I can see where she's coming from."

"Where are you?" Thomas asked.

"Home. The Loot's going to meet us at the 9th—that's your old stomping grounds, isn't it?"

His old stomping grounds, Thomas thought. The 9th Precinct included all those blighted lots and empty blocks of the Tombs. It was in there, smack in the middle of those dead lands, that he'd killed a man in the line of duty. It was funny, but he hadn't thought about that in a long time. That the man had deserved to die had never made Thomas feel any better about it.

"That's right," he said. "What was Papa Jo-el doing out there?"

"Brewer says there was voodoo shit lying all around," Frank said. He paused for a moment, then added. "Like I said, we're supposed to meet him at the 9th. Do you want me to pick you up, or will you meet us there?"

"I'll meet you there."

When he hung up, he found Angie looking at him in sympathy.

"He struck again?" she asked. There was no need to say who "he" was.

Thomas nodded. "In the Tombs this time. Three black men. One of them was a voodoo priest, the other two his bodyguards." He rubbed his palms against his face, then looked at her. "Do you see what I mean? It just gets worse."

"You can't just quit," she told him. "That's not who you are. See this thing through and then make your decision."

"I . . ."

What could he tell her? Thomas thought. His head was filled with wild ideas: evil spirits and dead men seeking vengeance or whatever it was that the Slasher was after. But it was all just bullshit, wasn't it?

Seems the Slasher caught them in the middle of some kind of ritual.

What the hell was that supposed to mean?

There was voodoo shit lying all around.

What was Papa Jo-el doing out in the Tombs at that time of night—calling up spirits? Is that what happened? Had he called up the Slasher's spirit—maybe planning to deal with him as he'd intimated he could yesterday afternoon—only the whole deal backfired on him and he got killed instead?

"Tom?"

He focused on his name, using it to draw him out of the spinning eddies of stray thoughts that were starting to give him a sense of vertigo.

"Are you all right?" Angie asked.

No, he wasn't even close to all right, but he found a weak smile and nodded. "Yeah. Just a little tired, that's all. But I think you're right; I have to see this thing through before I make any major decisions."

She followed him into the bathroom and leaned against the doorjamb while he washed up.

"You'll be careful, won't you?"

"I'm always careful," Thomas said. "Because I know I've got you to come home to."

She stepped closer and gave him a hug, ignoring the soap on his cheeks.

"I was such a shit last night," she said.

Thomas held her close, wishing the day would just go away and leave them alone. But it wouldn't. Out there, beyond the safe comfort of their apartment, shit happened. And he had to deal with it.

Sighing, he gave her a final squeeze, then turned back to the sink.

"I'll get you some breakfast," Angie said.

Mickey Flynn wasn't particularly happy about having to shift his bulk out of bed this early in the morning. He was even less happy with the crap Billy Ryan was trying to lay on him.

They sat in the main suite of Mickey's penthouse. The remains of Mickey's breakfast lay on the glass coffee table between them. All Ryan had had was some coffee and about a hundred cigarettes.

"So some jigs got themselves killed," Mickey said. "What's it to us?"

"I'm telling you, Mickey, the thing that killed them wasn't even fucking human."

Mickey studied his lieutenant with a touch of concern—not so much for Ryan himself, as for what it would mean to him if Ryan really was losing it. Ryan looked like he was wired: chain-smoking, twitching in his chair. What the fuck was he *on* anyway? And when did Ryan start sampling the merchandise?

"You know what you sound like?" Mickey asked, keeping his voice mild.

"I know what I fucking sound like," Ryan said. He lit another cigarette from the butt of the one he was smoking, then crushed the butt in the ashtray. "I sound like a goddamn lunatic, is what I sound like. But I was *there*, Mickey. I saw it happen."

"Some . . . what do you call it? Some ghost killed Papa Jo-el and the Etienne brothers. He just stepped right up to them, cut 'em up, and then took off."

"Vanished."

"Don't give me any of this fucking 'vanished' crap. Jesus, Billy. You sound so full of shit, I swear your eyes're turning brown."

Those pale blue eyes Mickey had referred to narrowed dangerously.

"Look," Ryan said. "You asked me to look into this Slasher business, so that's what I did. You don't like what I found, what am I supposed to do?"

Mickey shrugged expansively. "I'm just saying I find it hard to buy." He paused, then leaned forward. "What the fuck are you *on*, Billy?"

"That's it?" Ryan said. "You think I'm popping pills, maybe doing a few too many lines?"

"I think you're fucked up, is what I think."

"You wanted me to deal with it, so—"

Mickey cut him off. "So deal with it."

For a long moment the two men stared at each other. Slowly Ryan reached behind his back, under his jacket. When his hand came back out it was holding his .38. He pointed the weapon at Mickey.

"Easy now," Mickey said.

Jesus, he thought. What a fucking way to start the day. First Ryan shows up, doped to the gills, and now he's waving a piece around like he can scare me into believing his shit.

"Give me the gun, Billy," he added.

He never thought for a moment that Billy would actually shoot. There just weren't the percentages in it for Billy.

The first bullet took him by surprise. It hit him in the chest like a sledgehammer, driving his bulk back into the couch. The pain was more than he thought it'd be, but then he'd always been on the firing end of a gun. He'd never been the victim.

"Jes—" he began.

The second bullet tore into his cheek, glanced off the bone and took out his right eye along with half the temple. He was dead before his enormous body rolled off the couch and thudded onto the floor.

"You see?" Ryan said. "I'm dealing with it, Mickey."

He was breathing heavily. The whispering voice in his head whined like a buzz saw. He'd risen to his feet, swaying where he stood. He kept the muzzle of the .38 pointed at Mickey's inert corpse for long minutes, then slowly lowered his arm. He sat down again. Laying the .38 down on the glass coffee table, he shook another cigarette free from the pack and lit it with a shaking hand.

There'd been a kind of gauze across his mind ever since he'd seen Papa Jo-el die. He didn't know what he'd hoped to gain by coming to Mickey and telling him about what he'd seen. He'd known what Mickey's reaction would be. Christ, someone came to him with a story like he had to tell and he'd be showing the poor fuck out the door, too.

Except he knew that what he'd seen was real. And if it was real, then that changed everything. It meant you couldn't trust anything to be the way you'd always expected it to be.

The whisper in his mind seemed to be laughing at him.

"Fuck you, too," he said.

All Mickey'd had to do was listen with a sympathetic ear. All Mickey'd had to do was treat him with a little respect—allow Ryan the benefit of the doubt—and he wouldn't be dead. It was just that simple. Ryan knew he had to talk to someone about it—someone had to believe him—or he was going to go right out of his mind.

He looked down at his boss's corpse.

What the fuck was he thinking? he thought. Mrs. Ryan's boy was already a little too far gone as it was.

He closed his eyes and all he could see was that . . . *thing* killing Papa Jo-el and his boys. They were physically dead, but there was a kind of death in him, too. An emptiness filled only by the sound of a midnight wind that whispered across the flat wasteland that his mind had become.

He focused on Mickey's corpse again and took a long drag from his cigarette.

Okay, he told himself. You're on the edge. Just stay cool. Don't move, don't step off.

Whispering laughter woke a pain behind his eyes.

The first thing to do was get rid of Mickey's corpse. He'd cut it up into a hundred little pieces and scatter them all over hell and back again. No body, no crime.

See, Mickey? I learned real quick.

Then he was going back to the Tombs, going back with a fucking payload of weapons and see if he couldn't shake that ghost down. Because he knew that if he didn't, he was never going to get its fucking voice out of his head.

Okay. Get rid of the body, load up a car with little bits of Mickey Flynn, all bite-sized and ready for the rats in the Tombs. Get himself some heavy artillery. And then what?

Then he'd get himself some hoodoo worker to call that ghost up for him. Call it up and get it the fuck out of his head.

He finished his cigarette and smoked another. Finally he got up.

He dragged Mickey's body into the bathroom and manhandled the corpse into the tub. On the way to the kitchen for a butcher's knife and the small saw he knew Mickey kept in a toolbox under the sink, he paused to look at the couch. Messy. He'd have to get rid of the cushions and carpet, too.

He looked up at the ceiling. There was a bullet hole in it just above the sofa. He'd have to dig the slug out—and find the other one, which'd be in the sofa if it wasn't still stuck in Mickey's fat corpse.

He pushed his palms against his temples, trying to stem the ache that was burning back in behind his eyes.

Fuck this, he thought. Get moving. Get doing. Don't even think about it.

But the whole time he worked on Mickey's body, all he could think of was that monster last night, that killing machine. And whispering in his head was a sound like a midnight wind, sharp and thin, a mean, cutting wind, whining through the city like it was looking for him.

Viewing Papa Jo-el's corpse before it was taken away, Thomas felt an unaccountable sympathy for the man. 'It wasn't that Thomas had liked him—he hadn't even respected the little *houngan*. But Papa Jo-el hadn't deserved to die like this. Nobody deserved to die like this.

Detectives from the 9th were in charge of the case. The police cruisers, ambulances, media vans, and the men and women who'd come in them were the only sign of movement or color in all the endless blocks of abandoned buildings and lots that surrounded the intersection where the bodies had been discovered. A slate gray sky that promised rain only added to the sense of desolation.

Thomas found himself remembering another crime scene in the Tombs, some two years back. The circus was much the same—cops and media crawling all over everything; he was the one playing a different role then.

It wasn't a good memory.

Thomas had assumed that Brewer would have Frank and him take over the investigation, but once they'd viewed the crime scene, the lieutenant took them aside, leaving the men from the 9th to continue the investigation on their own.

"What do you think?" Brewer asked.

Thomas shrugged. That this was the work of the Slasher was too obvious to bother replying. He stepped to one side, to move away from the smoke as Brewer lit a cigarette, and looked back at the crime scene. He believed he knew what Papa Jo-el had been doing. Would the *houngan* still be alive if he and Frank had helped him?

"It's connected, all right," Frank said, "and the perp's just upped the stakes. It's not just blonde hookers now, and the hunting ground's widening."

"You talked to Papa Jo-el yesterday," Brewer said. "Did he give any indication that he'd be coming here last night?"

"He said he wanted to help," Thomas offered.

Frank made a derisive noise. "Like we need help from slime."

"Right now," Brewer said, "I'll take what I can get—from any source."

Frank gave the lieutenant a quick rundown of their conversation with Papa Jo-el yesterday.

"That fits with the voodoo paraphernalia lying around the bodies," Brewer said thoughtfully.

Frank just shook his head. "Don't tell me you're buying into this crap, too?"

"Buying into what?"

"Evil spirits and all that shit."

"No," Brewer said. "But if Papa Jo-el was sincere in his beliefs, and we've no reason to suspect otherwise, it explains what he was doing out here."

"Well, why didn't he do his little ceremony in the Zone?" Frank wanted to know. "That's where the Slasher was doing his hunting."

Brewer shrugged. "Maybe the privacy this place offers was something he knew he just couldn't get in the Zone. The thing we have to ask is, how did the Slasher know to find Pilione here?"

Because the Slasher is a spirit and he was called to this place, Thomas thought, unable to stop the conviction that was growing in him. Called by Papa Jo-el's ceremony.

"We'll need to talk to his people—friends, associates, whoever we can run down," Brewer went on. "My gut feeling says the Slasher's somebody Papa Jo-el knew. That's the only way he could've known about what Papa Jo-el was planning."

"I don't get it," Frank said. "Why should he give a shit what Papa Jo-el was doing down here?"

"Maybe our perp's a believer, too," Brewer said.

Or maybe, Thomas thought, Papa Jo-el was onto something and the Slasher knew it was kill or be . . . what? What could you do to something that was already dead? Banish its spirit?

He knew he shouldn't be letting this take over his view of the case. That was one of the first things you learned: Keep an open mind, don't narrow your investigation down to one pet theory, or you could easily blind yourself to the real solution. It was good advice in a normal situation. But then, the instructors at the academy had never dealt with a spirit of the dead before—had they?

"The place it gets complicated," Brewer added, "is that I was going over the surveillance reports on our witness, Mr. Michael 'Twitchy-eye' Fisher. Seems he had himself a visitor yesterday. The name Billy Ryan ring any bells?"

"Mickey Flynn's Ryan?" Thomas asked.

Brewer nodded. "The officer on stakeout got a photo of him. It's Billy Ryan all right."

"The Irish mob doesn't leave bodies around," Thomas said, nodding toward the ambulances. Attendants were in the process of loading the body bags. "That isn't the way they work."

"Except," Frank said thoughtfully, "what if they're trying to leave a message to someone?"

"Or maybe it's a third party," Brewer offered, "playing the two gangs off each other. You see what I mean about complications?"

Thomas and Frank nodded.

"Have we picked up Ryan?" Thomas asked.

Brewer shook his head. "We've got an APB out on him, so it shouldn't be long—unless he knows we're on to him. In the meantime, why don't we get to work on Papa Jo-el's people?"

Thomas and Frank spent a fruitless afternoon interviewing Papa Jo-el's relatives and business associates. By the time midafternoon rolled around, they'd talked to everyone except for Isabeau Fontenot, the woman who helped the *houngan* in his voodoo ceremonies. From descriptions they got of Fontenot, Thomas doubted she could be responsible for the killings—she just wasn't big enough. Calling up her driver's license on the computer just confirmed what they'd been told.

Fontenot was a slight, striking woman, weighing in at just over a hundred pounds. She simply couldn't have the brute strength required to have killed the Slasher's first victim, let alone be responsible for the carnage in the Tombs. They still had to talk to her, so they put an all-points bulletin out on her, to add to the one they already had out on Billy Ryan. While her sudden disappearance awakened Frank's suspicions, it struck Thomas as ominous.

There was something building—not just the tension that had a death grip on Thomas's neck and shoulders, but something in the city itself. Throughout the frustration of the afternoon, as they'd gone from one low-rent apartment to another in Upper Foxville, he'd been all too aware of a sense of oppression that seemed to be gathering over the city. It was aided in part, he knew, by overcast skies, but the gloom of the cloud cover alone couldn't explain the foreboding that had settled on him.

He wasn't alone in feeling it. In the squad room of the 12th Precinct, where he, Frank, and Brewer had met to compare notes, conversations were carried on in hushed tones by the other officers and suspects alike. The media people, while clamoring for information on the killings in the Tombs—and thank Christ, they hadn't made a connection to the Friday Slasher yet—were oddly subdued in their own pursuit for information.

Thomas and Frank were just finishing up their meeting, when the desk sergeant brought Thomas's brother into the squad room. For one shocked moment, Thomas thought John had been arrested, but then he saw the visitor badge he was wearing and realized that his brother was here to see him.

That, in itself, was unusual enough.

John paused in the doorway. He was taller than anyone else in the squad room, broader-shouldered, his face wider, an impassive expression in his dark eyes. Except for the lack of his hunting knife, he was dressed much the same as he'd been last night—sweatband with the eagle's feather, the long black braids, flannel shirt, jeans, and boots.

He looked about the room slowly until his gaze reached the desk where Thomas was sitting. Thomas found his own gaze sliding from his brother's features to take in the reaction of his fellow officers. They were looking at John as though his brother were some new low form of life, not bothering to hide their dislike.

"They're always going to look on us as second-class citizens," John had told him once. "Why would you want to be one of them?"

But he didn't, Thomas tried to explain. I want them to see that we're no different from them. We can do the same jobs; we've got the same needs and desires.

"The only thing they want," John had concluded, "is to keep us as far from them as they can."

That was the look Thomas saw now in the eyes of his fellow officers. They didn't see a man; they didn't see his brother. Never mind that John was clean and sober; all they could see was a dirty, drunk Indian lying in a downtown gutter, shouting abuse at passersby, or maybe some young brave down from the reserve, trying a little B&E, hitting a gas station, picking a fight in a bar. If he's got to be here, they seemed to be thinking, then why isn't he in cuffs?

They don't look at me like that, Thomas thought. But the ugly realization came to him as he was standing there: not anymore they don't. Not to his face they didn't.

He turned to Brewer and Frank.

"Are we about finished up here?" he asked.

The lieutenant nodded. "Sure. Take a break." His glance encompassed Frank as well. "Both of you."

"What's your brother doing here?" Frank asked.

"I guess we'll find out," Thomas said. "Do you want to grab something to eat with us?"

Frank shook his head. "I think he wants to talk to you on your own."

"Okay," Thomas said. "I'll see you in an hour or so," he added, then crossed the squad room to join his brother.

"Do you want to get something to eat?" he asked John as they shook hands.

"Let's just walk," John said. "Outside somewhere."

Once they had left the precinct, they walked west, toward Fitzhenry Park. John seemed wrapped in his own thoughts, but Thomas could be patient. He'd just wait until John was ready. When they reached the park, Thomas got himself a couple of hot dogs and a Coke at one of the concession stands that lined Palm Street on the park side. John settled for just a black coffee. When he brought it over to the bench to which Thomas led them, he popped the plastic lid, tore a small triangle from it and then replaced the lid. He fingered the little wedge of leftover plastic for a long moment, then stowed it away in the pocket of his shirt.

"So what brings you to town?" Thomas asked as the silence continued to lengthen.

"You do," John said. "I'm here to help you with your case."

Thomas shook his head. "I can't let you get involved in a police matter. This isn't the reserve, John."

"I can see that."

"Look, it's not that I don't appreciate the offer, but there's nothing you can do to help."

John took a sip of his coffee and said nothing. Thomas had to smile. It seemed he wasn't the only person who'd learned something from their mother. He was tempted just to let the silence lie there between them, but he realized that'd be about as childish as when they were boys, trying to stare each other down.

"What did you have in mind?" he asked.

"You and me," John said. "We're going to bring the Slasher to us and deal with him."

"What're you talking about?"

But Thomas knew before his brother replied. A picture flashed in his mind—three dead black men, lying sprawled amid the debris of their voodoo ceremony.

"You know," John said.

Thomas nodded. "But we can't do it."

"Why? Because you think it's all crap?"

"No, because I think it'll work," Thomas replied. "I shouldn't be telling you this," he added, but he went ahead and told his brother about Papa Jo-el's death, how it connected to the Slasher, what Thomas thought the *houngan* had been doing.

"I'll be damned," John said softly.

"So don't you see?" Thomas said. "I can't let you throw your life away. There's no percentage in it."

"And what about all the others who are going to die if we don't do something about this spirit?"

"What do you care?" Thomas said. "It's not like they're from the reserve."

John was silent for a long moment. When Thomas glanced at him, the hurt in his brother's eyes surprised him.

"They're still people," John said.

Thomas nodded. "I was out of line. It's just . . . you and the rest of the Warriors. You're all so hard-line."

"That won't change," John told him. "We just want what's rightfully ours and we'll fight to get it; the time for waiting's long past. But that doesn't mean I don't care about people. When we finally reach a solution, Tom, it's going to have to include both Natives and whites in the equation."

"Okay."

"So what time do you get off today?" John asked.

Thomas had only got halfway through his first hot dog. He set it down now beside the other one, his appetite gone.

"I . . . ," he began.

"It's the whole rules and regulations trip, right?" John said. "You're afraid of what'll happen if we fuck up. How your lieutenant'll call you up on the carpet, maybe put a couple of demerit points on your record, is that it? Well, sometimes you can't go by the rules, Tom," he added before Thomas could respond. "Especially when you're from the reserve. We don't mean shit to them and never will. Don't you remember what happened to Ronnie Bobbish?"

Thomas couldn't place the name at first, but then his mind went back, fifteen, almost twenty years into the past to when he was still living on the reserve. Once the memory came to him, he wondered how he could ever have forgotten. Sitting here in the park, he could still hear the arguments between John and their father, the final decision of the clan mothers, how John's justifiable fury had turned to a cold anger. That was the year John had turned his back on talk of moderation and negotiation and joined the Warrior Lodge. He was thirteen years old.

"He was the boy you said got—"

"Not *said*," John corrected him. "I saw him get shot. By a cop. I was there, Tom. I saw it happen. Ronnie didn't run away like some people would like us to believe. And if somebody—*Nos* or the aunts—had just had the guts to demand an inquiry . . ."

The anger Thomas heard in his brother's voice was as bitter now as it had been all those years ago.

"But you have to see it from their point of view," Thomas said. "There was no body and the band was negotiating those logging rights which—"

"We got screwed on, just as we always get screwed—Ronnie most of all—because nobody wanted to make waves. Nobody wanted the white man mad at us and maybe having their support cheques cut off."

Thomas sighed. "Okay. You've made that point before."

"That's what hurt me the most when you first told me you wanted to be a cop," John said. "It was like you were saying, who cares about Ronnie? It was like you were joining the enemy."

"You know that's not true."

"My head knows," John said, "but not my heart. Sometimes, like when I was standing in your precinct just now and saw you there, just one more cop among all the others, all I wanted to do was hit something."

"They—"

"Couldn't you see the way they were looking at me?"

"Yeah, but—"

"That's the same attitude that let Ronnie's killer go unpunished. Jesus, I . . ." John shook his head. "Oh, what's the use?"

He slumped back against the bench. His gaze went out to the traffic going by on Palm Street, but Thomas knew he didn't see the city; John was in the past, a thirteen-year-old again, helpless with his frustrated anger.

"I'll never forget that day," John said after a few moments. His voice was so soft the words almost went unheard. "I don't *want* to forget it."

The depression that Thomas had been fighting all day dropped like a thick blanket over him. It seemed no matter which way he turned, there was something to remind him of just how crappy the world was. The teachings handed down from the old Kickaha spoke of the world's Beauty, how it must be preserved, how it lay all around one, if one would only look for it.

Thomas couldn't see it. He found it hard to remember if he ever had. He slouched beside his brother, the oppressive skies above just adding to his depression. There had to be a way to get away from it all, but he just couldn't see it. No matter what John said, no matter his own mixed feelings about the job, he knew he had to see this thing through, and knew as well—by the hollow feeling in his stomach, the coldness in his chest—that Beauty was going to slip further and further away with each step he took. When it was all done, he'd be left here in the city with the taste of ashes in his mouth and all hope turned to sand, its last grains just slipping away through his fingers.

The Slasher had seven victims to his credit now—at least seven that they knew of—but right now Thomas's thoughts kept circling, whirling, around the memory of Ronnie Bobbish's death.

He'd never realized how much that old wound still hurt his brother. As John had said, it was one of the main reasons John had argued against Thomas becoming a cop, but it was also one of the reasons that Thomas had become one.

Ronnie Bobbish. And John, so impassioned, asking, if there wasn't going to be justice for Ronnie, then how could they ever expect justice for anything?

Years fell away until it felt as if that day had only been yesterday. That was the trick the mind could play on you; in your mind there was no past, present or future. Everything existed at the same time.

It had been in the early spring, when everyone felt a little light-headed after all the dreary months of winter. John and Ronnie had taken off from the reserve and headed into town—just a couple of kids, not meaning any real harm, just goofing off, running through backyards and alleyways like a pair of high-spirited colts trying to outrun all the energy that the winter had pent up inside them.

They ran into a cop in one downtown alleyway and knocked him down—not on purpose; they just came around a corner and there he was. Before they could stop, they had knocked him to the ground. And then they panicked. They took off, running side by side, ignoring the cop's cry to stop. The gunshot had been very loud. Ronnie was running ahead of John. The bullet took him in the back of the head and dropped him in his tracks.

John fell over him, the two of them landing in a pile, John's head close to the back of Ronnie's head—or at least where the back of Ronnie's head should have been. John had scrambled back from the awful sight. Lifting his gaze, he saw the cop standing with his gun pointed straight at him.

The tableau held for long moments, John related later, as though neither of them could quite believe what had happened. Then John bolted again.

He cleaned himself up in a subway toilet, but he was still a mess when he got back home. Their father looked into his story, but there was no report of a shooting incident anywhere in the city, no young Native boy brought into any area hospital, nothing to back up John's story at all except for Ronnie's disappearance and the fact that John simply did not lie.

And that wasn't enough. So nothing was ever done.

But thinking about it now, Thomas realized that the patrolman, panicked, scared, could easily have just taken a page from the Irish mob's book. Without a body, there was no crime. . . .

Christ, he wished John had never brought up that memory. Not now, not when his own faith in the job was so unstable.

"I'm sorry," his brother said then. "I came here to help you, not drag up old pain."

Thomas nodded slowly. "I know you did."

"So what happens now?" John asked.

"You still want to help?"

"That's what I came for," John said.

"I just don't know what we *can* do," Thomas said. "Papa Jo-el didn't do so well with what he tried last night."

"That's because he went about it wrong," John said. "Strong as it's grown, I'm not sure that even Whiteduck could banish it now. We've got to lower our sights. We might not be able to banish it, but I still think we can imprison it—bind it into one place so that it's at least harmless."

"Where?"

John nodded his head northward. "In the Tombs."

"And it won't get free again?"

"I can't make promises," John replied, "but once it's bound, we can get Whiteduck to advise us what to do with it then. The old people had ways of dealing with *windigo*."

Thomas tossed the uneaten remains of his meal into the nearby trash. He stood up and looked down at his brother.

"Then let's do it," he said.

"What about your job?"

"I'll call in sick."

"But—"

"Let's just do it," Thomas said.

John nodded slowly. He took a final sip from his coffee and tossed it into the trash as well.

"Welcome back, Wabinose," he said.

Thomas started at the sound of his Kickaha name. John had it wrong. Thomas wasn't giving up and coming back home, defeated by the white man's world; he was fighting back.

But he merely nodded in response to his brother's comment, saying nothing.

EIGHTEEN

They were coming for him now, the murderer and the whore with their mumbo jumbo and their guns. They couldn't hide from him anymore, nothing could hide from him, he could see everywhere, he knew just what to do to make it all right again.

They thought they were going to hurt him, but he couldn't be hurt anymore. He was past hurt. He'd had his little girl taken away, and survived. He'd been shot, shot dead, bullet in the head, bits of brain splattered everywhere, and survived. He'd lived in the cold, silent dark, and survived. He'd become the nightmare man. His voice was the midnight wind, his touch cold like the ice that burns, and shadows lived in his heart, making him strong.

He was past hurt, and now that he knew all the secrets of getting there from here and back again, no one was ever going to send him away, not any of them, not ever again. Not a cop with his gun. Not some pickle-in-the-ass concerned for his well-being court-appointed

psychiatrist, who was the really crazy one, not him—the little children loved him, they wanted him, he was sane. Not some witchy
black man who thought he could call up the nightmare man like he
was some kind of spook, like mumbo-jumbo words were all you
needed to make the nightmare go away, but he'd showed him,
showed him good, and he was never going away again.

He was stronger than them all. And if they'd didn't believe it, he'd
show them, wouldn't he show them, just like he did the witchy man,
showed *him*. He'd show them just as often as they wanted, because
he liked the way the blade went in, liked the way it cut through skin
to bone, liked the dying in their eyes and the blood on his hands.
They could come chasing after him all they wanted, because he
didn't care, he'd show them, show them both, the little whore who
pretended to be his Niki and the cop who thought he was going to kill
the nightmare man again, show them all.

He shifted his enormous bulk in the cold place, hands opening
and closing where they lay on his fat belly, testing the strength of his
grip. He was strong, stronger than them all, getting stronger, ready,
he was ready for them, teach them a lesson that they'd never forget.
And once they learned, he'd have time to find his Niki, his real Niki,
not one that turned into dead meat as soon as you stuck a little knife
into her.

He'd have time for her.

And the little children.

All the little children with her face, waiting for him, for the midnight man, the nightmare man, all of them, standing in a row, little
faces smiling, little bodies trembling, eager and happy.

They were all going to live so happily ever after.

That's the way the story would end, the good story, the real story
that belonged to him, the midnight man who lived forever, not dying
in some empty lot, shot in the head, kill that cop and see how he likes

it, but living forever and always happy, happy *ever after*, because he deserved to have a happy story now, after all the hurt, all the years of no one understanding, not really understanding, how good he was, a good person, good with children, a happy man, and strong now, strong then, but stronger now, a good father, the best father, just ask his darling Niki.

Ask any of the little children.

They loved him the best. He could see it in their eyes, always saw it, just before they went away, that shining light, that love for him.

They died so happy, ever after, but they weren't gone, not gone forever, because he kept them all inside, had them stored up, all their happy smiling faces, locked away inside him, inside the midnight man who lived forever, strong and good, ever after, happy when the story ends.

He rose in the cold dark, his enormous body light as a feather, but strong, like steel girders, like a diesel engine, like a wronged man who knew he'd been served unjustly and finally saw that recompense would be his.

Time now for the happy ending.

NINETEEN

Jim found the whole situation far too awkward at first. He felt disjointed from reality. It wasn't simply the supernatural aspect of what had brought them all together, but that his companions were basically all strangers. He didn't know Niki at all except from her pictures and their brief unfortunate meeting outside the restaurant last night, and he barely knew Ti Beau, while Cindy, the most familiar of the three women who were suddenly ensconced in his apartment's small living room, he'd only just met the day before.

Of the three, Ti Beau seemed the most at ease, as though she found herself in such situations all the time—which, Jim thought, considering her profession, might not be so far off the mark. Niki perched on the edge of the sofa and kept her backpack between her feet. She looked as though she was about to bolt at any minute. Cindy seemed to be having second thoughts concerning not so much what she was doing with Jim, per se, but the wisdom of involving herself in the whole affair.

It would have taken them longer to put the situation into some kind of understandable perspective except that Ti Beau seemed to have a gift not just for making *gris-gris* that actually worked, but also for chairing what had become a conference of war. She was the one who told Cindy and Niki about Papa Jo-el's death the previous night and, with the skill of a born diplomat, extracted the unhappy, but necessary, information about Niki's background. And she was the one who then went on to connect what they learned to the overall problem of the Slasher.

Jim was more than content to let her take charge. Everything that was going on had taken him too far from familiar territory. So he just sat on the floor beside the chair Cindy was in, holding her hand and fingering the small pouch that dangled from his neck. He wasn't sure which gave him more comfort.

He concentrated hard on what was being said, trying to ignore the voice of reason that said it was all impossible. But he'd seen what he'd seen last night, and he knew what would happen if he took off the charm that Ti Beau had given him. That *other* voice would be back again. . . .

Even when Niki wasn't talking, he found himself unable to stop studying her. His heart went out to her as the story of her past unfolded. He couldn't imagine going through the kinds of things she had and still holding on to any piece of the belief that the world wasn't all just darkness and despair.

"He's my father," Niki said when Ti Beau spoke of the Slasher's identity. "His name's Teddy Bird."

Though the events that had led to Bird's death had occurred two years ago, Jim was still familiar with the name. It was like Charles Manson or the Son of Sam—some names you just didn't forget.

They'd become icons, synonymous with the psychotic evil that seemed to plague the last few decades. He'd still been working free-lance when he'd photographed that crime scene in the Tombs on the day of Bird's death.

"I was there," he said. "Just after he died. I was monitoring the police band and I heard the call go in. I got there just before the TV vans."

"He's not dead," Niki said.

Jim pointed toward his spare bedroom. "He's dead. I've got a picture of the body somewhere in my files."

"He's not dead," Niki repeated. "Not anymore."

"You are both correct," Ti Beau said. "He died and he has returned."

Jim could feel Cindy shiver through her hand. He gave it a tighter squeeze.

"You told me your surname was Adams," Cindy said. "But that's not your name, is it? You're not Chelsea Adams."

"Adams is my mom's maiden name. And Chelsea's my middle name. I could . . . I could never use . . . his . . ."

Her brow furrowed with pain and she lifted her hands to her temples. Jim knew what she was going through. He'd had that voice in his head all morning, until Ti Beau had given him the charm. He'd thought it was going to drive him crazy. When he realized how long Niki had been enduring it . . .

"Can't you do something for her?" he asked Ti Beau. He loosened his grip on the *gris-gris* pouch and bounced it lightly in the palm of his hand. "Would this help her?"

The *mambo* shook her head. "It does not have the strength to combat what assails her."

"Well, we've got to do something."

Ti Beau nodded in agreement. "We must do what Papa Jo-el attempted last night."

"But—"

"It comes down to blood," Ti Beau said, interrupting him. "We have what Papa Jo-el didn't—the blood of the one the spirit would possess."

Jim looked slowly from the *mambo* to Niki. "You're not planning to—"

"Sacrifice her?" Ti Beau gave a short hard laugh, devoid of humor. "Hardly. We will need just a few drops of her blood—enough to bind him into the room where we call him."

"I'm not sure I'm following you," Jim said.

He glanced up at Cindy. Her lips were drawn into a tight line, her eyes large and serious. Shifting his gaze to Niki, he saw that she was still pressing her temples, fighting the midnight whisper of her father's voice.

"I mean," he added. "Even if we trap him, won't he still be dangerous?"

Ti Beau nodded. "Very much so. But we will be careful." She leaned forward. "A spirit such as this exists for a purpose. We must discover that purpose and then—"

"I know what he wants," Niki interrupted. "He wants to kill me."

"And then," Ti Beau went on as though Niki hadn't spoken, "we can consider how best to deal with him. It is possible that *les invisibles* can help us, once we know what it is that has brought his spirit back, where his strength lies."

"And if . . . if they can't?" Cindy asked.

"Let us not consider failure," Ti Beau said. "It is of prime importance that we put forward a brave show. If we allow our fear to rule us, the *baka* will feed upon it and so grow stronger."

Niki let her hands drop and looked at Ti Beau then.

"I know why Cindy's doing this," she said, "and I figure Jim's reasons are much the same, but what's in it for you?"

"Because, as I told Jim earlier," Ti Beau replied, "the *loa* that speaks through me is Zaka, the Spirit of the Land. He is a healer, he wakes the harvest; to him was given the task to see that the harmony of sowing and growth, reaping and rest, follows its patterns. Your father disrupts the cycle. Because of who I am, because of He Who Speaks Through Me, I must do what I can to see that harmony is restored."

No one spoke for a long time. For all their varying degrees of belief in what was happening to them, Jim realized that none of them was that comfortable with the metaphysics of the *mambo*'s beliefs.

"I must return to my apartment to collect what we will need for tonight," Ti Beau added.

"Where are we going to . . . you know, do this?" Jim asked.

"Where her father died."

Frank Sarrantonio set down the phone receiver and looked across the desk at the lieutenant. He cleared his throat.

"That was Tom," he said. "He's calling in sick."

"He didn't look sick to me," Brewer said.

Thomas hadn't looked sick to Frank either, but what could he do? The man was his partner. And knowing Thomas as well as he did, Frank knew that he'd have a damned good reason for pulling a stunt like this. He just wished Thomas had let him in on what it was before he took off, leaving Frank to hold the bag with the lieutenant.

"We've got a meeting with the DA in ten minutes," Brewer said.

"He had to have a good reason," Frank began. "Couldn't we cover for him?"

He knew he was treading dangerous ground here, but he felt he owed it to his partner to make the attempt. He tried to read Brewer's mood, but the lieutenant's features were like a mask.

"Why should we?" Brewer finally asked.

"Because he's always played it by the book before," Frank said. "Because he wouldn't be doing whatever he's doing unless it was important for the department or the case. Because"—Frank hesitated for a moment—"he'd do it for us."

Brewer regarded Frank steadily, gaze unblinking. After a moment that seemed to go on forever, he shook a cigarette out of his pack, got it lit and took a long drag.

"Okay," Brewer said slowly. "We'll cover for him. For now."

Tom, Frank thought. You owe me. And you've got some heavy-duty explaining to do.

"In the meantime," Brewer went on, "let's get these reports ready for the DA. We can start with—"

The sudden appearance of a uniformed patrolman interrupted him.

"Billy Ryan's been picked up, Loot," the patrolman told them.

Brewer looked up. "Where?" he asked.

"They took him into the 14th," the patrolman said. "He was picked up in back of the Ritz by the hotel's receiving bays."

"What was he doing there?" Brewer asked.

"According to the arresting officers," the patrolman said, "he was loading garbage bags into the back of his Camaro."

"Garbage?"

"Garbage bags," the patrolman repeated. "He had a body in them—all cut up to shit."

"Jesus."

The patrolman nodded. "They've had to put him in restraints. He's raving like he's gone off the deep end."

"What? For a lawyer?"

"No. Something about a monster in the Tombs that won't get out of his head. Crazy talk."

"Any ID on the body?" Brewer asked.

The patrolman shook his head. "Apparently, he really did a number on it, Loot. It's all in pieces"—he held up his hand, thumb and forefinger separated by about an inch of air—"about so big."

"This monster," Frank began. He was starting to get an awful feeling.

"Ryan's the fucking monster," Brewer said, getting to his feet. "But trying to cop an insanity plea isn't going to cut it. Sounds like we've got him dead to rights for a change."

Frank rose from the desk as well. He couldn't shake the word "monster" out of his head. Everywhere he turned these days, things were turning spacy. Papa Jo-el's jujus and the way he'd died, their witness's weird description of the Slasher, his partner's talk about Indian curses. The whole city seemed to be turning into a Twilight Zone overnight.

"You think this is connected to what we're working on?" he asked.

Brewer shrugged. "Only one way to find out." He turned to the patrolman. "Tell them to hold Ryan," Brewer ordered as they started for the door. "Put him in a cell and let him stew until we get there."

"You got it, Loot."

Ti Beau needed a hand with the gear she was picking up from her apartment, and Jim found himself elected by default to help her, since Niki wouldn't be separated from Cindy, and the *mambo* insisted that he and Niki keep apart as much as possible until they actually set about summoning the spirit.

"The *baka* has got a fingerhold in both of you," she explained. "His hold is stronger on the girl, but if you stay together my *gris-gris* is going to weaken and you'll find him back in your head, too, Jim. That'll be good when we're ready to call him—it will make it easier to draw him to us—but right now we don't want him thinking about us any more than he already might be."

"Why?" Cindy asked.

"Knowledge is power," Ti Beau explained, "for spirits as well as humans. If this *baka* learns what we are up to before we attempt the summoning, he could well prepare his own surprise for us. Why allow him any advantage?"

The plan was for Cindy and Niki to make their own way to the building where they'd both been squatting, while Jim drove Ti Beau to her apartment. They would all meet up again in the Tombs, once Jim and Ti Beau had collected the things the *mambo* needed.

"So is this . . . uh, something you do a lot of?" Jim asked, making conversation as they drove toward Upper Foxville.

He knew what he'd seen; he'd felt the creature's voice in his head, but despite the proof, it all still seemed farfetched to him. The rational part of his mind was offended at his reluctant acceptance.

Ti Beau shook her head in response to his question. "*Voudoun* is a religion much like any other," she said. "Its followers derive comfort from its services in the same way a Catholic does from mass."

"You don't much hear about priests doing exorcisms and stuff like that except in the movies," Jim said.

"Most of the commonly held beliefs concerning *voudoun* are only fit for fiction as well," Ti Beau said.

"So this isn't something you do a lot of?"

"I have never summoned an errant spirit, nor attempted to banish it from this world."

"But—"

"Yet I have seen it done," she went on, before he could interrupt. "In Haiti. The *houngan* who first sponsored me into the Society had a patient who was possessed by such a *baka*. She was a little girl— about ten or eleven."

"What happened?"

"The spirit was successfully banished, but the little girl died."

Oh, wasn't that just great, Jim thought.

They couldn't find a parking spot near her building and had to leave the car almost a block away. The inconvenience proved fortuitous, for as they began the walk back to her building, they were stopped by a young black woman carrying a skateboard.

"Police be looking for you, missy," she told Ti Beau in a thick Caribbean accent. "They do leave a man to watch your door."

"Thank you, Rosa," Ti Beau said.

The girl gave Jim a questioning look, then smiled at the *mambo*. Dropping her board to the pavement, she put a foot on it and pushed herself off with the other leg. Once she had some momentum, she slalomed on down the sidewalk, both feet on the board, body swaying like a skier's.

Jim watched her go, then turned back to his companion.

"Why would the police be looking for you?" he asked.

"Because of what happened to Papa Jo-el last night, I would suppose. They would question everyone he knows."

"God, this'll take forever," Jim said.

He was thinking of Cindy and Niki, waiting for them in the Tombs.

"Unless I do not speak to them," Ti Beau said.

Before Jim could ask how she was going to manage that, she led him back to an alleyway that they'd passed a moment ago. Garbage crunched underfoot, and something made a noise in the alley's depths as they entered. A rat or some old tom, Jim thought. Halfway down the alley they came to a door set in the wall on their right. Opening it, Ti Beau stepped through the doorway.

"This isn't your building," Jim said as he followed her inside.

"The basements connect—all up and down the block."

It was like another world, Jim thought. Not quite the Tombs, but the rundown tenements weren't that far from being condemned en masse.

They didn't meet a soul as they stepped from one basement to another through makeshift doorways that seemed to owe their existence to some enterprising individual armed with a sledgehammer. The halls were empty in Ti Beau's building as well, though Jim could hear conversations and televisions as they passed by various doors.

In her apartment Ti Beau took just a few moments to gather what she needed, filling two backpacks. They each carried one back to where they'd left the car. Three quarters of an hour from when they'd first reached Ti Beau's street, they were heading for their rendezvous with Cindy and Niki in the Tombs.

Except for the straitjacket binding his arms to his torso and the wild light that came and went in his eyes, Billy Ryan seemed far calmer than either Frank and the lieutenant had been led to believe. He sat slumped in one of the four chairs around the table that took up the center of the interrogation room. A patrolman stood by the door, arms folded across his chest.

A one-way mirror separated the two detectives from the room. Joining them in the observation room were Andy Steel and Joe Walker, the detectives from the 14th in charge of the case, and Sarah Taylor from the DA's office.

"So," Brewer asked. "Did somebody read him his rights?"

"The arresting officer did when he was picked up," Walker said.

"Did he call his lawyer?"

Steel shook his head. "All he talks about is this monster he says he's got in his head."

"So what is he on?" Brewer asked. "PCP?"

"We ran some tests on him," Steel said. "Preliminary reports say he's clean."

"Any ID on the body yet?"

"What body?" Walker said. "All we've got is pieces."

"Wilkes from the ME's office found a finger pretty much in one piece," Steel added. "She managed to get a print from it and it's being run through the computer."

Brewer nodded thoughtfully, then turned to the assistant DA.

"Okay if we talk to him?" he asked.

Taylor nodded. "Evans said you have carte blanche, but I don't see the connection to your case."

Brewer had called Jim Evans, the DA, on their way to the 14th, to cancel their meeting and get the required permission.

"That's what we're going to find out," he said. He started for the door, pausing to look back and add, "Shall we?"

Frank and Sarah Taylor followed the lieutenant into the interrogation room, leaving the two detectives from the 14th to observe from the other side of the one-way mirror. Once the three had joined Ryan, they pulled up chairs around the table, on which Frank set a tape recorder. He gave it a quick test to make sure it was working, then set it on Record. He gave the date and who was present in the room, then pushed Pause.

"Anytime, Loot," he said.

Ryan had showed absolutely no interest in either their presence or the tape machine.

Brewer nodded. He'd turned his chair around so that he could fold his forearms on its backrest. He leaned forward and gave Ryan a prod with a stiff finger.

"Anybody home?" he asked.

Ryan jerked at the touch, his eyes going wide, then narrowing when they focused on the lieutenant. Brewer nodded to Frank, who turned on the tape player and then read Ryan his rights again.

"Do you understand your rights as they've been read to you?" Brewer asked.

Ryan nodded.

"Do you want your lawyer present?"

Ryan shook his head.

"Are you willing to answer questions without having an attorney present?" Brewer asked.

"Yeah. Sure."

"That's good, Billy. Why don't we start with what you were doing last night?"

Ryan suddenly lurched forward until his face was only inches from the lieutenant's. His eyes held a kind of frenzied light that made Frank shiver.

"You don't understand," Ryan said. He spoke too quickly, like a junkie still peaking. "There's not a fucking thing you can do to me. You can't touch me."

"Why's that, Billy?" Brewer asked, his voice mild.

"'Cause if you get in my way, I'll cut you into pieces—just like I did Mickey."

They all knew that "Mickey" could only mean Mickey Flynn, Ryan's boss.

Brewer never moved, but Frank glanced quickly to the mirror. If the detectives were any good at all, they'd be on the horn right now to have somebody pull Mickey Flynn's prints to match them against the one that Wilkes had found in the garbage bags.

"Are you saying you killed Mickey Flynn?" Brewer asked.

"He wouldn't listen to me."

"Well, I'm listening, Billy. What wouldn't he let you tell him?"

"Oh, I told him all right, but the stupid fuck just laughed at me. Nobody laughs at me."

"I'm not laughing, Billy. You can tell me."

For a long moment there was only the sound of the tape turning in its spools.

"What was it you wanted to tell Mickey?" Brewer prompted.

"I got this *thing* in my head," Ryan said. The wild light in his eyes seemed to grow even more frenzied as he spoke, but his voice was calm, almost expressionless. "I saw it last night in the Tombs, killing those three jigs. It was a fucking monster. It just stepped out of the night and cut 'em, and then it was gone."

Frank saw Brewer's gaze shift slightly to Taylor, as though to say, Now do you see the connection? But Taylor didn't see him. She seemed entranced by Ryan's madness. Frank found it hard to look away from the man himself.

"So you saw a murder committed last night," Brewer said, his attention back on Ryan. "Three murders. Could you identify the killer for us?"

Right, Frank thought. Like Ryan was suddenly going to turn stoolie, though the way things were going in this case, he didn't think he'd be surprised at anything that happened now.

Ryan was shaking his head. "You don't understand," he told Brewer. "You're just like Mickey."

"Am I laughing, Billy?"

"No. It's just . . ."

Ryan's voice trailed off and he lapsed back into silence. The tape continued to hiss through the spools.

"I want to understand," Brewer said, "but you've got to talk to me, Billy. What was it that made Mickey laugh?"

Fires flashed in Ryan's eyes. "Nobody laughs at me—you get that?"

Jesus, Frank thought. It was like talking to a toddler—a homicidal toddler, mind you.

"Nobody's laughing, Billy. Talk to me."

Ryan nodded slowly. His gaze was fixed on Brewer's face, but he seemed to be looking through the lieutenant.

"It's just . . . this *thing*," he said. "It wasn't real."

"I don't understand what you're saying, Billy. I'm not laughing, but I just don't understand."

"It, like, it just appeared out of nowhere and killed those jigs and then it was gone again. Vanished."

A cold chill went through Frank. The words of their witness to Leslie Wilson's killing returned to him, how the Slasher had stepped from a doorway when there was no door nearby and then as good as vanished.

"This happened at night, didn't it, Billy?"

"I'm telling you, he *vanished*!"

Veins popped out at Ryan's temples as he shouted the last word. Brewer held up a placating hand.

"Okay, okay. But isn't it possible that he could have just moved out of the firelight?"

"You're laughing at me."

"Look at my face, Billy. Do you see even a smile?"

Veins continued to throb at Ryan's temples, but a confused look moved across his features.

"No . . . ," he said, his voice soft.

"Okay. So is it possible?"

"No!"

As Brewer calmed Ryan down again and began to lead him step by step through how he'd killed Mickey Flynn, Frank found it harder and harder to concentrate on what was being said. He kept returning to their witness. Fisher's testimony about the Slasher and what Ryan had just said concerning the death of Papa Jo-el and the Etienne brothers.

His thoughts were taking him straight into a Twilight Zone—a place he'd fought hard to ignore, every time the case started pushing him in that direction—but this time he let himself go, because for all

that it went against everything he believed to be true, he was begin-
ning to think that something was going on that just couldn't be
rationally explained. He wished his partner were here, Tom with his
intuitive leaps and—

The realization of what Tom was up to came to him like a fist in his
gut. It all made a crazy kind of sense: Tom's brother John with his
Indian medicine man ways, what Papa Jo-el had been up to in the
Tombs last night. . . . Tom and his brother were going to try to duplicate what Papa Jo-el had attempted.

"Jesus," he said softly.

"You've got something you want to add?" Brewer asked.

Frank felt disoriented, and it took a moment for the lieutenant's
words to register. Then he realized where he was, that the tape
machine was still running.

"No, sir," he said.

Brewer gave him an odd look, then turned to the assistant DA.

"I guess we can wrap this up, then, Ms. Taylor—at least for the
time being. We'll have to check into a few of the things that Mr.
Ryan's told us and then—"

Ryan lunged at him suddenly. Trapped in the straitjacket; he
couldn't keep his balance, and his attack degenerated into a stumbling fall.

"You said you'd believe me!" he shouted as he went down.

Frank and the patrolman by the door helped Ryan back onto his
chair.

"I didn't say I'd believe you," Brewer said. "I told you I wouldn't
laugh. Do you see me laughing?"

"You're waiting until I'm back in my cell. You're just going to—"

"That's a great idea," Brewer said. He directed his attention to the
patrolman. "Put him back in his cell."

"You lying fuck!" Ryan cried.

Brewer ignored him. "And see that he undergoes psychiatric evaluation, ASAP."

Frank waited while Ryan was taken from the room, fiddling with the tape machine as he tried to figure out how to approach Brewer with what he had to tell him. The lieutenant and Taylor talked for a few moments longer, but since everything was going to hinge on the psychiatric evaluation, they didn't take long to wrap things up.

"Loot?" Frank said when Taylor finally left, catching Brewer before he stepped out of the room as well.

Brewer paused to look back. "What is it, Frank?"

"I've got something that needs looking into. . . ." Frank cleared his throat. "It's about Tom."

"What about him, Frank? I said we'd cover for him."

"I think I know what he's up to."

Brewer waited a long heartbeat, but Frank didn't say anything else. How could he? It sounded crazy to him. If he told the Loot, Brewer'd have men all over the Tombs looking for Tom. Somehow, Frank didn't think that was going to be such a good idea. He wasn't saying he actually *believed* there was some kind of real-life boogeyman running around the Tombs, but right now he wasn't willing to take the chance that he was wrong. Not without talking to his partner first.

"Okay," Brewer said finally. "So tell me."

"I can't."

"Frank . . ."

"I just can't, Loot. You've got to trust me on this."

Brewer shook his head. "I've already got my neck out on a limb for your partner, Frank. Don't ask me to—"

"I'm walking out of here," Frank said.

Brewer shook his head. "Don't do this. I've already got one of my main investigators out running around without a leash. There's no way I'm letting both of you hotdog it."

"I'm sorry, Lieutenant, but this is something I've got to do. I owe it to my partner."

"I can't cover for you."

Frank understood what that meant. He and Brewer were due at the DA's office for the meeting they'd missed earlier. It was bad enough with Tom gone. The DA'd be all over Brewer's ass unless he showed up with at least one of them. Frank knew he was looking at a suspension, maybe worse, but he didn't think he had a choice.

"I'm sorry, Loot," he said, "but he's my partner." The simple response said everything.

Then he walked. Out of the interrogation room and the precinct, to where he and Brewer had left the car. He drove back to the 12th, all the while trying not to think about what he'd just done. When he got there, he found that Tom's car was still parked in the lot behind the building.

All right, he thought. So they went in John's pickup. Only *where*? The city was so goddamn big, they could be anywhere, maybe even back on the reserve.

He could put out an APB on John's vehicle, but he didn't want to involve the department. He and Tom were already skating on ice so thin he didn't know what was keeping them from going through.

Think, he told himself. Where would they go?

Okay. If he went with the premise that Tom and his brother were going to try to duplicate Papa Jo-el's little ceremony—and he had to go with that, since he was betting all his cards on the one hand and he didn't think he'd get more than this one shot—then the answer was simple.

They'd go to the Tombs.

There'd be no sense in trying anything until nightfall, so they were probably holed up at the moment, somewhere around that intersection where Papa Jo-el and his bodyguards had bought it last night.

He thought it through for a few moments longer, then backed out of the parking lot and headed north to where the abandoned buildings and empty lots of the Tombs sat like the blight they were. It was the armpit of the city, a place to go when you got to the end of your rope, a place where hope died and there was nothing left to do but just let go.

His partner was somewhere in there. Frank thought. He couldn't have told anyone how he could be so sure. He just knew it.

Niki hadn't thought it could get any worse, but the closer she and Cindy got to the Tombs, the louder and more insistent her father's midnight voice became. It pounded in her head until all she wanted to do was just bang her forehead against a wall to make it go away.

Niki, Niki, Niki. . . .

It wouldn't ease, wouldn't give her a moment's respite.

NIKI.

She envied Jim for the little charm that the voodoo woman had given him. She'd have given anything to get that cold and awful sound out of her head.

By the time they got to the building where she'd been squatting, it was all she could do to shuffle one foot in front of the other. Cindy put an arm around her shoulder, partly for support, more for comfort.

"Are you going to be okay?" Cindy asked.

No, Niki thought. I'm never going to be okay again.

But she nodded dully.

"Well, ladies," Bobby Brown greeted them as they entered the building's foyer.

He had the place to himself, although the marble floor was still littered with little islands of blankets, clothing, and other possessions too threadbare or cheap to be worth stealing, which the other squatters had left behind for the day.

"Into a little heavy shit, are we?" Bobby went on, as he took in Niki's condition. He stepped closer, in front of her and Cindy. "Like

I told your friend," he said to Niki, "I don't much appreciate your trying to move in on my turf, see? The problem is, there's only so much
to go around and—"

"Get the fuck out of my face," Niki told him.

Here was something she could take out her anger on. She shook
herself free of Cindy's arm and took a step forward. Something in her
eyes made Bobby back up quickly.

"Hey, chill. Everything's cool. We'll talk when you're not so
fucked up."

Niki had started to take another step toward him, reaching into
her pocket for her blade, when Cindy touched her arm.

"He's not worth getting messed up over," Cindy said.

Niki turned, ready to turn the blind anger on her companion, but
she stopped herself in time. It was the voice that was screwing her
up, she told herself.

Niki, Niki. . . .

Her old man, mindfucking her because he couldn't get his hands
on her body. Cindy was just here to help. It wasn't her fault. It wasn't
even Bobby's fault, for all that he was an asshole.

She nodded and turned from the dealer, heading for the stairs.

I've got something for you, Niki.

Beside her, Cindy wrinkled her nose at the stink in the stairwell,
but Niki wasn't even aware of it.

It's here in my pants. . . .

She needed Cindy's support going up the stairs. The walls were a
blur of graffiti that wouldn't come into focus.

A great big surprise. . . .

At the top of the stairs, the hall seemed to go on forever. Niki
leaned against the wall. She closed her eyes, trying to cover the cold
whispering in her head with a sheet of silence.

Niki, little Niki. . . .

But it wouldn't go away.

Go ahead and touch it.

Her father's voice went on and on, cutting through her like an icy wind. It was like she'd never been away from him, like she'd never escaped.

You know how you like to touch it.

It was like she was still trapped in that dingy apartment, her mother pretending to be asleep in the next room as her father approached her own bed, zipper open, playing with himself.

You can kiss it, Niki.

The bedsprings creaked as they took his weight.

Don't you want to kiss it?

She shook her head.

Open wide, now, sweetie.

Her face was up against the flaking plaster of the wall, but she was no longer sure if it was the wall of her bedroom or that of the squat in the Tombs.

Time to take your medicine.

"No," she said.

She felt someone beside her, someone putting an arm around her, and she shook it off.

Don't fight it, Niki.

"Get away from me!" she cried, stumbling down the hallway, weaving back and forth along its length like a drunk.

Daddy knows best.

She came up against a wall and banged her head against it. Once, twice. The pain made the voice recede for a moment, long enough for her to turn around. Back to the wall, she watched Cindy approaching her, her features strobing. She was Niki's father, herself, Niki's father. . . .

Niki, little Niki. . . .

Niki brought her hands up to her ears, covered them.

Niki.

She rocked her head back and forth.

"I . . . I'll tell," she said. Her voice was small, faint. "I swear . . . I'll tell. . . ."

It's too late to tell, sweetie. Everybody knows you want me to do this to you. Everybody knows that you beg me. To. Do. This.

Her head filled with a rhythmic grunting that kept time to the words. Familiar. It was so painfully familiar.

Beg. Me.

"Fuck you!" she screamed. "Just leave me alone, you fucking pervert."

For a long moment there was silence inside her head. She opened her eyes to find Cindy regarding her, her face drawn with worry. Her mind felt as though it held a vacuum. She trembled, shaking and shivering as though the chill that he'd put inside her would never go away.

"I . . . I don't think coming here was such a good idea," Niki said slowly.

She heard a vague, whispering sound in her mind—not quite words, more like a shallow kind of breathing.

"He's so . . . strong," she added.

Cindy swallowed nervously. She looked up and down the hallway, but Niki knew there was nothing to see. It was all in her head—real, but invisible.

"Do you want to wait for the others outside?" Cindy asked. "Would that be better?"

Niki gave a small nod in reply. "Yeah. Maybe, he won't be able to—"

BITCH!

She gave a sudden shriek and dropped to her knees at the force of the word. Her gaze locked on the wall behind Cindy. Panic froze her throat as she tried to warn her companion.

"Sih . . . sih . . ." was all that would come out.

A face was forming in the plaster, lifting from its flat surface like a bas-relief. The features were terrifyingly familiar. On either side of the face were palms, taking three-dimensional form, becoming hands, attached to wrists, attached to arms, pushing out and reaching.

God help her, but Niki knew that face, knew those hands. They were her childhood night fears given physical shape, but unlike those of most children, her nightmares had always been real.

Again she tried to speak. "Sih . . ."

Cindy started to bend down toward her.

"Niki," she said. "What's the—"

The arms grabbed Cindy, cutting off her question, transforming it into a wail of fear. Cindy struggled as she was pulled back toward the wall, but her strength wasn't up to the contest. She was dragged back, inch by inch, until she came up hard against the surface of the wall.

Her scream was a long, wordless wail that was almost eloquent in its single note of terror. There was no sense, no reason, to that sound. The scream would have kept Niki frozen, but the expression of need, the sheer desperation in Cindy's eyes galvanized her.

"You stupid fuck!" she shouted at her father.

She lunged to her feet and grabbed at the steel cords of his cold flesh, trying to pry Cindy loose from his grip. But it was like trying to take apart steel girders that had been welded together. Niki had always known her father to be strong. Dead, he'd become superhumanly so.

Still she wasn't about to give up. Cindy was here because of her. She was going to die, just like all those other girls had died, because she had blonde hair and looked like what Niki's father thought Niki would look like now that she'd grown up.

"It's dyed!" she cried as she continued to pummel the impossible presence of those arms that were pulling Cindy into the wall from which they'd come.

She looked into the plaster bas-relief of her father's face that still thrust out from the wall.

"You hear me, you dumb pervert? My hair's dyed."

She'd dyed it black because blonde meant pretty, blonde meant dumb. She didn't want to be pretty and she sure as shit wasn't dumb.

BITCH! the cold voice roared in her mind. *YOU'RE A FILTHY LYING LITTLE BITCH. YOU LIKED IT. YOU WANTED IT. YOU BEGGED ME TO GIVE IT TO YOU.*

Niki's head rocked under the onslaught of his voice. The hands were slowly withdrawing into the wall, crushing Cindy against its hard surface. Her voice was silent—throat still working, but no sound coming out. Her face was starting to darken, to turn blue as she fought for air.

"Look at me!" Niki cried, trying to force the monstrous bas-relief's attention to her. "*I'm* the one you want, you dumb pervert."

She used the epithet deliberately, having already discovered how much it angered him.

DON'T CALL ME—

"Pervert, pervert, pervert!" Niki shouted.

And finally the face looked her way, its strange dead eyes focused on her. As it reached for her, Cindy fell like a loose bundle from its grip. Niki ducked the hands to grab hold of Cindy's arms.

TEACH YOU. BITCH. LESSON.

It wasn't supposed to be active during the day, she thought, remembering what Ti Beau had told them. It needed the night. Maybe that was why it was so slow. She realized that she didn't much give a shit what the reason was, just so long as she could get Cindy out of there.

KILL YOU.

The voice roared in Niki's head, and it was all she could do to haul her companion down the hall, grateful that Cindy's limp form slid as easily as it did along the floor. The creature followed them as a rippling effect in the wall. Sometimes the face was visible, sometimes a hand reaching, a knee lifting, a foot coming down. And all the time the voice howled in Niki's head.

She got to the stairwell before the creature did, but saw no way she could get Cindy down before the creature would be upon them. The stairwell was simply too narrow. No matter where you were in it, you'd be within the creature's reach.

And what if it could step right out of the wall? Niki thought, a hopeless feeling rising up inside her. Why the hell shouldn't it be able to do that? Hadn't it moved freely enough on the street to kill all those girls?

But that was at night.

Uh-huh. And still here it was, big as life, moving slowly, perhaps, but moving all the same.

KILL YOU LYING BITCH YOU LIKED IT KILL YOU.

Whatever Ti Beau knew about these things, right now all bets were off. Cindy stirred, at Niki's feet, choking for breath. Niki bent down beside her, holding her both to give and take comfort, trying to shut the awful roaring from her own mind.

She was beyond fear now, she realized with surprise. What she was experiencing was impossible, but instead of it shutting her down as it had just a moment before, already she was handling it—at least she was handling the idea of it. When it came to how to deal with the situation, how she and Cindy were going to survive, only one useless thought came to mind:

Basically, they were screwed.

The rippling effect had disappeared from the walls, though the voice railed on. Then, as though to punctuate her despair, hands appeared on either side of Niki and grabbed hold of her ankles.

TWENTY

John told Thomas that they had everything they were going to need in the back of his pickup, so when they got back to the precinct, they drove directly to the intersection in the Tombs where Papa Jo-el had died. Only the detritus of the morning's investigation remained—chalk outlines on the cracked pavement, the scattered ashes of the fire that Forensics had poked through, and the general debris, like styrofoam coffee cups, that investigating officers were liable to leave behind in a place like this, where they assumed that another handful of garbage wasn't going to make a bit of difference.

John shook his head at the mess. Shifting into four-wheel drive, he steered the pickup across the bumpy terrain of the deserted lot that lay north of the intersection and tucked the vehicle away between some buildings, where it could be parked out of sight. Thomas joined him outside by the bed of the truck, where he helped John peel back the canvas covering.

"Jesus," he said. "What is all this stuff?"

Lying in the truck bed was a bundle of poles tied together with thongs, two big blue water jugs, rolls of canvas, a half-dozen plastic bags from various department stores, bulging and fat with their contents, and even a heap of firewood. John reached into the bed and passed one of the plastic bags to Thomas.

"There's jeans and a jacket in here," he said. "You'll probably feel more comfortable in them."

Thomas nodded. He'd just paid a couple of hundred bucks for the suit he was wearing; scrabbling around in the Tombs wasn't going to do it any good at all.

"This other stuff," he said, nodding to the bed of the pickup, "is this what I think it's for?"

"We're going to build a sweat lodge," John said.

"Oh for—"

John cut him off. "If we're going to do this at all, we're doing it my way. You don't go talking to spirits without the proper preparation."

"No way I'm going to sit around chanting or doing some war dance," Thomas told him. "I'd feel like an ass."

John smiled. "Just get out of the suit, would you?"

While Thomas changed, John started setting up the sweat lodge in a clear spot that was still hidden from general view. He lashed the poles together at the top, then fastened the canvas at the top and wrapped the thick fabric around the poles to make a small tepee. By the time Thomas finished changing, John had started to build a fire.

"People will see the smoke," Thomas said.

"They'll just think it's some hoboes, cooking up their lunch," John replied. "Why don't you collect some rocks?"

"Sure," Thomas said.

As he went about his task, he couldn't help wondering if he'd really lost it. It was bad enough that he half-believed all this talk of spirits, but building a sweat lodge in the middle of the Tombs . . . If any of his fellow officers saw him doing this, he'd never hear the end of it.

They sat near the fire while they waited for the rocks to warm up. Thomas found himself fidgeting.

"Here," John said suddenly. From his pocket he pulled a small leather pouch attached to a thong and handed it over to his brother. "Put this around your neck."

Thomas regarded it suspiciously. "What is it?"

"A medicine bundle."

"Yeah, but what's in it?"

John sighed. "Look, Tom. I know all of this is making you uncomfortable, but why don't you just try to go with the flow? I'm here to help, so why don't you take advantage of my expertise?"

Because it made him feel like a fool, Thomas thought, but he accepted the medicine bundle and slipped the thong over his head. The bundle was a lighter weight lying against his chest than he'd estimated.

"You have to think of this as a kind of meditation," John went on. "When we sweat the poisons out of our bodies, we're sweating poisons out of our minds as well. That way we can approach the spirit world with purity and strength. It opens us up to the presences of those who live in the Otherworld, but keeps us firmly rooted in our own as well."

"You're the chief," Thomas said, trying to keep his voice light.

"No," John said. "I'm just an adviser. You don't *have* to do any of this."

"I know. It just feels . . . strange."

"Why? Because we used to play at this, but now you're supposed to take it seriously?"

"Something like that."

John just shrugged. He held his palm near one of the stones to feel its heat.

"This is good enough," he said.

Standing, he began to strip off his clothes, and continued until he was standing there in just his jockey shorts. He gave Thomas an expectant look.

"First you want me to dress, now you want me to strip," Thomas complained, but he followed suit.

Putting on a pair of gloves, John began to move the hot stones into the sweat lodge. When he had a half-dozen inside, he moved some others closer to the fire for them to heat up. Hefting one of the big water jugs, he turned to his brother.

"Let's go," he said.

It was dark and close inside the small tepee. Before Thomas had a chance to adjust to the dimness, John was pouring water onto the hot stones. Steam rose up in clouds, enveloping them both. Thomas choked as he involuntarily inhaled a sudden lungful of the steaming vapor.

"Don't fight it," John's voice came to him in the steamy dark. "Just relax. Let the poisons go."

Poisons, Thomas thought. That was about as apt a description as any for the sources of his tension: the case gone bad, then worse, gone spacey; the frightening possibility of him and Angie falling into that old trap that affected so many cops and their spouses; the fact that he wasn't sure he and Frank were doing any real good anymore.

He couldn't figure out how he was supposed to just let it all go. His worries were too deeply rooted in his being. He didn't want them there, but they were like leeches, burrowed deep under the skin of his thoughts, feeding on his insecurities and frustrations, adding to the tension.

"I . . . I don't know how," he admitted to his brother.

"Concentrate on your body," John said. "Your breathing, the heat, the sweat. . . ."

Breathing? It was hard to breathe. He found himself taking quick, shallow breaths to keep the stinging heat out of his lungs, but listening to John, he could hear his brother's slow, steady intakes of air and even slower exhalations. He tried to copy John's rhythm and found it easier than he had thought.

John began to chant, a soft hypnotic sound. Thomas's hand stole up to close around the medicine bundle his brother had given him, and he nodded his head slowly in time to the rhythmic flow of the sound. His breathing fell into time with the chanting, and soon he wasn't thinking of anything at all.

Jim left his car in the parking lot of the Yo Man Club on Gracie Street. With each of them carrying a backpack, he and Ti Beau continued into the Tombs on foot. They followed Niki's directions, but there was too much of a sameness to every part of the area. The streets, littered with abandoned vehicles and refuse, just like the derelict buildings and empty lots, were all too similar. Street signs had long since disappeared. With the sun hidden behind a cloud cover, they soon lost all sense of direction.

"We're lost," Jim said finally.

Ti Beau nodded. "I know."

"Well, can't you use some of your hocus-pocus to just . . ."

His voice trailed off as she raised her hand for silence. Her eyes took on a glazed, distant look, and she cocked her head as though listening to something faint that only she could hear. Jim tried to be patient, but he was too much on edge to do more than pay lip service to Ti Beau's request.

"What is it?" he asked as the minutes dragged by. "Can you . . . sense them?"

Jesus, what was he thinking? But he remembered that voice in his head and shivered. He lifted a hand to cup the *gris-gris* bundle hanging from his neck.

Whatever worked, he thought. Let's just get this over with.

"Ti Beau?" he tried again when there was no response to his first question.

"Not your friends," Ti Beau replied. She spoke slowly as though she was in a light trance. "But I sense him—his *guédé*. He is far more . . . present than should be possible." Her dark eyes opened suddenly, locking their gaze on his. "He is far stronger than I imagined he could be."

Jim was already nervous. What the *mambo* was telling him wasn't helping at all.

"What . . . what are you saying?" he asked.

"I fear he's too strong for us."

Great. And meanwhile, Cindy and Niki were out there somewhere, waiting for them.

"Can't we call in the cavalry?" Jim asked, trying to keep his tone light for all that he was serious about their trying to get some help.

"What cavalry?"

Right. They were on their own.

"The good thing," Ti Beau added, "is that the *guédé* presence is so strong that I can lead us to where he has manifested."

"So what's the bad news?"

"The *guédé* will lead us to Niki and Cindy."

Jim gripped her arm. A knot formed in his chest.

"What are you telling me?" he asked.

Ti Beau ignored the painful tightening of his grip. "The *guédé* has manifested in their presence. They are in grave danger."

For a long moment Jim couldn't speak, couldn't even move. All he could think of was the last of the Slasher's female victims. The image rose up in his mind and lay there like a photograph; the sprawled and broken body, the pools of blood, the blonde hair fanned out upon the pavement—only this time Cindy's features were superimposed upon those of the victim. She was the one who lay dead there.

He shook his head, trying to shake the image away. He couldn't imagine her dead. If she died, it'd be all his fault. She was so full of life—how the hell could he live with her death on his conscience?

"What the hell are we waiting for?" he demanded of his companion.

Ti Beau pried his hand from her arm. Her eyes were dark with worry and sympathy.

"Come," she said and set off at a quick jog down the rubble-strewn street.

Jim hesitated for a moment. It didn't seem right that it was just them there, that there was no one to help. But he and Ti Beau were all that Cindy and Niki had.

He caught up to the *mambo*, then matched her pace as she led them deeper into the Tombs.

The more Bobby Brown thought about it, the more it had rankled. Who'd that dumb chick think she was, coming on all heavy to him like she had?

He was halfway to the stairwell, intent on going upstairs and putting her in her place, when the screaming started.

What the—?

He froze in the middle of the foyer and stared up at the ceiling. Niki'd looked bad, he thought, but he didn't think she'd been this out of it. It sounded like somebody was getting killed up there. Maybe Niki was having a go at her friend. The idea of the two of them fighting brought a bulge to the groin of his jeans. He pictured the two of them rolling around on the floor, pulling each other's hair, maybe tearing off each other's clothes. . . .

The screams trailed off.

Maybe they were making up. Kissing, hands on breasts, stiff fingers slipping into each other. . . .

His hard-on was starting to get a little painful. He stuck a hand down the front of his pants, adjusting his penis so that it lay against his abdomen, pressed in there tightly by the pressure of his jeans.

Maybe they wanted some company.

He started up the stairs at a quick trot, a half-dozen horny fantasies running through his mind, all of them centered on him and the two of them, hot for him, crawling all over him. . . .

He heard shouting while he was still in the stairwell, but he couldn't make out the words. Then the top of the landing came into view, and he halted abruptly.

Niki was there. And her friend. They were huddled against each other, looking down the hall like some ax murderer was coming for them.

Maybe this wasn't such a good idea, Bobby thought.

Then the arms came up out of the floor and grabbed Niki's ankles, and it was like Bobby's mind shut down. Those arms weren't reaching up through a hole; they came right *out* of the floor, seemed to be made of the same material.

"Oh, fuck . . . ," he mumbled.

There was no way this was real. But the arms were pulling Niki back down against the floor. They just disappeared to wherever it was that they were coming from, but Niki's body didn't have the same bizarre property. Her body came up sharp against the floor. The hands—all that was visible now of her attacker—kept up their pressure. Niki was wailing. Her friend was trying to tug her free.

All Bobby could do was stare. Niki's friend looked down toward him, her gaze catching his.

"H-help us. . . ."

Bobby shook his head. Something was happening to both Niki and her friend. They seemed to be . . . changing. Niki's black hair went white; her face went black. The whites of her eyes darkened; her pupils turned white. It was the same with her friend. They were like negatives, light and dark all reversed.

"P-please. . . ."

There was the opposite of a light flash then—a flare of darkness, just as blinding as if it had been light. Bobby's eyes watered. Spots danced in his vision. When he could see clearly, both women were gone. All that remained of their presence was a shadow on the floor.

He could feel his muscles turning to jelly. In another moment he was going to collapse there on the stairs like a puddle and just ooze downward, step by step. But then he saw that the shadow was growing.

It spread out, expanding like a stain, turning the floor black. When it touched the top of the stairs, Bobby reached out and grabbed the banister, hugged his body toward it. Slowly he eased his way down, moving backward, gaze locked on the shadow at the top of the landing, watching the uppermost step turn black. It was only when the landing was finally out of his vision that he could find the strength to bolt the rest of the way down the stairs and out across the foyer.

Behind him the shadow continued to spread.

John changed the stones in the sweat lodge three times in all. He poured water on their hot surfaces each time, sending up clouds of fiery steam to fill the small enclosed area where the two of them sat. Light crept in through the canvas, but it was diffused and dim. In the shadowy dark, wreathed in the hot steam, Thomas listened to his brother's soft chanting and felt the pores of his skin open and release their poisons. Unexpectedly, he discovered that his mind had pores of a kind as well. They, too, discharged poisons, of a different sort.

His hair clung wetly to his scalp; sweat beaded on his skin. When they finally emerged from the sweat lodge, blinking in the brighter light outside, he felt light-headed and clean in a way he'd never experienced before. Even the grimness of the Tombs and the brooding sky above them couldn't diminish the sense of well-being that had crept over him in the hot darkness of the lodge.

Once outside, they used the remaining water in the jugs to rinse themselves, taking turns upending the jugs over each other. Toweling themselves dry, they stripped off their wet jockey shorts, then dressed in silence.

"Can you feel it?" John asked when they were both done.

Thomas blinked, still feeling a little light-headed. "Feel what?"

"The spirit."

Reality began its relentless inroads through Thomas's consciousness once more. For a time there he'd been able to put it all out of his mind—the Slasher, Brewer's betrayal, his questions about his job, Angie. Now, with John's reminder as to why they were here in the Tombs, those anxieties were all back again, scrabbling for his attention.

Thomas sighed. "Don't start with the mumbo jumbo, John. Just come out and say what's going on."

"The *windigo* spirit," John explained. "I can feel its presence."

"So now what? Do we . . . uh, call it to us?"

John shook his head. "No, it's calling us."

"I don't hear anything," Thomas said.

But that wasn't true. There, behind his clamoring anxieties, he could feel an alien presence in his mind. It was a soft, whispering noise, like the barely audible rasp of a cold wind breathing through the rooms of an abandoned building at midnight. Thomas found himself not wanting to find out what kind of a creature could originate a sound like that.

"Why . . . why's it calling us?" he asked.

"It knows you, Tom."

"Because I'm investigating the murders?"

John shrugged. "Maybe."

"What other reason could it have to concentrate on me?"

"A spirit usually turns its attention on those who wronged it while it was alive," John said.

An uneasy feeling started up deep in Thomas's chest.

"Wronged," he said. "You mean, I knew the Slasher before it died?"

He was beyond questioning the impossibility of what he'd just said. The reality he knew, his accepted preconceptions of how the world was supposed to work, how he'd always believed it did, had slipped askew ever since he'd talked with Papa Jo-el.

John gave him a long, considering look. "You only ever killed the one man—right?"

Thomas stared back at him. As the memories John's words called up rose in his mind, the dark whisper inside him seemed to grow colder, more malevolent. Thomas could see the body of the overweight pedophile he'd shot, lying there in the empty lot. The moment that always first came to mind when he remembered that day, the moment that was frozen into the very core of his memory, was before the backup arrived and the crime scene turned into a zoo.

He was always alone with the body, just the two of them, the dead man and himself.

Teddy Bird.

He remembered going to the man's funeral, standing there, grave side, just himself and the gravediggers. And the coffin. And later, trying to explain it to Brewer:

I had to see them put him in the ground.

He had to *know* Bird was dead, because no matter which way you turned it, he was one sick fuck. He didn't think he could live in a world where a man like that still existed.

And now he was back.

The cold whispering voice in his head—who else could it belong to? Why else should it feel so familiar? Head shot, dead, buried—all two years past—but here he was, back again. Teddy Bird.

"Jesus," he said softly.

John gave him a sympathetic look. "It makes sense," he said. "It explains the peculiar intensity of the *windigo*'s attention on you right now."

Thomas knew John was right, with a gut instinct that sent an immediate affirmation coursing through every nerve end. But he didn't want to believe it.

"All . . . all those girls it's killed . . . ," he said. "What's that got to do with me?"

"Who says it's only going to have one thing on its agenda?" John replied.

He went over to the bed of the pickup then and took out another of the plastic grocery-store bags. This one was full of an off-white powder. He mixed it with water in a small bowl.

"What's that?" Thomas asked, joining him.

He was trying to concentrate on something else, wanting to put Teddy Bird out of his mind, but once called up, the dead man was hard to ignore. He could hear the shot, see the man fall, remember standing over his corpse, hear the dirt falling on his coffin. . . .

The midnight voice hissed in the back of his mind.

"Clay," his brother told him.

John held the bowl in one hand, then, using the side mirror on the driver's side, daubed the clay on his face. The clay quickly dried, hiding his features behind a gray-white mask.

"John," Thomas began.

"Come here," John said.

Thomas backed away. "I don't—"

"It's just a ghost mask," his brother explained.

"Yeah, but—"

"You're going to need its protection, where we're going."

"I—"

"Trust me in this, Tom."

Thomas hesitated a moment longer, then let his brother daub the mixture on his own face. It felt cool against the skin, prickling when it dried and hardened.

"Looks good on you," John said. "Now we just have to—"

"Jesus!"

Thomas and John turned to find Thomas's partner looking at them from the end of the alleyway.

"Look at the pair of you," Frank went on. "What the hell are you doing, going on the warpath?"

"Frank. What're you—"

"You put your job on the line—Christ, *I* put my job on the line—and it's for this? You better have one fuck of a good explanation for what's going down . . . partner. I mean, if this is your idea of a joke, I'm not laughing."

Frank's anger hurt, but Thomas understood it perfectly. He knew what he and John looked like—a couple of fools.

"This isn't a game," John said.

"Yeah? Then what the fuck is it?"

"We're going after the Slasher," Thomas said, knowing how lame it sounded.

Frank just shook his head. "As what? A pair of vigilante Indians? What happened to rules and regs, man?"

"They can't cover what we're up against."

Frank said nothing for a long moment. Then he seemed to deflate. His anger washed away, replaced by confusion.

"So . . . so you're buying into the weird shit?" he asked.

"I don't have any choice."

As he spoke, Thomas realized that something had changed in his partner.

"What's happened, Frank?" he added.

"We picked up Billy Ryan. He . . . he's lost it. He's talking wild, killed Mickey Flynn—cut him up into a couple hundred little pieces—and all he talks about is monsters."

John's eyes kindled with interest. "What kind of monsters?"

"He says it killed Papa Jo-el, says it's in his head now. . . ." Frank's voice trailed off. He moved closer to them, gaze locked on the white masks of their faces. "It's all for real, isn't it? All this Twilight Zone shit?"

Thomas focused on what his partner had just said about Ryan hearing a voice in his head. The midnight wind stirred in his own thoughts, and he realized now that it was a voice, too. A whispering cold voice, summoning him. . . .

"I . . . I don't know," Thomas said. "I just—"

"It's real," John said brusquely. "And we're running out of time."

Thomas turned to him. "What do you mean?"

"If we wait any longer, we're going to lose the advantage of choosing our battleground. It's going to come to us. I can feel it growing stronger every minute."

"We've got to go, Frank," Thomas told his partner.

As Thomas picked up his shoulder holster and put it on, John went to the cab of the pickup. He reached behind the seat and brought out a hunting rifle. Frank stood there, looking at the pair of them.

"You," he began. "You're really . . ."

"Get out of here, Frank. I'll give you a call later."

Frank shook his head. "I'm in."

"You don't have to do this," Thomas told him.

"What? We're not partners anymore?"

"It's not that. It's just—"

"Let's go!" John broke in.

Without waiting to see if they would follow, he set off down the alleyway, cutting across a litter-covered lot. Thomas and Frank regarded each other for a long moment. They both realized suddenly that there was too much lying unspoken between them.

"Later," Frank said.

It was half a question, half a promise.

When Thomas nodded in agreement, the two of them jogged after John, hurrying to catch up.

There was no longer even a hint of hesitation in Ti Beau's manner. She led Jim unerringly through the jungle of abandoned buildings that made up the Tombs, until they both came up short at the end of yet another long, deserted block. The hulk of an old school bus lay rusting to one side of them, half on the sidewalk, half on the street. On the other side, a brownstone stood tumbled in upon itself.

They gave the street only a cursory look, the whole of their attention drawn, then locked onto, one building that stood halfway down the block. It seemed to have a water stain on it, turning the brickwork dark, but as they watched, the stain spread, throwing more and more of the structure into shadow.

It was, Jim thought, as though the building's polarities of light and dark were being exchanged. The light sandstone brickwork turned black; the dark trim grew paler: black and white reversing like—like a photographic negative.

"That," he began, pointing to the building.

"Is where the *guédé* is," Ti Beau finished.

"But what's happening to the building?"

The *mambo* slowly shook her head. "I don't know."

This time Jim took the lead. Just as they reached the front of the building, a teenager burst through the front doors. For one moment he was framed in the doorway, and in that moment, he, too, was like a negative: black skin, black eye whites, white pupils. All color was gone, and he stood there in sharp contrasts of black and white.

Then he stepped out, stumbled and fell, and his reversed polarities of light and dark regained their proper equilibrium. Black skin became white; eyes returned to normal. Color returned to his clothing.

But the building remained unchanged.

"This is too fucking weird," Jim said with a catch in his throat. "I . . ."

All he wanted to do was bolt. Somehow this was worse than last night. He was numb with fear, frozen in place, desperate just to run as far from what he was seeing as he could. But then Ti Beau spoke, and he knew what he had to do.

"They're in there," she said. "Niki and your friend and the *guédé*. He has them."

Jim started for the building.

"Wait!" Ti Beau called. "We must work from outside where we have the freedom of our minds."

Jim shook his head and kept on going. "I'm not leaving them in there on their own," he called back over his shoulder.

Ti Beau hurried to catch up. "He will work his way into your mind if you go inside. You won't be able to do a thing."

Jim continued to walk toward the building, but he turned to her.

"Do you know what the fuck's going on here?" he demanded.

The rage he'd felt earlier in the day was building up inside him once again, for all that he was still wearing Ti Beau's *gris-gris* charm, but this time it had a focus, a logical focus, and he let it build. He didn't know from ghosts or walking dead men or whatever it was that the monster he'd seen last night might be. All he knew was that it was threatening Cindy and Niki. He was tired of running around, of feeling ineffectual. It was time to *do* something.

"Have you ever seen or heard of anything like this before?"

Ti Beau shook her head. "No, but—"

"Then you're no more of an expert than I am."

"That's true, but—"

"So either lend me a hand or keep out of my way."

They'd reached the building's stoop, where the teenager was getting to his feet. The boy looked like any one of the hundred or so kids that Jim had seen yesterday when he was trying to track Niki down. Except for his eyes. They were dull with shock.

"Is there anybody inside?" Jim asked the boy.

The boy's dull gaze shifted toward him.

"It . . . it ate them," he said slowly, as though he couldn't quite believe what he was saying, what he had seen. "The fucking floor *ate* them, man!"

Jim didn't know what the kid was trying to say. All he could think of was Cindy and Niki, trapped inside with that *thing* that had killed Papa Jo-el last night.

He moved around the boy, but the kid grabbed at one of his legs as he went by, fingers catching onto the cloth to hold Jim back.

"You . . . you don't want to go in there," the boy said.

"Jim, wait!" Ti Beau added.

But Jim just shook off the boy's grip, ignored Ti Beau and stepped through the door.

John, Thomas, and Frank had arrived at the other end of the street about the time Bobby Brown stepped out of the building. They, too, were shocked into immobility by the weird sight of the shifted black-and-white polarities of the boy and the building.

John nodded to himself. "That's the place," he said.

"Oh, Christ," Frank asked softly. "What the hell's going on? I knew there was weird shit going on in the Tombs, but I've never seen *anything* like this. What is it?"

Thomas didn't have an answer for either Frank or himself. He looked to John, who just shook his head. Both Thomas and Frank drew their handguns; then the three of them jogged toward the building, with John slightly in the lead.

A man and a woman had also approached the building, from the other side of the street. Thomas placed the man as a photographer from one of the daily papers—he'd seen him at enough crime scenes. It took him a moment longer to recognize the woman as Papa Jo-el's assistant.

They didn't arrive in time to stop the man from entering. The woman and the kid on the steps looked up at their approach. Their attention focused first on Thomas and John's painted faces, then on the weapons they were carrying.

"Police officers," Frank said, more from habit Thomas realized than out of an attempt to follow procedure.

"Yeah, right," the boy said.

Thomas had to agree with the boy's incredulity. All the kid was seeing was two Natives with painted faces and a guy in a suit.

"And my old man's the Pope," the kid added.

He vaulted over the stoop's railing and was pelting down the street before anyone thought to stop him. Frank started in pursuit.

"Let him go," John said.

Frank hesitated, then came back when Thomas nodded in agreement. John and Papa Jo-el's assistant, Thomas decided, were regarding each other as though they recognized not exactly who, but at least what, the other was. They cut straight through what normal people would have done in a situation such as this, getting right to the point.

John laid his rifle on the steps and stepped back to study the building.

"Do you understand any of this?" he asked Ti Beau.

The *mambo* shook her head. "It seemed a simple thing to begin with: a restless *guédé*—a ghost—turned evil. I knew it was strong, but I didn't doubt that we could exorcise it so that its influence would no longer be felt in this world. But this . . . this singularity . . . for it I have no explanation whatsoever."

"But the spirit is responsible," John said. Thomas couldn't tell if his brother was stating a fact or asking the woman her opinion.

"Without question."

John turned to look at the building. "It's as though the spirit has brought a piece of the Place Between back into this world."

Ti Beau nodded. "It shouldn't be possible, but he's creating a piece of limbo in the world of the living."

Thomas looked down at the gun in his hand, then holstered it. Whatever was going on here wasn't going to be solved with a gun. Beside him, Frank followed suit.

"And it's spreading," John said.

"Will one of you tell me what's going on here?" Thomas asked.

His brother pointed to where the side of the building joined the ground. The entire structure had transformed into a negative aspect of itself; now the effect was spreading. The darkness was like a stain as it extended from where the foundation sunk into the ground.

"We can put up wards to hold it back," Ti Beau said, "but they won't last long."

"And will they even be strong enough?" John asked.

"We can only try. If I had some of my parishioners here to help with chanting, and a few drummers, I could guarantee to at least—"

"There's people in there, right?" Thomas said, breaking in. "More than just the guy we saw run in?"

Ti Beau nodded. "There are also two women for certain, perhaps some of the other transients who use the place as a squat."

"What's happening to them?"

"The *guédé* has them."

"What are you saying? That they're dead?"

"I don't know. Perhaps not yet, but they will be."

"Then we've got to go in after them," Thomas said.

John shook his head. "It's too dangerous. You can't even be sure that anyone's still alive."

"And once inside," Ti Beau added, "you will be susceptible to the *guédé*'s influence. It will get into your mind—perhaps even control it."

"Then what was all this shit for?" Thomas asked.

With one hand he held up the little medicine bag that hung from his neck and touched a forefinger against his clay-daubed face.

"The situation's changed," John said. "Those were to help protect you against the creature's influence in *this* world. They won't be of much help in there because he's changed that building into a piece of the world that belongs to the dead. Masks and little pieces of good medicine don't hold for a whole lot there."

"What you're saying is—"

"What I'm saying is we have to stop it *here*. If we don't do something right now, this thing could spread out and cover the whole city. Do you understand?"

Thomas shook his head. "Nothing's changed. The only reason I'm here is to stop that creature. That's my job. Just like protecting the city's citizens is—even if they're in limbo or whatever the hell you call what's spreading from that building. I don't get to choose which jobs I'll take and which I won't; I just take what's handed to me."

"You're not going in there alone," Frank said.

"It can't work that way," Thomas said. "Someone's got to stay out here to look out for my brother and Ms. Fontenot while they do whatever it is they're planning to try to stop that shit from spreading."

"Bull," Frank told him. "You know you're not coming back and you just don't want to drag me down with you, but it isn't going to work, Tom."

"I'm coming back out," Thomas told him.

"Then I'll be coming out with you."

Thomas shook his head. "I need to know someone's watching out for things out here while I'm inside. You're all I've got, Frank."

"But—"

"Do I have to pull rank?"

Frank gave a short, humorless laugh. "Ask the Loot how well pulling rank's working these days."

"How about if I ask you as a friend, then?"

"Aw, shit, Tom. I . . ."

Thomas put his hand on his partner's shoulder and gave it a squeeze. "Thanks, partner."

Before Frank could say anything, Thomas turned to Ti Beau and his brother.

"That stain's spreading," he said, indicating the stoop, where the darkness was spreading away from the building. "You'd better get to work with whatever the hell it is that you're planning to do."

He started for the doorway then, pausing when his brother called him back.

"Everybody's got their job to do, John," he said. "This is mine."

Then he stepped inside.

A long, desperate moment of silence held after Thomas stepped inside. Frank watched the negative effect take his partner and shivered. He felt so far out of his own depths that he thought his mind was just going to shut down. He tried to figure out what was being said as Thomas's brother and the hoodoo woman brainstormed, but their conversation seemed to be in a foreign language, or some kind of shorthand, and he had trouble following it.

". . . isn't absolutely necessary," Ti Beau was saying. "The rituals certainly help, but it's more a way of focusing one's intent."

"I couldn't be more focused," John said.

She nodded. "*Les invisibles* are always close by, always watching."

"The manitou."

"Different names for the same spirits?"

John frowned thoughtfully. "I'm not sure. Elemental forces, basic mysteries, but different, if only in how we perceive them."

"Semantics."

"Maybe." He looked to the building. "We're wasting time."

Ti Beau reached for him. "Give me your hand."

Her right in his left, flesh joined, mysteries mingling. Her eyes closed, breath deepening; his eyes open, swallowing light. Frank shivered again as an eerie blue aura began to glow about their free hands. The pale light waterfalled to the ground, where it pooled at their feet. Tendrils broke free and snaked left and right, encircling the building with a thin band that glowed blue, pale.

When the shadow stain that gripped the building oozed out, touching that blue ribbon, it held. The shadows thickened, grew darker, strained against the thin, pale barrier, but the glow held.

"You're doing it," Frank said, hope in his voice. He wasn't exactly sure just what it was they were doing, or what would happen if they failed, but excitement built up in him all the same. "You're stopping it."

"We're only holding it back," John said. "Barely."

"We can do nothing for those trapped within," Ti Beau added.

Her eyes remained closed. A vein pulsed in one temple. The strain of their effort showed in both their faces.

Frank shifted nervously. He felt useless, wanted to help, wanted to run. A supernatural dread traveled up and down his spine. They were alone, just the three of them outside this transformed building, but he didn't feel alone.

He felt a pressure all around them, the way the air seems overcharged with ions just before an electrical storm. His heartbeat sounded loud, like drumming, like it wasn't coming from inside him, but from somewhere beyond, from something that lay just out of sight behind the ruined buildings that surrounded them. He looked around. The air on either side seemed to pulse with heat shimmers. He got the strangest feeling that there was something in there behind the shimmering. And then, for a moment, it was as though he could see past a veil, as though a wind had lifted it for a moment, revealing strange tableaus, alike but different in their similarity.

To his left he thought he saw a tall figure, skin black as midnight, wearing a straw hat, denim shirt, pants, and old worn sandals. He had a machete thrust into a loop of his belt and was smoking a short clay pipe. Around him four small dark figures crouched, three of them tapping a rhythm from drums that ranged from small to large, while the fourth woke a counter rhythm from an iron bar.

To the right stood another figure, just as tall, but broader-shouldered. He wore a bear's head on top of his own like some strange kind of hood. Long braids hung below, falling against a buckskin vest with intricate beadwork designs. The skin of his arms and chest was a smoky red; his face was covered with a mask of white chalky mud, just as John and Tom's were. Small figures surrounded him as well, also playing drums, but there was no pretense of humanity about them. Their bodies were manlike enough, but their heads— one had a wolf's head, one a toad's; one looked like a mink or a weasel, and the last was some kind of hawk.

Frank stared, mouth open, but then the lifted veil fell back once more, the shimmering effect in the air returned, and only the sound of the drumming remained, twinning the sound of his heartbeat—or rather, he realized, his heartbeat had taken up the rhythm of the invisible drummers. Oddly, when he just let himself go with the sound, let his breathing join the rhythm, he felt calmer, more capable, though of what he didn't know until he turned to look at the door of the building, the door through which Thomas had disappeared. Ti Beau's words echoed inside him.

We can do nothing for those trapped within.

His partner trapped inside.

We can do nothing.

Tom.

Nothing.

Christ, how could he have let his partner go in there alone?

He started for the door, but was brought up short by John's sharp admonishment.

"Don't cross the ward line."

"But Tom's in there. Christ, what was I thinking? I should never have let—"

"If you break the barrier we have erected," Ti Beau said, "all our work will have been for nothing. The singularity will overrun the city."

Frank shook his head. "I've got to do something."

"There is something you can do," Ti Beau said.

Her voice seemed strained, which wasn't that big a surprise, Frank thought, considering the energy she and John had to be expending on keeping the shadow back.

"Anything," he said.

"We need help." She gave him a phone number. "Call that number and ask for Clarvius Jones. Tell him he is needed here."

"Isn't he your rival in the, you know, voodoo trade?"

"He was Papa Jo-el's rival. For me there is no rivalry in *voudoun*."

"I've got someone for you to call as well," John said, "though it's going to be a little harder to get hold of him. His name's Jack White-duck. You could try calling my dad, see if he can send someone out to his camp."

Frank memorized the number that John gave him as well.

"That's it?" he asked them. "Just these two guys are going to be enough?"

John and the *mambo* exchanged glances.

"It's all we've got," John said.

"Okay. I'm on it."

It was make-work, Frank realized as he headed back through the Tombs to where he'd left his car, but he was grateful for it all the same. Just standing there, watching the other two working their hoodoo, knowing Tom was trapped inside with who the hell knew what . . .

He couldn't believe that he'd let Tom convince him to stay behind. It had all just happened so fast—one minute Tom's talking, the next he's inside, and he could be so damned persuasive. But that was still no excuse. He should've gone in there.

Christ, some partner he'd turned out to be. If anything happened to Tom while he was in there, he didn't know how he was going to live with himself.

Pausing at the end of the block, he looked back at the building.

Don't you die, Tom, he thought. Don't you up and fucking die on me.

TWENTY-ONE

Inside.

They stood in a line, four of them, two women and two men, but they were the size of children when compared to the enormous bulk of Teddy Bird, not one of their little heads rising higher than his waist. He loomed over them, towered, the feared figure of authority, the upper hand his not because of wisdom or earned respect, but only because he was stronger. Jungle law.

The dark was all around them, but not so vast now. He could see an end to it, could see walls like they were standing in a giant warehouse, the dark place reduced to manageable size. And not so dark now. Too dark and you couldn't see, you need to see to play, even the midnight man knew that, and he was in charge now, the power was his, hoodoo in his veins, back from the dead, big as life, and strong, so very strong, but gentle, too. He could be gentle to the little darlings,

Santa Claus jolly, funny clown happy, got a sweet for the sweeties, but only in the not-so-dark, don't want our secret to escape, oh no.

He'd gathered them to him, here where he was the nightmare man, his voice a cold, midnight wind, gathered them, these little children, here to please him, to pleasure him.

I love you so much, he told them.

But did he, did he really love them, these little children, strangers some, see them tremble, anticipating pleasure, his pleasure, their pleasure, but not all strangers, oh no, not all. There, child of his flesh and blood who had denied him, who told secrets, who ran away, woke rage in him until he had to use the knife, didn't want to, didn't like the rage. There, policeman with his gun, punished him, shot him, killed him, could he still love them?

Could, did, the midnight man loved all the little children, loved them forever, because that was how he was, big hearted, had a heart so big it could love all the little children, each and every one.

When you try to hurt me, you only hurt yourselves, he explained. *Be sweet. Touch me here. Let me touch you there. This is love, true love, I love you all, don't you want to love me?*

Spare the rod and spoil the child, so true, he never spared the rod, watch it grow in his pants, hard and strong, a midnight rod, kiss it happy, don't be shy, don't spare the rod, don't spare your love.

Who wants to be first to make Teddy oh so very happy? Don't be shy, shy's sweet, shy's very sweet, but too shy spoils the fun, don't you want to have some fun?

Who wants to be first?

Inside.

None of this was real, Cindy told herself. It *couldn't* be.

From the moment the arms had come out of the wall and tried to crush the life out of her, she hadn't been able to accept any of it as real. It was just a dream, a bad dream, a nightmare, but it wasn't bona fide, right here and now, indubitably true. Couldn't be. Not for a moment.

But she'd almost died—if you die in a dream, do you die for real?—would have died, no question, if Niki hadn't stopped him, it, the thing in the wall, from killing her. And then it was pulling Niki into its awful embrace, changing her, making her into a negative image of herself, black hair white, pale skin dark, jean jacket bled of color. Pulling her into the floor, *right* into the floor.

It wasn't real, couldn't be, but her dream-self knew that she had to try and help the dream-Niki all the same, or the nightmare would kill her, could kill them both. . . .

It was the boy on the stairs that had convinced her. He wasn't changed. He had color, his black-and-white contrasts weren't reversed. He'd stood there on the stairs, the horror of what he was seeing etched across his features. Her throat was locked, voice trapped, so she'd called out to him with her eyes—*Help us*—knew he understood, but was too scared to help, why should he, who were they to him—

And then they were gone, her dream-self and the dream-Niki. The nightmare in the wall had stolen them away into some dark place, an *other* place, a place so *other*, dark and chill, that only a nightmare could be real here. The monstrous man loomed over them, twice their height, talking to them as though they were children, and the things it was saying, the awful things . . .

This was Niki's father, she realized.

Real.

In his eyes a dark glee, remembering all the children he'd tormented with his sickness.

Real.

She wanted to fight him, to shut the slippery wet sound of his voice out of her mind, to make him pay for all he'd done, but in his presence she was just a child again, helpless and small. Superimposed over his features were another father's features, *her* father's features. The air was heavy with the smell of cigarette smoke, the stink of burned flesh.

Her flesh.

She could feel the pain erupt across her lower torso, red-hot embers pressed against the skin, awful voice cutting through every defense she tried to raise to shut it out—

teach you, teach you, little cunt, teach you, who the fuck do they think they are, laying me off, teach you

—the stinging slap of an open hand across her face.

"Please God . . . ," she murmured through lips that memory recalled as swollen.

—the closed fist that pummeled her soft belly—

". . . don't let this . . ."

—tied to the bed, an army of sewing pins marching up her forearms, each waking one tiny drop of red, so red, blood on the pale skin—

". . . be real."

The memories were too powerful. Standing before the monstrous nightmare man, trapped in his world, child-sized and helpless, listening to his madness as it spewed from between those blubbery lips, all her hard years of trying to forget, of learning to be strong, of prevailing with dignity, hard-earned self-esteem, were stripped away, and she was the helpless child again that her father, in *his* madness, had tormented in his bouts of drunken rage.

She was the world once again, microcosm reflecting the macrocosm, on which he took out all his anger.

Real. It seemed so real.

She was the helpless child, beaten into submission.

It was all too real.

The nightmare man's gaze locked on hers, trapping her in place. She couldn't move, couldn't cry out. In her head—

"Please, don't . . ."

—a small voice—

". . . hurt me . . ."

—pleading as she waited for the pain to come again.

Inside.

It wasn't just because Jim was brave, not even that he felt responsible for Cindy, that he—maybe—loved her, was for sure infatuated with her, that he had left Ti Beau behind and gone through that door. A deeper need rode him as he stepped inside the building, a need to strike back.

Injustice had been too much a part of his life for too long. He was always the observer, distanced by the camera lens, freezing the moment, safe behind his refuge of camera angles and f-stops and film speeds, standing apart from the accident victim, corrupt politician, abused child, murder victim, grief-stricken family, brave kid dying of leukemia, desecrated graveyard, rape victim, drunk driver without a scratch on him, abused wife, corporate executive shrugging shoulders at the chemical spill, AIDS victim, homeless family, racial intolerance, all the thousand and one sorrows and terrors that had grown so commonplace that, unless you were on the receiving end, you had to just shut it all out. Or you couldn't live a normal life.

But what kind of normal life was it, where this shit went on, day after day, the endless litany, newspapers, TV, radio all deploring it in their editorials while it was the very lifeblood of their business?

It wasn't sane, not even close to normal.

Horror and pain and hurting and grief—they were now the norm.

No matter where you turned, or how hard you looked to escape it, injustice bred like a cancer in the heart of *normal*.

It was because of injustice that Jim went through that door. It was because he couldn't stand aside and observe the news, edit it into bite-sized chunks with his photographs anymore. It was time to shit or get off the pot, time to take a stand.

The stand he chose was to fight back.

For Cindy and Niki.

For the Slasher's victims.

For everyone touched by the despair of injustice.

He wasn't a hero; he was just a man who knew he couldn't stand by any longer.

So he went in, into the nightmare land that this abandoned building had become, and injustice caught him as well. The midnight man loomed over him, twice his size, reducing him to the vulnerability of a child.

Jim's fingers reached up to close around the *gris-gris* pouch that Ti Beau had given him, but it fell apart in his hand when he touched it, became dust and ash and lost hope. The midnight man's gaze grabbed Jim's, and rage though Jim did, he was made helpless with just that one cold dark blaze of the monster's eyes.

Inside.

It was the same man, Thomas realized with shock as the bulk of the nightmare man arose before him. Unhurt, alive, and twice his natural size.

Thomas's mind went back two years, present dissolving, past and present mingling. He saw again—

The traffic violator turning in the rubble-strewn field, gun in hand.

The bullet fired from Thomas's gun that took out the back of the man's head.

The fat corpse lying in a porcine heap, sprawled in the dirt at his feet.

The autopsy.

The burial.

Himself, up before the Police Commission, being cleared of any possible charges for killing the man.

The first of the Slasher's victims. And the subsequent victims, one by one.

He heard the voice of Wilkes, the woman from the ME's office, as though she were standing right behind him. *He seems to be getting stronger with each attack. Not just more brutal, but actually physically stronger.*

Teddy Bird towered over Thomas as if he were a child.

And then Papa Jo-el's voice, a hollow sound as though it spoke not just from memory, but from beyond the grave: *What walks the night streets is an* esprit—*a spirit of the dead. An evil spirit, what we call a* baka.

Teddy Bird, back from the dead, bigger and better than life.

And then Jack Whiteduck: *You can carve yourself out a piece of the day and call it your own, but no one owns the dark. . . . The night belongs to the* windigo.

Teddy Bird, a corpulent whale of a monster, here in the alien dark that held sway inside this building. An urban *windigo*, born of the injustice that bred freely in the inner city's streets.

Two years ago, Thomas had drawn his weapon in self-defense, shot and killed a monster.

Today Thomas drew his weapon in frustrated anger, confronting a distilled essence of all that was wrong with the city that he'd claimed as his own, to serve and protect, life on the line, day in day out, trying to make a difference. He'd made no difference. If this monster could come back from the grave and carry on with its evil, then the rule book had to go out the door. The concept of right and wrong, the judicial system that tried so hard for all its flaws, justice itself, had become a mockery. Only vigilante justice remained.

So he drew his weapon and took aim at the monster looming over him, but before he could fire, the midnight man slapped the gun from his hand. His .38 went skittering off into the dark. The corpulent face pressed close to his own, pig-eye gaze locking onto his gaze, freezing him in place.

Naughty, naughty boy.

The sensation of that voice filling his head was like putting his hand in a deep puddle of wet vomit. His fingers went up to the medicine pouch his brother had given him, but like Jim's *gris-gris*, it had never been meant to protect against such an intense confrontation. The pouch came apart in his hands. He could feel the clay mask cracking, flakes falling off.

How many times do you have to be told that it isn't polite to point a gun at someone, even if it is just a toy?

This was madness. How could Bird be so large?

It's not a nice thing to do at all.

He was dwarfed by the monster's awful bulk. Helpless.

Teddy's going to have to teach you a lesson.

Inside.

After ten years, Niki was finally face-to-face with her father once again. Ten long years, but it was as though no time had passed at all. He was still twice her size, still had the power because he was stronger. She might as well have been a toddler again, because there was no difference, no difference at all, except for one thing.

This time Niki wasn't scared.

TWENTY-TWO

Outside.

Frank made the two calls at a pay phone on Gracie Street. He considered making a third, to the local precinct to ask for backup, but he hung up the receiver and went back to his car instead.

What was he going to tell them? How was he supposed to explain what had happened to the building when he couldn't even come close to understanding it himself? And if he did try, he'd be lucky if the backup he called in didn't just take him in, wrapped up in a straitjacket, a direct run to the Zebrowski Institute for testing.

He drove back to the building where he'd left the others. When he first got out of the car, nothing seemed to have changed. But then he took a closer look at Thomas's brother and Ti Beau. Whatever mojo juice they had looked like it was running out. Veins stood out at their temples, their arms were corded with muscle strain, their bodies shaking.

"Look," he said, nervous, but approaching them all the same. "You've got to let me help."

And do what?

Ti Beau's eyes were closed. John's were rolled back in his head, only the whites showing. The sound of Frank's voice triggered a reaction from them. They began to speak, each taking a turn, as though sharing the one voice.

"Something . . ."

". . . happening now . . ."

". . . so . . ."

". . . too . . ."

". . . strong . . ."

". . . in my . . ."

". . . God . . ."

". . . head . . ."

Ti Beau suddenly drew back her head and screamed. The flickering ribbon of their protective barrier flared with an explosion of blue light. Frank jumped back, then moved forward as Ti Beau and John collapsed.

He managed to grab enough of a hold on each of them to be able to ease their bodies to the ground. Kneeling beside them, he lifted his head. The protective barrier was gone. The building was the same except that its stain was slowly spreading outward again.

Then he realized that the drumming was gone.

He looked to each end of the street, but the strange mystic shimmering that had once hidden the two spectral figures had vanished as well. Utter silence grabbed the street and held it in a choking grip.

Frank got his arms under Ti Beau's shoulders and half-carried, half-dragged her back to the car, away from the insidious spread of shadow that continued to grow from the sides of the building. He went back and got John, then stood there by the car, staring at the building.

He should be in there. With Tom. He trusted his partner and Tom had asked him to look after things out here, but that didn't cut much anymore.

His gaze went to the spreading stain as it continued to inch away from the side of the building. He had to get John and Ti Beau farther away. Had to figure a way to help Tom. Had to figure some way to stop all of this. . . .

Christ, it made his head hurt.

There came a sudden rumbling from underfoot, a deep underground murmur like·an earthquake tremor. Frank's gaze shot back to the building. He could actually see it shaking. A large crack appeared in the facing wall and traveled down the side. A deep, hollow grinding sound came from the foundation.

TWENTY-THREE

Inside.

Finally she was here, right at hand, the errant daughter, disguised behind a tough veneer of street punk, hair dyed, angry eyes, all a lie. He could see through the lie, see the little girl trapped behind the facade. Who had done this to his little girl? Harridan wife, do-good social workers, stole her away from a father's love, a father's influence, father knows best, always, always, little girls loved their daddies, loved them in special ways.

He reached out a hand to her and she spat at him.

"Keep the fuck away from me."

Foul-mouthed, voice hard. No, no, it was all wrong, all a lie. Where was the welcoming hug, the happy smile, the sweet lips, so sweet, kiss him here and here and here?

They've told you lies, filled your pretty head with ugly lies. Daddy loves you.

"Daddy's a fucking pervert."

Anger flash, red hot, scalding the cool logic of his reason. Take a breath, let it out, calm, be calm, don't scare her, they taught her fear, stole her love. It was up to him to win it back, but be firm, daddies are firm, hard, hard as rock, they don't spare the rod, feel it grow.

Little girls have to learn to respect their fathers.

Dark, dark hate in her eyes. Like a wild animal, scared, hurting, win her trust.

Daddy loves you.

"You just don't get it, do you?"

They told you lies.

"Nobody's told me anything I didn't already know. You're just a sick fuck. You're a slime."

Anger flash, no, stay calm, so hard to stay calm, so hard, hard, like a rock, needs her little fingers, sweet kisses. . . .

Don't—

"You're a pervert."

Anger flash, burns, burns. Why does she make it so hard? Hard to stay calm, hard in her hand, if she'd only take it in her hand. . . .

Don't—

"You're a fucking monster."

All wrong, all wrong. Hurtful words, lies, dirty lies, dirty words, stop telling Daddy lies.

He was the nightmare man, he was the midnight man, he loved all the little children, but he loved her best, needed her, needed her so bad, couldn't she see, couldn't she, couldn't she just put her mouth . . . there, stop the words, stop the lies. . . .

His gaze locked onto hers, holding her.

Your daddy's a good man. All the children love him, love him best of all.

Scorn in her eyes.

"Is that what they say when you kill them?"

I don't ... it's just ... they have to learn ... not to cry so much ... I don't mean to hurt them ... I never hurt them. ...

"Maybe it's better when they die, then they don't have to live remembering what some sick fuck of a pervert did to them."

Don't—

"But you like to hurt them, don't you?"

I—

"That gets you off the most, right?"

Stop—

"Because you're just a pervert."

The power in his gaze, the nightmare man's hoodoo, the midnight man's cold control, bore down on her.

Shut up, shut up, SHUT UP!

"A sick pervert."

Anger, red hot, cold hot, blade sharp hot, cut through skin to bone hot.

LIAR!

"Oh right. Like you're normal."

Calm, calm, baby's head is filled with lies, not her fault, don't hurt her, hold her, put her little mouth ... there. ...

But he couldn't move any more than she could. The hoodoo in his eyes arced back and forth between them, a fiery burning witchy power. He fought for control, but that just seemed to make her stronger.

"You're dead. What are you doing here, when you're supposed to be dead?"

Too much love in me. ...

"So if you can come back, what's to stop them from coming back too?"

Them ... ?

"All your little friends."

They . . . they're . . .

"Let's ask them how much they love you."

Can't. They're all gone . . . gone away. . . .

"But you came back."

Special. I'm special. I'm the midnight man.

"I can hear them."

Can't. They're all gone. . . .

But he heard a playground sound, little voices, dozens of little voices. It was distant, but it seemed to come closer. And behind it, behind all those little voices, he heard another sound, a rhythmical slapping sound. . . .

"Maybe they're midnight people, too."

Can't be. There's only . . .

The voices were growing closer. Behind him, he could feel something behind him. . . .

. . . one midnight man.

Inside.

Niki stood up to her father, for all that the hoodoo in his eyes had trapped her just as it had her companions. And the longer she stood up to him, the easier it got. She didn't know why the others fell prey so easily to his power, while she could resist. Maybe it was genetic, his power, his tainted, sick blood running in her veins; maybe her anger, her *need*, ran that much deeper than theirs. She didn't really care how it worked, just so long as it did. Just so long as she could finally put to rest the specter of despair that he'd laid over her life.

She didn't care if she had to die to do it. There was no fear left in her at all. Just that *need*.

But then she saw the children. They came out of the darkness behind her father, almost two dozen small children, the youngest three, oldest nine. The sound of playground voices rang in her head, but the children themselves were motionless, speechless. They stood silent, big eyes staring, bodies spectral, ghostly, spooky.

And they weren't alone.

Behind the children were some adults—just a handful of them. Four women, all of a kind, blonde and well built, dressed like hookers in fishnet, shiny shorts, micro skirts, tank tops, heels. And three men, black men, two of them built like linebackers and almost identical, bent slightly over, hands slapping against their thighs, waking an eerie counterpoint rhythm to the schoolyard sound, the other a thin little guy but with the look of a man who was usually in charge of any situation.

Her father turned slowly to face them.

Make . . . make them go away. . . .

Niki found that she could move again, found that she wasn't so small anymore. She still wasn't as big as the obese monster that was her father, but then she wasn't, wouldn't want to be, that fat mountain of sick flesh.

She reached in her pocket.

I don't want them here. . . .

Her father's slimy voice was petulant now, like a little boy who wasn't getting his own way.

Niki's hand came out of her pocket.

The ghostly crowd of her father's victims moved with shuffling steps, approaching. As they drew closer, Niki could see their death wounds upon them. Holes in torsos from which hung matter never meant to see the light of day. One had a crushed head. Another a slit throat.

Niki swallowed thickly. It was wrong, so wrong what her father had done to them.

They're not supposed to be here. They . . . they're dead. . . .

"Like you."

I'm not—

His enormous bulk turned to face her, gaze traveling down to the switchblade in her hand. She thumbed the release and the blade leapt out of the handle with a sharp *snick*.

What are you . . . doing. . . ?

"Making things right."

She saw fear in the monster's face, indecision, then a hardening of resolve. He shook his head.

You can't hurt the midnight man.

"Maybe, maybe not. But I'm sure as hell going to give it my best shot."

I'll come back. No matter what you do, I'll come back. He seemed to grow taller as he spoke, resolve filling him with strength. *Bigger and stronger than ever. You can't kill the nightmare man.*

"He's right."

Niki turned to see that the ghost of the little black guy was standing beside her.

"Who the fuck are you?"

"My name was Papa Jo-el. I tried to stop him, but he killed me for my effort. He's too strong."

Listen to him, little Niki. Come back to Daddy.

"He's come back for you," Papa Jo-el told her.

"I know. But if you think I'm letting him get near me again, there's a place you can shove it, pal."

Daddy loves you, Niki.

"There's only one way to stop him."

Niki looked from the ghost to her father. He had grown taller again, towering over her like the monstrous nightmare man he claimed to be. But she still wasn't afraid.

"Oh yeah?" she asked the ghost. "And what's that? Give him a blow job?"

Daddy wants you with him, forever and always.

Papa Jo-el shook his head. "You must forgive him."

Niki laughed. There, in that dark place, with the cold creeping into her bones, the ghosts of her father's dead all around her and her father himself grown to monstrous heights, it was all she could do.

"Forgive him? Jesus, no wonder you're dead—with an attitude like that."

Papa Jo-el accepted her mockery without a change of expression. "Trust me, child."

"Trust you? I don't even fucking know you. I don't *want* to know you."

"You must forgive him, complete the circle. Otherwise he *will* return."

Niki shook her head. "I don't think so. You're right about one thing—he came back because of me— but you've got the reason all ass-backwards."

I know you love me, little Niki.

"He's a monster, you see, and he can't ever be forgiven for what he's done, both to me and . . . to them." She nodded at the silent crowd of ghostly children. "I've lived in fear of him all my life. He really is the midnight man. He comes creeping into your bedroom late at night and makes you do shit that you shouldn't even know about when you're that young. Even when my mom took me away from him, even when we lived right across the country, I was afraid I'd hear the floorboards creak and he'd be there."

Loving you, always loving you in special ways. . . .

"The real reason he's back, is because I brought him back."

She hefted the switchblade in her hand, turning away from Papa Jo-el's ghost.

"I always believed he'd come back."

Nothing can keep me from you, my sweet little darling.

"But I don't believe it anymore."

She thrust up with the blade of the switchblade, puncturing the expanse of pale flesh that formed a band between his low-hanging jeans and his high-riding T-shirt.

The midnight man screamed.

"There's nothing inside of him."

Blood didn't gush from the hole in his gut. Instead, hot, fetid air streamed out of the wound.

"He's a hollow *thing*. A bad memory. A construct of all those years that I've been so scared of him."

He clapped his hands across the wound, but the foul air continued to escape. He began to deflate, like a balloon with a slow leak.

"He didn't call me back to this city. I called him back with my belief in him."

The nightmare man was just a puddle of skin on the floor now, a face in its center, eyes pleading.

Please. Help me . . . little Niki. . . .

"The only people I have to ask for forgiveness"—she looked up from what remained of her father to where the four ghostly women stood behind the children—"are you."

The women nodded slowly. Their features were so battered that Niki couldn't read the expression in them, but she thought they understood. She prayed they accepted her apology. They regarded her for long, silent moments; then with the help of the two large black men, they took the youngest children by the hand, ushering the others ahead of them, and slowly walked away until the darkness swallowed them. Only Papa Jo-el's ghost remained.

"Do you see?" Niki asked him.

"How . . . how could you know?"

Niki looked down at the knife in her hand. She let it fall to the ground. It clattered once, then lay still. Of her father, there was no trace except for a dark wet stain from which arose a foul stench. She lifted her gaze to look at the ghost, but he, too, was gone now.

"I don't know," she said.

The walls of the vast cavern of the dark place closed in on her, drawing nearer and nearer. She knew a moment of vertigo, as though the world shifted underfoot and she stood, for that one brief instant, over some depthless abyss; then she found herself standing in the boiler room of the building from which she and Cindy had been taken.

She crossed the room to where Cindy crouched on the floor and slowly lifted the blonde woman's head.

"What . . . what happened?" Cindy asked in a halting voice. "I had the most awful . . . dreams. . . ."

Niki couldn't speak. Her throat was too thick with emotion. All she could do was hold Cindy in a comforting embrace.

Other figures stirred in the murk. Niki recognized Jim. She started for a moment at the ghostly features of the other man's face before she realized it was just a kind of mask he was wearing—gray-white clay, hardened over his features, now cracked and flaking.

"It wasn't a dream," the stranger said.

"No dream," Niki agreed.

"Is it over?" Jim asked. "Is everything back to normal?"

Niki slowly nodded, though she wasn't so sure about what was normal anymore. All she knew was that, inside her, something had changed. She wasn't afraid anymore. But was it finished? It was over for her, but the real horror was that every day, every hour, what her father had done to her was happening to some other little kid who was just as helpless, just as hurt, just as alone and lost, as she had been. That was the real horror.

Maybe she should become a social worker. At least she'd *know* what those kids were going through.

"Let's get out of here," the stranger with the masked face said.

Niki nodded slowly. She helped Cindy to her feet and supported her as they went upstairs.

———

Outside.

Frank held his breath, waiting for the building to come down. Instead, the tremors died and the crack stopped halfway down the side of the building. An almost reverent silence fell; then a weird flickering covered the entire face of the building. Its polarities reversed once more, light to dark, dark to light, color returning. He started, nerves jumping, when something moved in the doorway.

Four figures emerged onto the stoop: two women Frank didn't recognize, the photographer they'd seen run into the building just as they arrived, and—

"Tom!" he cried, running for the door. He wrapped his arms around Thomas, enfolding him in a hug. "Jesus Christ, man, you had me worried."

"You and me both, partner."

By the side of the unmarked police car, John and the *mambo* woman were sitting up. They looked worn to the bone and dazed, utterly beat. John lifted a weak hand to give his brother a thumbs up. Thomas returned the gesture over his partner's shoulder and stepped back from Frank.

"What the hell happened in there?" Frank asked.

"Hell's about as apt a description as we're going to come up with. The Slasher's gone."

"You killed him?"

Thomas shook his head. "He's just . . . gone. I can't explain it any better than that."

"Gone . . . ?" Frank repeated.

Thomas looked back at the building. Slowly he nodded his head. "I don't know where, but this time I don't think he's coming back."

TWENTY-FOUR

Jim and his companions slipped away while the two policemen were talking and made their way back to where he and Ti Beau had left the car. They let the *mambo* off a block or so from her building so that she could circumvent the plainclothes policeman who was still keeping watch on her front door. Throughout the walk to the car and the drive there, not one of them had seemed willing, or perhaps able, to speak about what they had so recently experienced.

"Go with God," Ti Beau said as they got out of the car.

Jim thought it was an odd thing for her to say, considering her own religious beliefs, but then there hadn't been anything normal about the weekend to begin with and what did he really know about voodoo anyway?

Niki needed to pick up her things at his apartment, but Cindy asked to be dropped off at Meg's on the way.

"I'll see you later?" Jim said when they pulled up to the curb in front of Meg's apartment.

The haunted look in her eyes troubled him, but with Niki there he didn't feel right trying to talk about what had happened in that boiler room which hadn't seemed like a boiler room for most of the time they'd been in it.

"I . . . suppose," Cindy said, closing the door before he could say anything else.

He drove back to his own apartment more quickly than he should have, but it being a Sunday, the traffic was light and they made it in one piece. He felt uncomfortable with Niki. She'd had such a shitty life, he thought, remembering what he'd learned from the conversation between her and . . . her father? Already the details were sliding away from his consciousness.

"Are you going to be okay?" he asked Niki after they'd fetched her pack.

She nodded. "I'm out from under the shadow now."

"Back there," he began. "What really hap—"

"I don't want to talk about it," she said.

She left him standing on the curb beside his car and walked away. Jim hesitated for a long moment. He knew she was living on the street, knew she didn't have anybody, but the haunted look in Cindy's eyes returned to him and he just let Niki go. She was out of danger now, and if he had to pick priorities, his lay with Cindy.

But she was gone by the time he got to Meg's.

"How could you let her *go*?" he said.

Meg caught hold of his arm and pulled him in from the hall, steering him to a chair in the living room.

"What was I supposed to do?" she asked. "Tie her down?"

"No. It's just . . ."

The night before, the day—everything caught up to him and he leaned back in the chair, deflated, a vast weariness weighing down his limbs. His head felt completely empty.

"You don't look so good," Meg said. "And neither did Cindy. Just what exactly did you guys do today?"

Dozens of vague images crisscrossed through Jim's mind: strange, confusing images of ghosts and a monstrous man and a dark room that just seemed to go forever. . . .

"We . . . we found him. The Slasher."

Meg leaned in toward him. "My God. What happened?"

"I . . . I'm not so sure anymore. He . . ."

What could he say? That it had turned out the Slasher was a dead man? That Niki stuck him with a knife and he deflated like a balloon? Had any of that even happened?

"It's all confusing," he said finally. "None of it makes a whole lot of sense."

"Cindy didn't have much to say about it either."

"Did she say where she was going?"

"No. Just that she had to go. Jim, will you please *tell* me what happened?"

He met her worried gaze. "I wish I could. We found the Slasher and . . . and I guess Niki . . . killed him. . . ."

"You're not telling me everything."

"I can't," Jim said, helplessly. "None of it seems real. There were cops there. . . ."

But it had been a couple of hours now since they'd left the Tombs, and Meg told him there'd been nothing on the news.

"Did you get any pictures?" she asked.

He shook his head. "I don't think I can take that kind of picture anymore."

"Jim, you're—"

He sat up suddenly, then rose to his feet. What the hell was he doing, sitting here, when Cindy was gone? Out there on her own somewhere, lost, hurting . . .

"I've got to go, Meg. I'll call you."

She tried to hold him back. "You're in no shape to go anywhere. Why don't you just bed down in my spare room?"

"I've got to find Cindy. I . . . I've got a weird kind of hurt inside me—an emptiness—and I know it's a lot worse for her. She shouldn't be out on her own right now. She needs someone; maybe it isn't me, not for always, but she needs someone right now and I think I'm all she's got."

He thought of Niki, her small figure as she walked off on her own down the street, and felt a pang of guilt. But it was short-lived. Out of all of them he believed that Niki had come out the strongest from their ordeal.

Meg followed him to the door.

"We have to talk," she said. "About what happened, about you quitting your work."

He nodded. "We will."

She gave him a hug. "Good luck," she said.

Jim thought of the size of the city. Christ, Cindy could be any-where. Where was he supposed to start?

"You might try the bus station," Meg said, as though reading his mind.

And that was where he found her.

He sat down beside her on the bench, glanced at the ticket in her hand.

"So . . . you're going?"

She nodded.

"You don't have to."

She turned to him, that haunted look still darkening her gaze.

"I . . . I thought I was strong," she said. "I thought I could make my own way, could put all the bad shit behind me, but he . . . he just cut me down like I was nothing."

Jim didn't have to ask who "he" was.

"He did it to all of us," he said.

"I didn't see Niki's father," Cindy said, her voice dull. "I saw my own. He was an alcoholic and he used to"—she took an unsteady breath—"beat me."

"Oh, Jesus."

"I just feel . . . so ashamed. Niki . . . Niki stood up to her father, but I just . . . ran away from mine. . . ."

Jim felt more helpless at that moment than he had confronting the awful monstrosity that had been Niki's father. The station's intercom crackled, announcing the departure of Cindy's bus.

As she started to rise, Jim touched her arm.

"Don't go," he said.

She shook her head. "You don't want me."

"But—"

"I find it hard enough to live with myself; I couldn't live with pity."

The thought of her leaving made Jim's stomach tense into knots.

"It's not that," he said. "We hardly know each other, but I know . . . I know I'd like to know you better."

Her knuckles were white around the handle of her sax case.

"What are you saying?"

"I'm asking you to stay—like before, no strings. I just don't think I could handle you walking out of my life without us at least giving things a try."

"But now that you know—"

"What's happened to you before is in the past. Jesus, it's not like it was your fault."

"But, I just ran. . . ."

"There's running, and then there's running. There's things you have to face up to, and then there's things that you can't ever change; trying to just hurts you more. For that kind of thing, making a clean break is the only solution."

"You're not just feeling—"

"Sorry for you?" Jim shook his head. "No way. There was something happening between us right from the start—don't tell me you didn't feel it."

She lowered her head, hiding her face behind a curtain of hair.

"Let me take you back to Meg's and then we can try to start over again."

She looked up at him. "I don't want to go to Meg's."

"But—"

"If you . . . if you really mean what you've been saying, take me home."

Jim sat in stunned silence. Then a slow smile spread over his features. He reached over and picked up her duffel and sax.

"I liked that picture in today's paper," she said as they went to cash in her ticket.

"So what happens now?" Frank asked. "With the Slasher case?"

They were standing outside the 12th Precinct. John was waiting for Thomas in the pickup, parked by the curb.

"We keep working it until it plays itself out and something else comes up to take away the manpower. There aren't going to be any more deaths, but there's no way we can put what happened inside that building in a report."

"What *did* happen in there?"

Thomas shook his head. "I'm not really sure. All I know is that the kid—the Slasher called her Niki, so we were right about the graffiti being connected—she dealt with him."

Frank realized he wasn't going to get any more out of his partner, not right now. But he could give it time. Besides, there were some more immediate concerns that had to be dealt with.

"And the Loot? He's going to want some answers."

"I know," Thomas said. "But I can't deal with that right now. Tell him I'll be in tomorrow morning, first thing."

There was no way they could foresee how it was going to play out, Frank thought, but taking in the shape his partner was in, considering how he'd stayed outside while Tom had gone into the building, he figured he could take the heat for now.

"Are you going to be okay?" he asked.

"Yeah. I'm going to go home to Angie and try to connect myself back into the real world."

Frank put a hand on his shoulder and gave it a squeeze, then stepped aside so that Thomas could join his brother in the pickup.

"I'll see you tomorrow, Frank," Thomas said.

John drove slowly to Thomas and Angie's apartment.

"So," John said after a time. "Does this change anything?"

Thomas looked at him. "What? You mean the fact that all that mumbo jumbo's for real?"

John shrugged.

"Or about my being a cop?"

John nodded.

Thomas looked out the windshield for the longest time, then slowly shook his head.

"I'm a good cop," he said. "I know sometimes it doesn't seem like what Frank and I do makes much of a difference, but the times when we do do some good make up for the times that we don't. And I believe that I make a good role model for other Kickaha who can't find a way to fit in on the reserve." He glanced at his brother. "There's got to be room for both; people have to choose for themselves. And just because I chose this life, it doesn't mean I'm any less a Kickaha than someone who stays on the reserve."

John made no reply. He concentrated on his driving, until he finally gave a grudging nod of agreement.

"We could still use you full-time," he said. "But we'll take what we can get. You won't be a stranger?"

"You think you can get Dad to lay back a little?"

John laughed. "Hell, I'm going to be chief."

"Like that'd make a difference to him."

"You're right. We'll get Mom to work on him."

First thing Monday morning, the receptionist for the social services center on Peel Street glanced up to find a young girl standing at her desk. She was a little scruffy-looking with that untidy thatch of short black hair, but at least she was dressed neatly. She didn't seem to have that finger-to-authority attitude that so many teenagers who came in there had.

"Can I help you?" the receptionist asked.

"I'd like to go back to school."

Well, that was nice for a change. The girl actually sounded as though she meant it.

"I'll see if there's a caseworker free," the receptionist said as she took a form from a slot and put it into her typewriter. "Meanwhile, let's get these forms filled out. What's your name?"

"Niki. Nicola Chelsea Adams."